Praise for *The Kings of Cool*

"My beef with Don Winslow comes down to this: He can't write these books as quickly as I rip through them. Though good lord, he's tryin'. . . . As always with Winslow, the savage delight is in the details. . . . Throw in the usual array of crooked cops, stone-cold killers and Magic Mountain sex, and you have another Cherry Garcia reading experience."

—*The Oregonian*

"Wordplay is a hallmark of Winslow's distinctive narrative voice . . . [He] maintains a loose, witty stream-of-consciousness banter laced with puns and pop-culture-fueled digressions."

—*Entertainment Weekly*

"An inventive writer . . . Winslow pushes the boundaries of prose in *The Kings of Cool,* supplementing a conventional story with haiku-like paragraphs, the occasional script and a stream of consciousness approach."

—*The Denver Post*

"All the snap and savvy of *Savages* but with even more ambition and heart . . . The money gets bigger, the stakes get higher and the violence turns from an off-screen flirtation into a live-in lover. . . . [Winslow has] graduated from well-reviewed writer to a name brand author who delivers the goods."

—*The Huffington Post*

"Blistering . . . Winslow serves up nonstop action, tempering the tension with his trademark razor-sharp wit. . . . This cool, clever entry is sure to be a royally popular summer read."

—*Booklist* (starred review)

"Another Winslow roller-coaster thriller."

—*Library Journal* (starred review)

Praise for *Savages*

"A revelation . . . Every bit as savage as its title . . . This is *Butch Cassidy and the Sundance Kid* on autoload."
—Stephen King, *Entertainment Weekly*

"*Savages* will jolt Mr. Winslow into a different league . . . [His] most boisterously stylish crime book, his gutsiest and most startling . . . its wisecracks are so sharp, its characters so mega-cool and its storytelling so ferocious that the risks pay off, thanks especially to Mr. Winslow's no-prisoners sense of humor. . . . The Winslow effect is to fuse the grave and the playful, the body blow and the joke, the nightmare and the pipe dream."
—Janet Maslin, *The New York Times*

"*Savages* is the book of my generation . . . Solidifies Winslow's reputation as not just one of the best crime writers working today, but one of the best writers, period. Jesus Christ, this book."
—Brendan Leonard, *January Magazine*

"Blisteringly original . . . Winslow's prose is so choppy and grammatically acrobatic that in lesser hands it would have obliterated the storytelling. Like his heroes, though, the only rules he plays by are his own, branding him a kind of Hunter Thompson for the fiction world. . . . The perfect meshing of style and substance."
—Jon Land, *Providence Journal-Bulletin*

"Winslow's marvelous, adrenaline-juiced roller coaster of a novel . . . is both a departure and a culmination, pyrotechnic braggadocio and deep meditation on contemporary American culture."
—Sarah Weinman, *Los Angeles Times*

"While the book is hip and slides along as smooth as a docile wave over sand, the stakes are extreme and the outcome fatalistic. This is the story of love's costs—and the acceptance of whatever that cost entails."
—Randy Michael Signor, *Chicago Sun-Times*

"*Savages* continues Don Winslow's streak of darkly funny Southern California novels. Winslow's short bursts of well-timed action, hipster dialogue and rat-a-tat prose are as addictive as ever."

—Adam Woog, *The Seattle Times*

"*Savages* is an unrelenting and entertaining summer read. And the fun—even in a novel where you can trust that few people end up in one piece—is flat-out contagious."

—Steve Duin, *The Oregonian*

"A spellbinding tour de force that is utterly impossible to put down. *Savages* is, bar none, the finest novel I have read in years."

—Christopher Reich

"*Savages* is Don Winslow's best book yet—a wickedly funny and smart novel, with a ripped-from-the-headlines story that gets your pulse racing as the action unfolds. Razor-sharp plot twists, a cast of ruthless antiheroes, and of course, Winslow's superb, adrenaline-fueled prose make this scorching, drug-infused thriller an addictive and entertaining read."

—Janet Evanovich

"A game-changer for the genre. This fascinating thriller is super hip, wildly funny, supremely smart and sexy. Don Winslow has actually invented a new kind of graphic novel by using uniquely formatted, vivid prose constructions instead of hand-drawn panels. It's a thrilling and brilliant tour de force, and it will produce many imitators."

—Joseph Wambaugh

ALSO BY DON WINSLOW

The Gentlemen's Hour

Satori

Savages

The Dawn Patrol

The Winter of Frankie Machine

The Power of the Dog

California Fire and Life

The Death and Life of Bobby Z

Isle of Joy

While Drowning in the Desert

A Long Walk up the Water Slide

Way Down on the High Lonely

The Trail to Buddha's Mirror

A Cool Breeze on the Underground

THE
KINGS
OF
COOL

A PREQUEL TO *SAVAGES*

DON WINSLOW

SIMON & SCHUSTER PAPERBACKS

NEW YORK   LONDON   TORONTO   SYDNEY   NEW DELHI

In the Bible, Mama, Cain slew Abel
And east of Eden, Mama, he was cast,
You're born into this life paying
For the sins of somebody else's past.

—BRUCE SPRINGSTEEN, "ADAM RAISED A CAIN"

Simon & Schuster Paperbacks
A Division of Simon & Schuster, Inc.
1230 Avenue of the Americas
New York, NY 10020

First Simon & Schuster trade paperback edition June 2013

SIMON & SCHUSTER PAPERBACKS and colophon are registered trademarks of Simon & Schuster, Inc.

For information about special discounts for bulk purchases, please contact Simon & Schuster Special Sales at 1-866-506-1949 or business@simonandschuster.com.

The Simon & Schuster Speakers Bureau can bring authors to your live event. For more information or to book an event contact the Simon & Schuster Speakers Bureau at 1-866-248-3049 or visit our website at www.simonspeakers.com.

Designed by Kyoko Watanabe

Manufactured in the United States of America

1 3 5 7 9 10 8 6 4 2

The Library of Congress has cataloged the hardcover edition as follows:
Winslow, Don.
The kings of cool / Don Winslow.
p. cm.
"A prequel to Savages."
1. Friendship—Fiction.   2. Conflict of generations—Fiction.
3. Laguna Beach (Calif.)—Fiction.   4. Domestic Fiction.   I. Title.
PS3573.I5326K56   2012
813'.54—dc23   2012010619
ISBN: 978-1-4516-6532-1
ISBN: 978-1-4516-6533-8 (pbk)
ISBN: 978-1-4516-6534-5 (ebook)

To Shane Salerno, for everything.
Anytime, anywhere, man.

THE
KINGS
OF
COOL

Fuck me.

Laguna Beach, California
2005

2

Is what O is thinking as she sits between Chon and Ben on a bench at Main Beach and picks out potential mates for them.

"*That* one?" she asks, pointing at a classic BB (Basically *Baywatch*) strolling down the boardwalk.

Chon shakes his head.

A little dismissively, O thinks. Chon is pretty choosy for a guy who spends most of his time in Afghanistan or Iraq and doesn't see much in the way of anything outside cammies or a burqa.

Actually, she can see how the burqa thing could be pretty hot if you played it off right.

Did, you know, the harem thing.

Yeah, no.

The burqa ain't gonna work for O. You don't want to hide that blonde hair, you don't want those bright eyes peeking out from behind a *niqab*.

O was made for sunshine.

California gurl.

Chon, he ain't small but he's thin. O thinks he looks even thinner than usual. He's always been cut, but now it looks like he's been carved with a scalpel. And she likes the short, almost shaved, hair.

"That one?" she asks, jutting her chin at a tourist-type brunette with really big tits and a retroussé nose.

Chon shakes his head.

Ben remains silent, sphinx-like, which is a role reversal, because Ben is usually the more verbal of the two. This isn't a high bar to jump, as Chon doesn't talk a lot, except when he goes off on a rant; then it's like you pulled the plug from a fire hose.

While Ben is the more verbal, O considers now, he's also the less promiscuous.

Ben is more Consecutive Monogamy while Chon is more Women Are To Be Served Concurrently. Although O knows for a fact that both of them—albeit Chon more than Ben—take full advantage of the Tourist Chicks who watch them play volleyball here at the beach, just a few convenient paces from the Hotel Laguna—encounters she refers to as FRSO.

Fuck—Room Service—Shower—Out.

"That pretty much sums it up," Chon has admitted.

Although at times he skips the room service.

Never the shower.

Basic rule of survival in the Greater Cross V Crescent Sandbox Tournament:

If there's a shower, take it.

He can't shake off the habit at home.

Anyway, Chon admits to doing matinees at the Hotel Laguna, the Ritz, the St. Regis, and the Montage with not only tourist women but also Orange County Trophy Wives and divorcées—the difference between the two being strictly temporary.

That's the thing about Chon—he's totally honest. No pretensions, no evasions, no apologies. O can't decide if that's because he's so ethical or because he just doesn't give a fuck.

Now he turns to her and says, "You have one strike left. Choose carefully."

It's a game they play—ODB—Offline Dating Baseball. Predicting each other's sexual preferences and hitting for a single, a double, a triple, or a Home Run. It's a really good game when you're high, which they are now, on some of Ben and Chon's supremo weed.

(Which is not weed at all, but a top-of-the-line hydro blend they call Saturday In The Park because if you take a hit of this stuff any day is Saturday and any place is the park.)

O is usually the Sammy Sosa of ODB, but now, with runners on first and third, she's striking out.

"Well?" Chon asks her.

"I'm waiting for a good pitch," she says, scanning the beach.

Chon's been in Iraq, he's been in Afghanistan . . .

. . . Go exotic.

She points to a beautiful South Asian girl with shimmering black hair setting off her white beach dress.

"Her."

"Strikeout," Chon answers. "Not my type."

"What *is* your type?" O asks, frustrated.

"Tan," Chon answers, "thin—sweet face—big brown eyes, long lashes."

O turns to Ben.

"Ben, Chon wants to fuck Bambi."

3

Ben's a little distracted.

Sort of following the game, but not really, because his mind is on something that happened this morning.

This morning, like most mornings, Ben eased into his day at the Coyote Grill.

He got a table on the open deck near the fireplace and ordered his usual pot of black coffee and the crazy-good eggs machaca (for those in the benighted regions east of I-5, that's scrambled eggs with chicken and salsa, a side of black beans, fried potatoes, and either corn or flour tortillas, which might be the best thing in the history of the universe), opened his laptop, and read the Gray Lady to see what Bush and his coconspirators were doing on that particular day to render the world uninhabitable.

This is his routine.

Ben's partner, Chon, has warned him against habits.

"It's not a 'habit,'" Ben answered. "It's a 'routine.'"

A habit is a matter of compulsion, a routine a matter of choice. The fact that it's the same choice every day is irrelevant.

"Whatever," Chon answered. "Break it up."

Cross the PCH to the Heidelberg Cafe, or drive down to Dana Point Harbor, check out the yummy-mummies jogging with their strollers, make a freaking pot of coffee at *home* for chrissakes. But do not do not do not do the same thing every day at the same time.

"It's how we nail some of these AQ clowns," Chon said.

"You shoot AQ guys while they eat eggs machaca at the Coyote Grill?" Ben asked. "Who knew?"

"Funny asshole."

Yeah, it was sort of funny but not really funny because Chon *has* smudged more than a few Al Qaeda, Taliban, and their assorted affiliates precisely because they fell into the bad habit of having a habit.

He either pulled the trigger himself or did it remote control by calling in a drone strike from some *Warmaster 3* prodigy sitting in a bunker in Nevada knocking back Mountain Dew while he smoked some unsuspecting *muj* with a keystroke.

The problem with contemporary warfare is that it has become a video game. (Unless you're on the actual ground and get shot, in which case it is most definitely not.)

Whether direct from Chon or run through the gamer, it had the same effect.

Hemingway-esque.

Blood and sand.

Without the bull(shit).

All true, but nevertheless Ben isn't going to get into this whole subterfuge thing any more than he has to. He's in the dope business to increase his freedom, not to limit it.

Make his life bigger, not smaller.

"What do you want me to do," he asked Chon, "live in a bunker?"

"While I'm gone," Chon answered. "Yeah, okay."

Yeah, *not* okay.

Ben sticks to his routine.

This particular morning Kari, the waitress of Eurasian Persuasion and almost reality-defying beauty—golden skin, almond eyes, sable hair, legs longer than a Wisconsin winter—poured his coffee.

"Hey, Ben."

"Hey, Kari."

Ben is seriously trying to get with her.

So fuck you, Chon.

Kari brought the food, Ben dug into the machaca and the *Times.*

Then he felt this guy sit down across from him.

4

Burly guy.

Big, sloping shoulders.

Sandy, receding hair combed straight back.

Kind of old school.

In fact, he was wearing one of those "Old Guys Rule" T-shirts, which totally miss the obvious point that if old guys really ruled, they wouldn't have to proclaim it on a cheap T-shirt.

They'd just, you know, rule.

These are guys who can't figure out social media technology, so Ben figures their days of rule have gone the way of the compact disc.

Anyway, this guy who looked to be in his fifties sat there staring at Ben.

Very high creepiness rating.

Ben was like, do I know you, am I supposed to know you, is this some sort of weird early-morning gay thing? Or is this guy just one of those "I'm a people person" tools who thinks it's his human duty to strike up conversations with people sitting alone at restaurants?

Ben is not I-like-to-meet-new-people guy. He's I'm-reading-my-freaking-newspaper-and-flirting-with-the-waitress-so-leave-me-the-fuck-alone guy.

So he said, "Bro, no offense, but I'm kind of into what I'm reading."

Like, there are five empty tables, why don't you sit down at one of them?

The guy said, "I'll only take a minute of your time, son."

"I'm not your son," Ben said. "Unless my mother has been deceiving me all these years."

"Shut your smartass mouth and listen," the guy said quietly. "We didn't mind when you were selling a little custom shit to your friends. But when it starts showing up in Albertsons, it's a *problem*."

"It's a free market," Ben answered, thinking he sounded like a Republican all of a sudden. Seeing as how Ben is generally to the left of Trotsky, this came as an unpleasant epiphany.

"There is no such thing as a 'free market,' " Old Guys Rule said. "The market costs—there are expenses. You want to sell up in L.A., compete with our little brown and black brothers, be our guest. Orange County, San Diego, Riverside—you pay a licensing fee. Are you paying attention?"

"I'm riveted."

"Are you clowning me?"

"No."

"Because I wouldn't like that."

"And I wouldn't blame you," Ben said. "So, for the sake of discussion, what happens if I don't pay this licensing fee?"

"You don't want to find out."

"Okay, but just for the sake of discussion."

Old Guys Rule looked at him like he was wondering if this kid was fucking with him, and then said, "We put you out of business."

"Who's 'we'?" Ben asked. He saw the look on the guy's face and said, "I know—I don't want to find out. And if I do pay this fee?"

OGR held out his hands and said, "Welcome to the market."

"Got it."

"So we have an understanding."

"We do," Ben said.

OGR smiled.

Satisfied.

Until Ben added, "We have an understanding you're an asshole."

Because it's also Ben's understanding that no one controls the marijuana market.

Cocaine—yes. That would be the Mexican cartels.

Heroin—ditto.

Meth—the biker gangs, more recently the Mexicans.

Prescription pills—the pharmaceutical industry.

But the 420?

Free market.

Which is excellent, because it runs by market rules—price point, quality, distribution.

The customer is king.

So Ben pretty much dismissed this guy as some whack-job trying to jerk his chain. Still, it's a little troubling, Ben thought—how does the guy know who I am?

And who *is* this guy?

Whoever he is, he gave Ben one of those old-school stares until Ben actually had to laugh.

OGR stood up and said, "You motherfuckers think you're the kings of cool, right? You know everything, no one can tell you anything? Well, let me tell you something—you don't know shit."

OGR gave Ben one more Bobby Badass look and then walked out.

The kings of cool, Ben thought.

He kind of liked it.

Now he turns his attention back to the game.

5

"I'm pretty sure that's illegal," Ben says, lacing his fingers behind his head and tilting his face to the sun.

"To have sex with a deer, or with a cartoon character?" Chon asks.

"Both," Ben says. "And may I point out that Bambi is an *underage* animated ungulate? Not to mention a male?"

"Bambi is a boy?" O asks.

"Again, Bambi is a *deer*," Ben clarifies, "but, yes, he's a *boy* deer."

"Then why are so many girls in *Playboy* named Bambi?" O asks.

She likes *Playboy* and is grateful that Stepfather Number Four keeps them in his "home office" desk drawer so Paqu—

Paqu is what O calls her mother, the

Passive Aggressive Queen of the Universe—

—doesn't see them and get pissy because she is an *older* version of the centerfolds who is constantly attempting to airbrush herself via expensive cosmetics and more expensive cosmetic surgery.

O is pretty sure that the National Geographic Channel is going to do an archaeological dig on her mother in a futile quest to find a single original body part, a private joke that explains why O gave Four a pith helmet for his last birthday.

("Why, thank you, Ophelia," a puzzled Four said.

"You're welcome."

"What's it for?" Paqu asked, icily.

"To keep the sun off your vagina," O answered.)

"Girls are named Bambi," Ben says now, "because we are culturally ignorant, of even *pop* culture, and because we crave the archetype of childlike innocence combined with adult sexuality."

His parents are both psychotherapists.

Ben, oh Ben, O thinks.

Hard body, soft heart.

Long brown hair, warm brown eyes.

"But that's *me,*" O tells him. "Childlike innocence combined with adult sexuality."

Short blonde hair, thin hips, no rack to speak of, tiny butt on her petite frame. And yes, big eyes—albeit blue, not brown.

"No," Ben says. "You're more adult innocence combined with childlike sexuality."

He has a point, O thinks. She does view sex mostly as play—a fun thing—not a job to be performed to prove one's love. This is why, she has opined, they're called sex "toys" instead of sex "tools."

"*Bambi* is a proto-fascist piece of work," Chon snarls. "It might as well have been shot by Leni Riefenstahl."

Chon reads books—Chon reads the *dictionary*—and also hits the Foreign Films/Classics section of Netflix. He could explain *8½* to you, except he won't.

"Speaking of gender ambiguity," O says, "I told Paqu that I'm thinking of becoming bisexual."

"What did she say?" Ben asks.

"She said, 'What?' " O answers. "Then I wussed out and said, 'I think I want a bicycle.' "

"To pedal to your girlfriend's house?" Ben asks.

"To pedal to *your* girlfriend's house," O counters.

She could play for either or both teams and would be heavily recruited because, at nineteen, she's drop-dead gorgeous.

But she doesn't know that yet.

O describes herself as "poly-sexual."

"Like Pollyanna, only *way* happier," she explains.

She would consider going LTG—

Lesbian Till Graduation—

—except she isn't in school, a fact that Paqu points out to her on a near daily basis. She tried junior college for a semester (okay, the first three weeks of a semester), but it was, well . . .

junior college.

Right now she's just glad to have her guys here. As for ODB, they can have any women they want, as long as one of them is her.

Check that, she thinks—

They can have any woman they want

as long as I'm the one they love.

The pain of it is

The *pain* of it is

Chon flies out tonight

This is his last day on the beach.

6

Specifically, Laguna Beach, California.

The brightest pearl in the SoCal necklace of coastal towns that stretches down that lovely neck from Newport Beach to Mexico.

Going along the strand (pun intended)—

—Newport Beach, Corona del Mar, Laguna Beach, Capistrano Beach, San Clemente (interrupt for Camp Pendleton), Oceanside, Carlsbad, Leucadia, Encinitas, Cardiff-by-the-Sea, Solana Beach, Del Mar, Torrey Pines, La Jolla Shores, La Jolla, Pacific Beach, Mission Beach, Ocean Beach, Coronado, Silver Strand, Imperial Beach.

All beautiful, all fine, but the best one is—

Lagoona—

—which was the name officially given to the town by the State of California until someone explained that there was no actual "lagoon," but that the name derived from "*canada de las lagunas*," which in Spanish means "canyon of the lakes." There are two lakes, up in the hills above said canyon, but Laguna isn't known for its lakes, it's known for its beaches and its beauty.

About which Ben, Chon, and O are a little blasé, because they grew up here and take it for granted.

Yeah, except Chon doesn't right now because his leave is up and he's about to go back to Afghanistan, aka Stanland.

Or, in the spirit of things—

Afgoonistan.

7

Chon tells Ben and O that he literally has to get packing.

He goes back to his efficiency apartment on Glenneyre and packs a baseball bat into his '68 green Mustang—

—in honor of Steve McQueen—

—*the* King of Cool—

—and drives down to San Clemente, not far from Richard Nixon's version of Elba and hence known in the latter half of the 1970s as

Sans Clemency.

(Nixon, poor Nixon, the only truly tragic hero in the American political theater; the only recent president more Aeschylus than Rodgers and Hammerstein. First there was *Camelot*, then *The Best Little Whorehouse in Texas*, then *Richard*?)

Chon drives not to the old Western White House

The real name of which was, with presumably unintended irony,

La Casa Pacifica

"Peaceful House."

There was Nixon in Exile, prowling around the Peaceful House chatting with paintings, while down on the actual Pacific, Secret Service agents chased surfers away from the nearby famous break at Upper Trestles lest they organize an assassination attempt, which is, it should be noted, probably the first time that the words "surfers" and "organize" have been used in the same paragraph.

Surfers? An assassination attempt?

Surfers?

California surfers?!

("Okay, let's coordinate our watches."

Uhhhhhh . . . watches?)

Anyway, Chon drives to the hospital.

8

"Who did this to you?" Chon asks.

Sam Casey, one of their best "sales partners," lies in bed with a broken jaw, a concussion, his right arm fractured in three places, and internal bleeding.

Someone beat the holy hell out of Sam.

"Brian Hennessy and three of his surfer buddies," Sam says through his wired jaw. "I was selling them a lousy QP and they ripped me off."

"You've sold to them before, right?" Chon asks.

One of Ben and Chon's cardinal rules: never sell to anyone you don't know.

Maybe only Chon would know that "cardinal rule" doesn't come from the Catholic religious official, but from the Latin "*cardo*," which means "hinge." So a cardinal rule is something that everything else hinges upon.

Everything hinges upon not selling dope to people you don't know.

And know well.

"I've sold to them a dozen times," Sam says. "Never any trouble."

"Okay, so look, the bills are covered," Chon says. Ben has set up a shell corporation through which he offers health insurance to sales partners who are fully vested. "I'll take care of Brian. Do me a favor, though? Don't mention this to Ben?"

Because Ben doesn't believe in violence.

9

Chon does.

10

It's an age-old debate, not to be rehashed here, but basically—
Ben believes that to answer violence with violence only begets more violence, while Chon believes that to answer violence with

nonviolence only begets more violence, his evidence being the entire history of humanity.

Oddly enough, they both believe in karma—what goes around comes around—except with Chon it comes around in a freaking hurry and usually with ill intent.

What Chon calls "microwave karma."

Together, Ben and Chon make up a collective pacifist.

Ben is the paci

Chon is the fist.

11

Rule of life—

Okay, more of a strong suggestion—

If you absolutely *have* to be an asshole?

Make yourself a *little* hard to find.

Go do your assholian bullshit and then lock yourself in your mother's basement and put a towel over the Xbox to block the light, but don't—

—beat someone up and then go surfing in your usual spot.

Just don't do it, asshole.

First of all, try not being a dick for a change and see how that works out, but in any case don't

park your van where you usually stick the piece of shit while you're out for one of your "sessions," bra, because

someone like Chon

or, in this case, Chon

might take a baseball bat to it.

Chon smashes out the headlights, the taillights, the windshield, and all the windows (baseball in the Steroid Era), then leans on the horn until Brian and his three buddies madly paddle in like "natives" in one of those old Tarzan movies.

Brian, who is a big freaking dude, comes out of the water first, screaming, "Dude, what the fuck?!"

Chon slides out of the car, drops the bat, and asks, "Are you Brian?"

"Yeah."

Bad answer.

Seriously.

Bad answer.

12

Billy Jack.

You've seen it, you know what I'm talking about, don't even try to pretend that . . .

Okay, fine—

Chon's sweeping inside roundhouse kick breaks Brian's jaw and gives him a concussion before he even hits the dirt unconscious, little pound signs in his eyes like it's a cartoon.

Chon steps over Brian's prone body and drives his fist into the solar plexus of Buddy One, bending him over. Chon grabs the back of Buddy One's head and pulls it down as he drives his knee up into Buddy One's face, then throws him away and moves on to Buddy Two, who lifts his fists up beside his face, which does no good at all as Chon sweep-kicks him in the lower right leg, knocking him off his feet. The back of Buddy Two's head hits the ground hard, but not as hard as the two side-blade kicks that Chon delivers to his face, shattering his nose and rendering him, as they say, unconscious, as Buddy Three . . .

Buddy Three . . .

Ahhh, Buddy Three.

13

Sad Fact of Life—

Smart people sometimes get stupid, but stupid people never get smart.

Never.

Ever.

"You can come *down* the evolutionary ladder," Chon has observed to Ben and O; "you can't climb up."

(Okay, there's always that ya-yo in the mall trying to run up the down escalator, but that just proves the point.)

So—

Buddy Three, having witnessed the utter destruction of his three pals in a matter of single-digit seconds, flees to the inside of the van (where, if he were smart, he would remain) and emerges (see?) with a pistol.

And says to Chon,

"*Now* what are you going to do, asshole?"

The prosecution rests.

God is God.

Darwin is Darwin.

EXT. BEACH PARKING LOT - DAY

An UNCONSCIOUS SURFER with a PISTOL (with the safety on) jammed in his mouth lies slumped out of the sliding door of a van. TWO OTHER SURFERS lie in fetal positions on the ground.

In their wet suits, they look like baby seals in a PETA clip.

CHON roots around in the console of the van and comes up with a plastic-wrapped QUARTER POUND of dope, which he jams into his jacket pocket.

Then he steps over to a fourth surfer, BRIAN, who is on all fours, trying unsuccessfully to get to his feet.

Chon kicks him in the ribs.

Several times.

Then grabs him by the collar and drags him over to the van.

> CHON
> Brian, let the word go forth from this time and place:
> It is not okay to steal our product. It is especially
> not okay to lay hands on our people. And one other
> thing—

Chon stretches Brian's right arm over the edge of the van's bumper, then picks up the baseball bat and

CRACK!

Brian screams.

—next time I'll kill you.

15

Time to go.

O's trying to get out of the fucking house.

Very expensive house in the exclusive gated community of Monarch Bay.

Except Paqu is, like, *on* it.

"What are you going to *do* with your life?" she asks.

"I dunno."

"Are you going back to school?"

"I dunno."

"Are you going to get a job?"

"I dunno."

Check Paqu out—

Blonde hair, perfectly coiffed.

Chiseled (not metaphorically) features.

Makeup *perrrfect.*

A couple of gr worth of clothing on her *perrrfectly* toned, sculpted body that features TTDF.

Tits To Die For.

(Many male ships have been wrecked on *those* cliffs, my friend. Crashed and broken apart. Y chromosomes flailing the crazy-bad whitewater waiting for a jet ski that ain't coming.)

Now she turns her formidable tits and formidabler eyes on O. "Well, you have to do *something.*"

"I dunno," O answers, wilting under the four-point gaze.

"You have thirty days," Paqu says.

"To . . ."

"Get a job or go back to school," Paqu answers, cutting up strawberries and putting the pieces into a blender with two scoops of protein powder.

She's been into "power smoothies" lately.

"Oh God," O answers, "have you been to one of those tough love seminars again?"

"DVD," Paqu answers.

"Did Four put you up to this?" O asks.

She *knows* that Four put her up to it because he doesn't want an "adult child" cluttering up the house he thinks is his just because he nails Paqu in it.

I was in this house before you were, O thinks.

Come to think of it, I was in *Paqu* before you were.

"Nobody put me up to it," Paqu yells over the whirl of the blender. "I have a mind of my own, you know. And if you go back to school, you have to take it seriously."

O had a 1.7 GPA at Saddleback before she gave up the charade entirely and just stopped going.

"What if I don't?" she asks.

"Don't what?"

"Will you shut that fucking thing off?"

Paqu turns off the blender and pours her power smoothie into a glass. O knows that in a half hour she'll go to the gym to work with her personal trainer for two hours, then drink a "meal replacement shake," then go to yoga before coming home for a power nap. Then she'll spend two hours getting herself ready for when Four comes home.

And she thinks *I'm* a useless cunt, O thinks.

"You have a power-smoothie mustache," O tells her.

"If you don't get a job or go back to school," Paqu says, wiping her upper lip with the back of her index finger, "you can't live here anymore. You'll have to find your own place."

"I don't have money for my own place."

"That is not my problem," Paqu says—obviously practiced from the DVD.

But they both know that it is.

Paqu's problem, that is.

She'll forget about it, O thinks, cognizant of Paqu's Bipolar Approach To Parenting.

Paqu has wide swings between

Absent Neglectful Mother and

Smothering Controlling Mother

So, like, Paqu will take off on—

—a European vacation

Rehab

Spiritual Retreat or just

Another Affair

And totally forget about O.

Then she'll come back, feel guilty, and go in the

Complete Other Direction

Micromanaging O's life down to the tiniest details of clothing, friends, education (or lack thereof), career (see "education"), and protein-carbohydrate balance, and was *literally* up her ass during a truly unfortunate "colonic" phase.

It's Either/Or

There is no middle ground, and it has been

Ever thus.

The worst is when Paqu comes back from rehab or a spiritual retreat. Having fixed herself, she sets out to fix O.

"I'm not broken," O argued one time.

"Oh, darling," Paqu answered, "we're *all* broken."

Indeed, O thought, Paqu does spend a lot of time in the body shop. Anyhoo, after a long discussion about O's denial regarding her "brokenness" it was decided that self-realization was a river that simply couldn't be pushed and that O would have to remain in the eddy of her own delusion. Which was just fine with O, although she was pretty sure that Delusional Eddy was a guy Paqu briefly dated.

But now this thirty-day thing.

O heads for the door.

"Where are you going?"

"To join the Peace Corps," O answers.

Or go see Chon.

Which is the

Exact opposite.

16

Actually it was the fact that O had no freaking idea what she was going to do with her life that led Ben and Chon into the marijuana business two years ago because it engendered a discussion of "vocation," and wordsmith Chon observed that "vocation" is merely one vowel removed from "vacation" yet could be considered an antonym.

That is—

vocation (n., from the Latin verb "to call"): an occupation to which a person is specially drawn or for which he or she is suited, trained, or qualified

vacation (n.): freedom from occupation

"But," Ben asked, "do you *want* freedom from something to which you're especially drawn? Probably not."

So, on his next deployment, Chon came home with—

A Purple Heart

A new set of nightmares and—

17

A seed.

The White Widow.

A particularly fine, THC-laden breed of cannabis.

When the seed of an idea meets the actual, physical seed it is

Seminal.

seminal (adj.)

1. Pertaining to, containing, or consisting of semen (uhhhh, no)
2. Botany: of or pertaining to seed (obviously)
3. Having possibilities of future development (oh, *hell* yes)
4. Highly original and influencing the development of future events (well, let's hope so)

Ben took this seminal seed and, actualizing the potential for future development, developed the hell out of it in highly original ways that would influence future events.

Ben started to breed a new plant.

First he separated the male plants from the female plants.

"Awww," O said, "that's kind of sad."

"We don't want accidental fertilization."

"Couldn't we just put tiny little condoms on the male plants?" O asked.

Ben told her that they couldn't.

O asked, "How can you tell the male from the female plants?"

"The stamens look like balls," Ben said.

"Well, there you go."

"We choose a male plant," Ben explained, "take its pollen, and pollinate the female plant."

"I might need a few minutes to myself here," O said.

O found it highly amusing that Ben created an Isle of Lesbos—a virtual Women's Prison Movie—marijuana farm. She also took a certain neo-feminist pride that the most powerful, juicy, THC-laden buds came from the females.

Anyway, Ben used the seed produced by the pollinated female to create what is known in genetics as the F1 hybrid. Then he grew that plant, took its seed, and bred it back with the parent plant.

"With the *parent*?" O asked.

"Yup."

"*Iiiiiccck*," O answered. "That's, like, *incest*."

"Not *like*. Is."

"Cue the banjo."

She came to refer to Ben's marijuana crop as "L.A."

Not "Los Angeles."

"Lesbian Appalachia."

Ben kept inbreeding like a European royal family, generation after generation, until he produced not a Tea Party member or a drooling pink-eyed idiot, but a female plant whose fecund buds veritably dripped (okay, not really) with THC.

Tetrahydrocannabinol.

Aka delta-9-tetrahydrocannabinol.

Aka dronabinol.

The main psychoactive substance in marijuana.

(For the blazers out there—it's why you're too high right now to understand "psychoactive substance.")

Ben the Mad Botanist didn't produce a Porsche, he produced a Lamborghini.

Not a Rolex but a Patek.

If Ben's blend were a horse, it would be Secretariat.

A mountain, Everest.

Michael Jordan.

Tiger Woods

(before).

The max.

The ult.

Cherry Garcia.

Hydroponic cannabis.

"Hydro," of course, means water, and there are many advantages to growing cannabis in water instead of in soil.

(For those of you paying close attention—it's tetra-*hydro*-cannabinol, remember?)

You get higher, faster yields because hydroponic cultivation bypasses the root web. A crop is usually ready in twelve weeks—four harvests a year—and you control your own "sunshine" and "weather." Therefore, you can rotate your cultivation from grow house to grow house so as to have a continuous yield.

You don't have soil-borne pests and parasites. You don't have to worry that you're going to wake up one morning and find that three months of work is being eaten or dying of a communicable disease. Ergo, you're not going to spray your plants with toxic pesticides and other shit.

Because it's more automated, hydroponic cultivation requires less labor. The greater automation requires a higher start-up cost, but it can be amortized over several years, and the higher yield more than makes up for the initial outlay.

Ben also had a philosophical reason for going hydro.

"Human beings are mostly water," he told Chon and O. "So it's like the hydro is going home."

"That's sweet," O said.

"Or stupid," Chon added.

In any case, it took a lot more than just water to get the business started.

It took money, and a lot of it.

Start-up costs.

They already had the big-ticket item—the primo plant—so then it was a matter of hardware.

The biggest item was a house.

The selection of which was tricky, because it's not so much the house, it's what they had to put *in* the house. Marijuana, yes, thank you—but to grow the marijuana required, among other things—

Grow lamps.

Metal halide for the vegetative stage.

(O assured them *she* could achieve a vegetative state *without* a grow lamp, although one of those sun reflectors was always nice.)

High-pressure sodium for the flowering phase.

Each lamp took a thousand-watt bulb.

Each bulb could light fifteen to twenty plants.

During the vegetative stage those lamps were going to be on sixteen to eighteen hours a day, so they were going to produce, in addition to light, a hell of a lot of heat, which, unless you're intending to do Bikram yoga in there, is a problem.

("I tried Bikram yoga," O told the boys.

"And?"

"I didn't like it."

"Because?"

"They *yelled* at me," she said. "If I wanted to get yelled at in high humidity, I'd just leave the shower on and wait for Paqu to show up.")

You can't have that kind of heat in a grow room because

(a) People have to work in there and

(b) It's bad for the plants.

Primo marijuana grows best in a controlled temperature of 75°F, so what they needed in addition to—in fact, *because* of—all those lamps was

Air-conditioning.

Every one of those lamps required 2,800 BTUs (British Thermal Units) of cooling, and a fan to circulate the cooled air.

So a fifty-light grow room—that's one thousand plants—needed 148,000 BTUs. Add to that the power needed to run the lamps and the fans, and you're talking 80 kilowatts of power.

Your average residential living room is wired to handle a single thousand-watt bulb.

So—they had to not only rewire the house, they had to find more power and do it

off the grid

Because the utility companies in addition to being rapacious, conscienceless sociopaths, are also . . .

Snitches.

If they notice an electric bill that is, say, twenty times what a normal house would use, they inform the police.

Oh, they'll take the money (natch), but they'll also drop a dime.

(The *only* dime to slip through their grasping grubby greedy fingers.)

Anyway, the grow house would need more power and would need that power secretly, so there were two ways to get it.

Steal it—which is a matter of drilling little holes in the meter (Google it), but the Gambino family is safer to steal from than the electric company, and Ben had a moral objection to theft.

("You can't steal from thieves," Chon argued.

"They are responsible for their karma," Ben countered, "I for mine."

"Can we get ice cream?" O asked.)

So the alternative was a generator.

This was not cheap—the generator needed to power a thousand-plant grow room cost between $10K and $20K and it
MADE NOISE
A lot of freaking noise
It practically screamed "Hey, there's a grow house in here! Hey! HEY!!!!"
So if they put that generator in the backyard, the neighbors were going to come over—and not to invite them to a cookout. They might have been able to assuage one or two of them with some homegrown product, but it was a drop-dead guarantee that one of the neighbors was going to make the call, not to mention some black-and-white happening to cruise by and hearing that thing rumbling "probable cause."

No, they had to put that generator down in the basement, and how many basements were there in Southern California?
Some.
Not many.
Ben and Chon went house hunting.

22

For a rental, not a purchase.
(Apologies to Tom Waits.)
For one thing, houses in SoCal—with or without basements—are expensive.
But the other thing
the other thing, the other *thing* is
under the tangled bowl of day-old schizophrenic spaghetti that

is the drug laws, if the cops bust your grow house and you own it, they can confiscate that $600,000 investment. So not only do you lose your dope and your freedom, you lose your down payment and every mortgage payment you've already made, and you still owe the bank the balance of the loan.

But if you rent the house and the landlord can reasonably claim he didn't know you were using it to cultivate a felony, he gets to keep his property and you go to jail free of *that* karma, anyway.

So Ben and Chon went looking to rent a house that

Had a basement

Wasn't too close to neighbors

Wasn't anywhere near a school or a playground (maximum sentencing under the guidelines)

Or a police station

Could be rewired

And where the landlord wouldn't be coming around every twenty-eight minutes

Or ever.

This narrowed down the possibilities.

You can't just put an ad in the paper stating your requirements, because the police will be happy to rent to you—they have some of these houses in stock—

You ain't gonna find it on Craigslist

(Well, not *that* Craigslist—see below.)

You need

A Realtor.

23

Fortunately, this was Orange County.

(Before the real estate market flopped like a European soccer player.)

Back in those halcyon "finance and flip" days, you could walk into any upscale OC hotel (the Ritz, St. Regis, or Montage) and drop something—anything—in the lobby—

Chances are, whoever picked it up would have been a real estate agent.

Or you could drive up (or down, didn't matter) the PCH and rear-end your ride into any BMW, Mercedes, Lexus, Audi, Porsche, Land Rover, Land Cruiser—actually any vehicle not a Mexican gardening truck. Just prison-shower that ride and the odds were that the person who got out of the other vehicle would have handed you a business card before the insurance information.

Everybody in the OC had a real estate license.

Everybody.

Every OC trophy wife who required a "career" for her self-esteem got a license. Every surf bum who needed a source of income (i.e., all of them) got a license. Dogs, cats, *gerbils* had real estate licenses.

If they weren't actually selling property, they were financing the mortgage, doing the title or the assessment, consulting on getting the property ready to show.

Others were involved in "creative financing," aka "fraud."

The entire economy then was based on swapping real estate around, boosting the price with every pass. Everyone was living off the ginormous Ponzi scheme that was the real estate market in those days, hoping they wouldn't get caught with the hot potato in their hands when the whistle blew.

People were using trash financing to buy three, four, five houses that they hoped to flip, so people had houses they needed to rent and there were real estate agents who specialized in rentals.

So finding a Realtor was no problem.

Finding the right Realtor was.

Because, generally speaking, Realtors hate dope growers.

24

You see, most dope growers don't have Ben's social conscience.

They trash a property out.

They rip it open and put in cheap, dangerous wiring that often sets the place on fire. Their power needs cause neighborhood brownouts. They tape plastic sheets over the windows to hide their nefarious activities. They have people coming and going all hours of the day and night. Their generators make noise; their dope smells. They not only take the value of a particular property down, they lower the value of the whole neighborhood.

They're dirtbags.

Rental Realtors and property managers properly shun them.

So Ben and Chon had to find one who was blissfully unaware.

The OC wife category was problematic because Chon had slept with probably half of them.

This is what Chon did between deployments—he read books, played volleyball, and fucked trophy wives, many of them (of course) real estate agents.

So he, Ben, and O went through the listings of Realtors.

"Mary Ingram," Ben read.

"Chonned," O said.

"Susan Janakowski."

"Chonned."

"Terri Madison."

Ben and O looked at Chon.

"You don't know?" Ben asked.

"I'm thinking."

"My *man*," O said.

They gave up on the OC wives and moved on to the surfer category.

"Here's our boy," Ben said.

He pointed to an ad for Craig Vetter.

"Is he a surfer?" Chon asked.

"Look at him."

Sun-bleached blond hair, deep tan, wide shoulders, vaguely vacant look in the eyes.

"He's been hit in the head a few times," O concluded.

They called him.

25

Craig assumed that they were a respectable gay couple.

A little younger than the usual Laguna Beach life partners, but Craig was your basic "whatever floats your boat, dude" dude.

Dude.

Duuuuuude.

"We need a basement," Ben told him.

"A basement."

"A basement," Chon affirmed.

Craig took a look at Chon and figured this was a dungeon sort of thing.

"Soundproof?" he asked.

"That would be good," Ben said.

Whatever floats your boat, dude.

Craig showed them five houses with basements. The gay guys rejected all of them—the neighbors were too close, the living room too small, there was a school nearby.

At this last thing, Craig got suspicious. "You guys aren't on one of those lists, are you?"

"What lists?" Ben asked.

"You know," Craig said. "Sex offender lists."

He'd hauled these two guys all over Laguna, Dana Point, Mission Viejo, and Laguna Niguel and they couldn't find a place they liked. He almost didn't care if he lost them now. Besides, the last thing he needed was neighbors picketing one of his properties.

"No," Ben said.

"We just hate kids," Chon added helpfully.

"You don't have something more rural, do you?" Ben asked.

"Rural?" Craig asked. Like farms and shit?

"Like maybe out in the East County," Ben suggested. "Modjeska Canyon?"

"Modjeska Canyon?" Craig repeated.

The lightbulb came on.

"You guys are looking for a *grow house*."

They smoked up on the ride to Modjeska Canyon.

Ben and Chon of course would not confirm that they were looking for a grow house, but now they and Craig had an understanding.

He showed them a fixer-upper on a cul-de-sac. Neighbors separated on each side by small strips of trees and brush. No sight lines. Single level with a basement. Below-market rent because the place was kind of a mess.

"Will the landlord be coming around?" Ben asked.

"Not for five to ten," Craig answered.

"Drugs?" Ben asked.

He didn't want to start his operation in a second-generation drug house that the cops already knew about.

Come *on*, Craig.

"He robbed a bank," Craig answered.

"Okay."

"In Arkansas."

Perfecto.

There was a lot to do to get the house ready.

Especially if you were Ben.

"*Solar panels?*" Chon asked.

"Do you know how much energy we're going to be using?" Ben

asked. Solar energy would supplement the generator and therefore use less natural gas.

"Do you know how much solar panels cost?" Chon countered.

"Do you?"

"No."

"Good."

Because they cost a lot.

Worth it to Ben—convictions are easy if they're cheap. Also, Ben wasn't going to trash out the house or the neighborhood.

On this topic, Ben and Chon had your Vulcan Mind Meld.

Ben had ethical concerns, Chon had security concerns, but they came to the same conclusion—do not make the grow house look like a grow house.

Chon did his due diligence as to what cops look for:

Condensation on the windows, or—

—the windows covered with black plastic or newspaper.

Sounds of an electric hum or constant fans.

Bright interior lights left on for long hours.

Local power failures.

(You cause a brownout while the wife next door is TiVo-ing *The Bachelorette,* she's going to turn your ass in.

"I would," O affirmed.)

Smell—a thousand marijuana plants smell like a Bard College dorm on a Friday night.

Residents in the home only occasionally.

People coming in and out at odd hours and staying only a few minutes.

"This is all handle-able," Ben said.

First they put in the solar panels to supplement the energy. Then they soundproofed the walls in the basement to cover the noise from the generator.

Then they went CGE. This came from Ben's research and it meant

Closed Growing Environment.

"I like the 'Closed' part," Chon said.

Indeed.

What CGE does is basically control the flow of air in and out of the grow room. It ain't cheap—they had to install aluminum and sheet metal vent pipes connected to a five-ton air-conditioning system fitted to forty-gallon coconut carbon charcoal filters.

"So the neighborhood is going to smell like coconuts?" O asked.

"It won't smell like anything," Ben said.

O was a little disappointed. She thought it would be fun to have a neighborhood that smelled like suntan lotion and drinks with umbrellas in them.

It's an article of faith with Ben that problems generate solutions, which generate more problems, which generate more solutions, and he labels this endless cycle "progress."

In this case, the five-ton AC unit solved the cooling and odor problem, but created another.

AC units are cooled by either air or water, and a lot of it.

If it's the former, it's pulling the air out of . . .

. . . well, the air . . .

and it makes a lot of noise.

If it's water, the water bill goes way up and you have the same utility-company-as-snitch problem.

The boys pondered this.

"A swimming pool," O suggested. "Put in one of those above-ground pools."

Genius.

A swimming pool is full of . . .

. . . water . . .

justifies the water bill, and besides . . .

"We could collect the condensation, pump it back into the pool, and recycle," added Ben.

Of course.

"Plus we could go swimming," O said.

In addition to the house renovation—

—and they hadn't even gotten to the rewiring—

they had to buy—

—metal halide lamps, high-pressure sodium lamps, thousand-watt bulbs, sixteen-inch oscillating fans, grow trays, reservoir trays for the nutrient mixture, the nutrient mixture, hundreds of feet of piping and tubing, pumps, timers for the pumps—

"And pool toys," O said. "Can't have a pool without toys."

They hadn't sold an eighth yet and they were already looking at a $70,000 outlay for start-up costs.

That was for one house, but they did it. Took Ben's savings, Chon's combat-pay bonuses, and then hit the volleyball courts in search of suckers to hustle. Fortunately, P. T. Barnum was right, and they raised the money in a few months of game, set, and match.

Grew primo product and reinvested the small profit into another house, then another and another, making Craig Vetter a very happy surfing Realtor.

Now they have five grow houses and are working on a sixth.

It costs money.

Which is why Chon doesn't let people rip them off.

Much less lay a violent hand on their people.

28

Now Chon, consumed with self-loathing because he feels a little winded after trashing four guys, gets back in the Mustang and drives home.

Grabs the bat, gets out of his car, and runs smack into

His father.

It happens every once in a while. Laguna is a small town and you run into people.

People you want to.

People you don't.

Chon's dad falls into the latter category, and the feeling is mutual. There's a seminal connection (see above), but that's about it. Big John was 404 for a lot of Chon's childhood, and when he wasn't Chon wished he was.

Ben and O both know that Chon's father is a subject Not To Be Discussed.

Ever.

They're aware, of course, that "Big John" was once a big-time Laguna dope dealer, a member of the storied "Association," that he went to prison and now is some kind of roofing contractor, but that's about it.

Big John looks startled to see his son.

And not very happy.

It's . . .

. . . awkward.

Big John, heavy shoulders, brown hair receding, a little jowly now, breaks the silence first.

"Hey."

"Hey."

"How's it going?"

"Okay. You?"

"Okay."

Big John looks at the bat, smirks, and asks, "You playing soft-ball now or something?"

"Hardball."

That's it. They stand there looking at each other for a second, then Big John says, "Well, okay . . ."

And walks away.

29

Duane Crowe finds a seat at the bar at T.G.I. Friday's (Thank God It's Friday's) and takes it.

T.G.I. Friday's is practically a club for fortysomething divorced guys. You get a burger, a beer, I don't know, some nachos, and kill time trying to find a fortysomething divorced woman who's as lonely and horny as you are. Which is a dubious proposition to begin with.

It ain't a great life, but it's the one he's got.

He's scoping the place out for possibilities when he sees Boland squeeze his way into the crowded bar. "Squeeze," because Bill Boland is built like a refrigerator and is one of the reasons that 24 Hour Fitness is open twenty-four hours.

Boland takes the stool next to Crowe and says, "Nice T-shirt. 'Old Guys Rule.' "

"My niece gave it to me for my birthday," Crowe says. "You get Hennessy straightened out?"

"He won't be waltzing through TSA anytime soon," Boland says. "They put a pin in his arm. Guy did a number on him."

They had worked dumbass Brian and his crew into ripping off one of Leonard's dealers to see what he'd do.

Now they knew.

Something else they know: before they make another move on Leonard, the other guy has to go.

"You get an ID?" Crowe asks.

"Working on it," Boland says. "Word is he's some kind of Special Forces stud. SEALs or Green Berets or something."

"Green Berets? They still got them?"

"I think."

The other reason they meet in T.G.I. Friday's is because it's crowded and loud. Television up high, people yapping—you get a mike on this place, all you're going to pick up is noise. And if someone's wearing a wire it's more likely to get some guy lying to a chick about his job than something a grand jury is going to get geeked about.

"What do the Powers That Be say?" Boland asks.

"What they always say," Crowe answers. " 'Deal with it.' "

Deal with it and send us our fucking money. The Powers That Be don't eat in franchises, they own them.

"This Leonard kid?" Crowe says. "He's a piece of work—a real cocky asshole. Get on him, see if he slips on the banana peel."

Boland looks at the menu. "You had the burgers here?"

Crowe surveys the line of divorcées at the bar.

"I've had everything here."

30

When Chon gets to his apartment, O is there.

She has a key because she looks after the place when he's gone.

Waters the single plant.

(No, not *that* kind of plant. Some innocuous plant, like a ficus or something.)

"I hope it's okay I let myself in," O says.

"Sure."

She gives him this weird, un-O-like vulnerable look. "Chon?"

"O?"

"Don't you think I'm sort of . . . Bambi-esque?"

31

"O," Chon says, buying time. They're pals, buddies. "We've known each other since we were kids."

"Maybe that will make it better," O says. "And I'm nineteen now."

Not a kid anymore.

"O—"

"Look, if you think I'm, like, hideous or something—"

"It's not that," Chon says. O is the opposite of hideous—whatever that is. "I think you're beautiful."

He means it.

"And you love me," she says.

He nods.

"And I love you, so . . ."

He shakes his head, smiles stupidly. "O . . . I don't know . . ."

"Chon," she says, "you're going away . . . and I don't know if . . . and it's my fault—"

"No, it isn't."

32

O's first conscious memory was of a boy pissing on marigolds.

"Ophelia" then—it would be years before she dropped the "phelia" and became just "O"—sat in the playground of the little school and watched the older boy water the plants.

The school in Laguna Canyon was one of those neo-one-room schoolhouses—kindergarten through eighth grade—that operated under the theory that children learn best when not arbitrarily separated into rigid grade groups but allowed to find their own levels among kids of various ages.

This was during one of Paqu's progressive phases, so every day she hauled her four-year-old daughter from their seven-digit home in gated Emerald Bay to the funkier environs of the canyon. The house and the money for the private school came from her settlement with O's father, who divorced her in the sixth month of her pregnancy.

Even the teachers at the school thought that Ophelia was too young to start kindergarten.

"She's precocious," her mother answered.

"But still four," the principal said.

"She's an old soul," the mother countered. Her psychic had told her that her daughter had had many previous incarnations and that her astral age wasn't four, but four *thousand*, which made her older than her mother by a good seven hundred years. "In very real ways, I'm actually *her* daughter."

The principal decided that Ophelia would probably benefit from getting out of the house for a few hours a day, and besides, the little girl was such a darling, already so beautiful, and so smart.

"I think we made a huge mistake sending you to that school," Paqu would say years later when O was flunking virtually every class at Laguna High.

By that time, Paqu was in one of her conservative phases. And, by that time, Ophelia had changed her name to O and had started calling her mother Paqu.

But that was all later, and right then O was watching the boy water the flowers. At first she thought it was just like the gardener at home, but then she observed that the boy wasn't holding a hose, but something else; then she heard a short, sharp shriek and a teacher ran over and grabbed the boy.

"John," the teacher said. "Our private parts are *what*?"

John didn't answer.

"*Private*," the teacher answered for him. "Now zip up your jeans and go play."

"I was just watering the flowers," John said.

O thought that was very fun, that this magical boy could water the plants all by himself.

"What's that boy's name?" she asked when the teacher came over to her.

"That's John."

"Chon," O mispronounced, and then got up to go look for the magical boy who, penis safely returned to his jeans, had wandered around toward the back fence searching for an escape route.

"Chon! Chon! Chon!" O hollered, wandering around in search of him. "Chon, play with me!"

The other kids quickly picked up the chant.

"Chon! Chon! Chon!"

The name stuck.

O became his shadow, followed him around like a baby duckling, a real pest, but it wasn't long before Chon learned to put up with her, to become her protector, even to like her a little. Chon wasn't particularly social, he didn't "play well with others," preferred to be alone, so the teachers were glad to see him make a connection.

O adored him.

The problem was that he disappeared from time to time—sometimes for a day, sometimes for a week—and then he'd be back at school again.

"Where you been, Chon?" she'd ask him.

Chon would make up fantastic stories for her:

He was out fishing and had been captured by pirates; elves who lived in the canyon took him for a trip to their secret world; aliens from another galaxy flew him into outer space and back again. Chon took the girl to China, to Africa, to Mars and the Mountains of the Moon, and he was her magic boy.

Then, one day, he disappeared for good.

When she realized that he wasn't coming back, O cried all night.

Her mother consoled her with the words "Men don't stay."

O already knew that.

33

"So you're saying, what?" she asks Chon now. "No?"

"No, I'm saying not now."

"What a totally wussy answer," she says.

"I'm a total wuss."

She backs off.

"Okay," she says, "you missed your chance, Chonny boy. That was it."

Chon smiles. "Got it."

34

It's funny Chon doesn't talk much, because he loves words and word origins.

He even knows the etymology of the word "etymology."

(Google it.)

But O gets that you protect what you love and hold it close. Defending his reticence one day, Chon posited a question to them—

"Words," he said, "are:

(a) A means of communication

(b) A means of *mis*communication

(c) Tools

(d) Weapons

(e) All of the above."

Ben answered (a), O answered (d)
>   (she is her mother's daughter),
Chon answered

(f) It doesn't matter.

Because there are things he will not talk about. Things he has seen, things he has done in IraqandAfghanistan. Things you don't burden other people with, memories that you try to prevent from overwhelming your brain and your nervous system, but that you can still feel on your skin. Movies that your mind privately screens on the inside of your eyelids.

These are things that you do not put into words.

They are ineffable.

Therefore, to fill the sad silence—

—underscored by O's chant of I hate this trip I hate this trip I hate this trip—

—on the ride to John Wayne–Orange County Airport (you cannot make this shit up) Chon goes neo–Spiro Agnew on the subject of neo-hippies.

35

Chon thinks that neo-hippies are grungy, pasty-faced-from-vegan-diets ("Eat a fucking cheeseburger, Casper"), patchouli-oil-stinking, Birkenstock-wearing, clogging up sidewalks playing hacky sack (why don't they save syllables and just *call* it a dirtbag), leaning their crappy single-gear bicycles against the doors of Starbucks, where they order Tazo green tea and borrow other people's laptops to check their e-mail, sitting there for hours and never leave a freaking tip, doing semi-naked yoga in parks so other people have to look at their pale, emaciated bodies, *parasites*.

Chon wishes Southern California would secede from the rest of the state so it could pass a law sending any white guy with dread-locks to a concentration camp.

"Where would the camp be?" Ben asks him.

This is known as "egging him on."

"I don't know," Chon mutters, still pissed. "Somewhere off the fifteen."

The problem (okay, *one* problem) with building concentra-tion camps in Southern California, Ben thinks, is that contractors would trip all over each other trying to rig the barbed-wire bid. Also that you have a governor whose accent is, well . . .

. . . uhhhh . . .

"Of course," Chon mumbles, "I suppose liberals would block it."

Chon also hates liberals.

The only liberal he doesn't hate is Ben.

(This is known as the Ben Exemption.)

Liberals, Chon will opine when he's on a rant—and he's on one now—

—are people who love their enemies more than their friends, prefer anyone else's culture to their own, are guilty of success but unashamed of failure, despise profit and punish achievement.

The men are dickless, sackless, self-castrated eunuchs cowed into shame of their own masculinity by joyless, anger-filled shrews consumed with bitter envy at the material possessions, not to men-tion multiple orgasms, of their conservative sisters—

("You should have stopped him buying *The Fountainhead*," Ben tells O.

"Who knew he was in the fiction section?")

Liberals took a pretty decent country and

Fucked It Up
to the point where
kids can't read *Huckleberry Finn* or play dodgeball—

—dodgeball, that perfectly Darwinian game meant to ensure the survival of the fittest because the others are too perpetually concussed to propagate—

—and any dune surfer with a grudge feels he can fly planes into our buildings without fear of the Big One being dropped on Mecca like it should have been five seconds after the towers came down—

(Nancy Reagan would have pressed her husband's finger on the button for him and turned the Saudi peninsula into the glass factory it deserves to be)

—except that liberals want to be *loved*.

Ben disagrees—

The liberals in the California State Legislature would *not* block a bill creating concentration camps as long as they got campaign contributions from the concrete manufacturers, the drivers hauling the inmates through the gates were unionized, and their trucks had the requisite minimum MPG standards and used the commuter lanes.

Ben knows California would be zapping guys at the pace of the Texas Versus Florida Bush Brothers Sibling Rivalry if the electric chair were solar powered.

"They don't use Sparky anymore," Chon tells him. "It's lethal injection."

Right.

Narcotics are illegal, so we use them to execute people.

For crimes.

36

Anyway, this is all well and good
verbal fun and games
but what matters isn't what Ben and Chon say to each other, it's
what they don't.

Chon doesn't tell Ben about Sam Casey getting ripped off and
beaten up, and his response to said provocation, because Ben
wouldn't approve and he'd get all bummed out about the necessity of force in a world that's supposed to be about love and peace,
blah blah.

Ben doesn't tell Chon about the weird interaction with OGR
because, well, it's just weird and random and probably nothing,
and besides, what's Chon supposed to do about it? He's on his way
to the Stan, he has enough to worry about (like staying alive), so
Ben doesn't want to bother him.

And so they miss this critical junction, this intersection of
events, this opportunity to put one and one together and get

One.

One same problem.

They're not stupid, they would have put it together, but "would
have" is just another way of saying

"didn't."

37

They walk Chon as far as the security line.

Where O hugs him and won't let go.

"I love you I love you I love you I love you I love you," she says, unable to stop the tears.

"I love you, too."

Ben pries her off, hugs Chon himself, and says, "Don't be a hero, bro."

As if, Ben thinks.

Chon's on his third deployment with a fucking SEAL team. He is a fucking hero and he can't be anything but.

Always has, always will.

"I'll be cowering at the bottom of the deepest foxhole," Chon says.

Yeah.

They watch him go through the line.

38

Boland gets on the phone.

"Good news," he says. "Leonard is putting the hard case on an airplane. Looks like he's deploying."

"You sure it's him?"

"He meets Hennessy's description of the guy who trashed him," Boland answers.

That is good news, Crowe thinks.

Very good news.

Well, not for Leonard.

39

Ben doesn't see the car that follows him out of John Wayne–Orange County Airport and stays behind him all the way to Laguna.

Why should he?

That isn't his world, he's bummed about Chon leaving, and then O drops this bombshell:

"I threw myself at him."

"Who?"

"Chon."

Boom.

He's not jealous—jealousy isn't in Ben's makeup—but Chon and O?

It's huge.

But Ben is cool. Ben is always cool. "And?"

"I bounced off."

The Wall of Chon.

"Oh."

"Rejected. Spurned. *Un*requited."

"You never hear about 'requited love,' " Ben says, because he doesn't know what else to say.

"*I* don't, anyway."

"Pouting doesn't look good on you."

"Really?" O says. "Because I thought it did."

A few seconds later she says, "I *hate* this *fucking* war."

She was fourteen, watching TV that morning, stalling going to school when she saw what she thought was cheesy CGI come across the screen.

An airliner. A building.

It didn't seem real and still doesn't.

But Chon was already in the service by then.

A fact for which she blames herself.

Ben knows what she's thinking.

"Don't," he says.

"Can't help it."

She can't because she doesn't know

It isn't her fault

It goes back

Generations.

Laguna Beach, California
1967

Said I'm going down to Yasgur's farm,
Going to join in a rock-and-roll band . . .

—JONI MITCHELL, "WOODSTOCK"

40

John McAlister rolls his skateboard down Ocean Avenue, then puts the board under his arm and walks along Main Beach up to the Taco Bell, because sometimes guys get their food, then go into the men's room and leave their tacos on the table.

The tacos and Johnny are both gone when they come out.

Dig young Johnny Mac.

Tall for his fourteen years, wide shoulders, long brown hair that looks like it was cut with hedge clippers. Your classic grem— T-shirt and board shorts, huaraches, shell necklace.

When he makes it up to Taco Bell there's a crowd standing around.

Big guy with long blond hair is buying food for everybody, handing out tacos and those little plastic packets of hot sauce to a bunch of surfers, hippies, homeless drug casualties, runaways, and those skinny girls with headbands and long straight hair who all look alike to John.

The guy looks like some kind of SoCal surfer version of a sea god. John wouldn't know Neptune or Poseidon from Scooby-Doo, but he recognizes the look of local royalty—the deep tan, the sun-bleached hair, the ropy muscles of a guy who can spend all day every day surfing and who has money anyway.

Not a surf bum, a surf god.

Now this god looks down on him with a friendly smile and warm blue eyes and asks, "You want a taco?"

"I don't have any money," John answers.

"You don't need money," the guy answers, his face breaking into a grin. "*I* have money."

"Okay," John says.

He's hungry.

Guy hands him two tacos and a packet of hot sauce.

"Thanks," John says.

"I'm Doc."

John doesn't say anything.

"You have a name?" Doc asks.

"John."

"Hi, John," Doc says. "Peace."

Then Doc moves along, handing out tacos like fishes and loaves. Like Jesus, except Jesus walked on water and Doc rides on it.

John takes his tacos before Doc changes his mind or anyone there makes him as the kid who filches food off tables, goes out into the parking lot, and sits down at the curb beside a girl who looks like she's nineteen or twenty.

She's carefully picking the beef out of her taco and laying it on the curb.

"The cow is sacred to the Hindus," she says to John.

"Are you a Hindu?" John asks.

He doesn't know what a Hindu is.

"No," the girl says, like his question makes no sense. Then she adds, "My name is Starshine."

No it isn't, John thinks. He's talked with plenty of hippie runaways before—Laguna is crawling with them—and they always call themselves Starshine or Moonbeam or Rainbow, and they're always really Rebecca or Karen or Susan.

Maybe a Holly, but that's about as crazy as it gets.

Hippie runaway girls annoy the shit out of John.

They all think they're Joni Mitchell, and he hates Joni Mitchell. John listens to the Stones, the Who, the Moody Blues.

Now he just wants to finish his tacos and get out of there.

Then Starshine says, "After you finish eating? I'd like to suck you off."

John doesn't go home.

Ever.

41

Ka

Boom.

Stan's head explodes.

It's like the sun rises in his skull and the warmth of the rays spreads to the smile on his face.

He looks at Diane and says, "Holy shit."

She knows—the blotter acid just melted on her tongue, too.

Not holy shit, holy *communion.*

Across the PCH, Taco Jesus is holding his daily service. Beyond that, the ocean rises in a blue so blue it outblues all other blues in this universe of blues.

"Look at the blue," she says to Stan.

Stan turns to look.

And starts to cry

it's so

bluetiful.

Stan and Diane

("This is a little ditty about Stan and Diane

Two American kids growing up in . . .")

Ah, fuck it)

Stan isn't your tall, stringy hippie—he's your shorter, plumper, Hostess Cupcakes and Twinkies hippie with a fat nose, Jewfro, full black beard, and beatific smile. Diane does have the skinny thing going—plus long, straight black hair that frizzes in the humidity, hips that hint at the earth-mother thing, and breasts that are at least partially responsible for Stan's beatific smile.

Now, cranked out of their minds, they stand on the porch of the decrepit building they want to turn into a bookstore. Recent immigrants from Haight-Ashbury, they knew that the scene was disintegrating up there so they're trying to replicate it down here.

Don't hate them—they never had a motherfucking chance.

East Coast leftie parents ("The Rosenbergs were innocent"), socialist summer camps ("The Rosenbergs were innocent"), Berkeley in the early sixties, Free Speech Movement, Stop the War, Ronald Reagan ("The Rosenbergs did it") Is the Devil, Haight-Ashbury, Summer of Love, they got married in a field on a farm in the Berkshires with garlands of flowers in their hair and some dipshit playing the sitar and they are

perfect products of their times

Baby Boomers

Hippies.

who came to Laguna to create a little utopia in the cheap rents of the canyon and spread the good word about love and peace by building a bookstore that will sell, in addition to *The Tibetan Book of the Dead, The Anarchist Cookbook,* and *On the Road,*

—incense, sandals, psychedelic posters, rock albums, tie-dyed T-shirts, macramé bracelets (again, try not to hate them), all that happy shit—

—and distribute acid to the turned-on.

There is a flaw in their plan.

Money.

More accurately, the lack thereof.

It takes money to buy even a shitty building, money to renovate it into even a hippie bookstore, and they ain't got none.

Which is the problem with socialism.

No capital.

Enter Taco Jesus, surfing in as a savior like a cowboy on his horse to . . .

Again, fuck it. The surfer/cowboy analogy, the end of the American West at the edge of the Pacific, Manifest Destiny reversing itself with the incoming tide—who gives a shit?

Suffice it to say that the Surfers met the Hippies in Laguna Beach.

It had to happen.

The difference between a Surfer and a Hippie?

A board.

They're the same cat, basically. The surfer was the original hippie; in fact, he was the original beatnik. Years before Jack and Dean hit the road searching for dharma, the surfer was cruising the PCH looking for a good wave.

Same thing.

But we're not going to get into all that. We could, we could, we're sorely tempted, but we have a story to tell, and the story is—

Stan, Diane, and the tribe are trying to build their store a block from one of the best breaks on the OC Coast—

—Brooks Street—

where Taco Jesus, aka "Doc," surfs and distributes free food to any and all

(socialism)

so Stan asks Diane, "Where does Taco Jesus get the money to be Taco Jesus?"

"Trust fund?"

"He doesn't look like the trust fund type."

In this Diane is intuitive, because Raymond "Doc" Halliday grew up in a blue-collar bungalow in Fontana and did two stretches in juvie for, respectively, burglary and assault. Ray Sr.—a roofer—left his son with certain skills with a hammer, but money?

No.

Eventually Doc migrated down to the south coast, where he discovered surfing and marijuana and also discovered that you could make enough money to support the former by selling the latter.

Now Stan and Diane watch him hand out tacos and decide to ask him where the bread for the loaves comes from. Crossing the PCH, which under the influence of blotter acid has become a river and its cars fish, they approach Doc.

"You want a taco?" Doc asks.

"You want some acid?" Diane replies.

Cue the *2001* theme.

This is a *moment*.

The seminal mind-fuck that gives birth to

the group that will become known as

The Association.

(And then along came Mary.)

42

Here's how it happens—

Doc gives Stan and Diane tacos.

Stan and Diane give Doc a tab of blotter acid.

Doc goes back into the water, gets into a wave, and discovers that the molecules that form the wave are the same molecules that form him, so that he does not need to *become* one with the wave, he is *already* one with the wave, in fact, we are *all* the *same wave* . . .

And goes and finds Stan and Diane and weepingly tells them so.

"I *know*," Diane gushes.

She can't know, she's never been on a board, but we're all on the same wave, so . . .

"I know you do," Doc says.

Doc comes back with his surfer buddies and they all turn on. Now you have Republican Orange County's baddest nightmare— the worst antisocial elements (surfers *and* hippies) gathered on one combination plate in a demonic, drug-induced love fest.

And planning to institutionalize it, because

Stan and Diane share their problem—lack of funds—with Doc and the boys

and Doc offers a solution.

"Grass," he says. "Dope."

Surfing and dope go together like . . .

like . . .

uhhhh . . .

. . . surfing and dope.

Surfers had been hauling grass back up from safaris in Mexico for years, the 1954 Plymouth station wagon being the smuggling vehicle of choice, because all of its interior panels could be removed, the insides stuffed with dope, and put back on.

"We can get you the money to fix up this place," Doc says, volunteering not only himself but his surfing buddies. "A few Baja runs and that's all you need."

Doc and the boys make the requisite runs, sell the product, and donate the proceeds to Stan, Diane, et al. to spread love, peace, and acid throughout Laguna Beach and its environs.

The Bread and Marigolds Bookstore opens in May of the year.

It sells *The Tibetan Book of the Dead, The Anarchist Cookbook, On the Road,* incense, sandals, psychedelic posters, rock albums, tie-dyed T-shirts, macramé bracelets (You know what? Go ahead and hate them), all that happy shit, and distributes acid to the turned-on.

Stan and Diane are happy.

43

The store opens, but—
—the guys keep making runs.
Because "enough" is a self-contradictory word.
Enough is never

           enough.

Finally—*finally*—surfers found something they could make money at without getting a j-o-b. And money they make. Fuck, they make money. Millions of dollars of the stuff. They even buy a yacht to hang out in and sail dope up in from Mexico.

Cool and cool.

But Doc—

Doc is a visionary.

A pioneer, an explorer.

Doc hops a plane to Germany, buys a VW van, and drives

drives

to Afghanistan.

Doc has heard stories about the amazing potency of Afghan hashish.

The stories turn out to be true.

Grass is fine, but Afghan hash?

Synaptic pinball, lighting all the lights, ringing all the bells.

Winner, winner, winner.

So Doc loads his van up with hash, drives back to Europe, and ships the van to California. Throws a few tasting parties, gives some samples away, and creates a market for his product.

It isn't long before the other Association boys follow Doc's footsteps to Afghanistan and load cars, trucks, and vans up with hash. The most ingenious smuggling vessel, though, is the surfboard. One genius ships a board to Kandahar, hollows it out, and stuffs it with hash, because nobody at the airport knows what a surfboard is or, critically, how much it should weigh. And no one even asks what a guy is doing with surfboards in a place where there's no ocean.

All this shit comes back to Laguna.

Pretty soon Laguna Canyon fills up with houses full of dope and houses full of dopers. The canyon is so full of outlaws that the cops dub it "Dodge City."

44

The little girl lives in a cave.

Not metaphorically—not a run-down house with no natural lighting source—a *cave*.

As in Neanderthal.

The cave is in the hills near the lakes that give Laguna its name.

A cave in Laguna in the summer isn't such a bad place—it's actually kind of congenial. The days are warm, the nights are merely cool, and the inhabitants of the cave do have some basic amenities.

They have candles for light and Sterno stoves for what little cooking they do. They have sleeping bags and blankets, rolled-up shirts and jeans for pillows. They shower and use the toilets at Main Beach, although they've dug a latrine down a path through the brush outside the cave.

The little girl, Kim, hates it.

Six years old, she already has a sense that there's something better out there.

Kim imagines a room (of her own, Ms. Woolf) with walls, pink wallpaper and bedspread, dolls lined up neatly along the big pillows, and one of those Easy-Bake Ovens where she can make tiny little cupcakes. She wants a real mirror to sit in front of and brush her long blonde hair. She wants a bathroom that is immaculate and a house that is . . .

. . . perfect.

None of this is going to happen—her mother's name is "Freaky Frederica."

A year ago, Freddie ran away from home and (abusive) husband in Redding and found her way to some shelter (and a new name) with the hippie commune in the cave. For her, it was the best thing that ever happened—for her daughter, not so much.

She hates the dirt.

She hates the lack of privacy.

She hates the chaos.

People come in and out—the commune's population is transient, to say the least. One frequent visitor to the cave is Doc.

He owns a house down in Dodge City, but sometimes he hangs out at the cave, smokes dope, and talks about the "revolution" and the "counterculture" and the revelatory powers of acid.

And fucks Freddie.

Kim lies there, still as a doll, pretending to sleep as her mother and Doc make love beside her. She shuts her eyes tight, tries to tune out the sounds, and imagines her new bedroom.

No one ever comes into it.

Sometimes the man with her mother isn't Doc but someone else. Sometimes it's several people.

But no one ever comes into Kim's "room."

Ever.

45

John likes living in the cave.

He started bunking with Starshine, but one night snuggled up with a runaway from New Jersey named Comet (presumably after the celestial phenomenon, not the household cleaner) and, as they were virtually indistinguishable, he didn't care.

It's just better than home.

The commune is a family in its own way, something John doesn't have a lot of experience with. They sit down to meals together, they talk together, they do common chores.

John's parents barely know that he no longer lives at home. He comes back every two or three days and leaves little traces of his existence, says hello to whichever parent is there at the moment, grabs a few clothes, maybe some food, and then goes back to the cave. His father is mostly living up in L.A. now, anyway, his mother is consumed with the details of the impending divorce, and it's summertime, and the livin' is easy.

John smokes grass, partakes in a little hash, but the LSD trips scare him.

"You lose control," he tells Doc.

"You lose it to find it," Doc says cryptically.

No thanks, John thinks, because he's had to talk people down from their trips, or sit there during tedious acid sessions while people freak out and Doc reads from *The Tibetan Book of the Dead*.

Other than that, there's nothing for a fourteen-year-old boy not to love living in the cave that summer. He goes down to the beach, Doc lends him a board to take out. He hangs out with the surfers and the hippies and gets high. He goes back to the cave and one of the hippie girls cuts him in on the free love buffet.

"It was like summer camp," John would say later, "with blow jobs."

Then summer ends and it's time for school.

46

John doesn't want to go home.

"You can't live in the cave year round," Doc says. Like, September through October would probably be fine, but then the weather changes and Laguna gets cold and damp at night. But cold and damp is exactly how John would describe the atmosphere at his house, his mother being remote and, more often than not, drunk.

What happens is, John moves mostly into Doc's house.

It's a gradual thing—John comes after school and hangs out, stays for the big spaghetti dinners, everybody gets stoned, John falls asleep on the couch or in one of the three bedrooms with one of the chicks who make up what is basically Doc's harem.

After a while, John is just there, a fixture, a mascot.

Doc's puppy.

He goes surfing with Doc, he helps Doc pass out tacos, he gradually comes to understand where Doc's money comes from.

Dope.

Just hanging out, John gets an idea what the Association is and who they are. The boys make thinly veiled references around him to their runs down to Mexico and the bigger expeditions to South Asia.

One day John tells Doc, "I want in."

"In on what?"

"You know," John says.

Doc gives him that charismatic, crooked grin and says, "You're fourteen."

"Almost fifteen," John says.

Doc looks him over. John is your basic grem, but there's something special about him—the kid has always been this little adult—the chicks around the place sure as hell treat him like a grown-up—and he's not so little anymore.

And Doc has a problem maybe John can help him with.

Money.

Doc has too much of it.

Well, not too much money per se—nobody has Too Much Money—but too much cash in small denominations.

So now you have to catch this image—

John skateboarding to banks in Laguna, Dana Point, and San Clemente with a backpack full of singles, fives, and tens that Doc gets from his street sales. John walking into the bank and exchanging the small bills for wrapped stacks of fifties and hundreds.

And John knows which tellers to go to, which ones get birthday presents and Christmas bonuses from Doc.

And if the cops see a skinny kid with long brown hair, a T-shirt, and board trunks pushing his street board along the sidewalk, he's just one of dozens of pain-in-the-ass skateboarders, and it doesn't occur to them that this one has thousands and thousands of dollars slung over his shoulder.

Some kids have paper routes—John has *cash* routes.

Doc kicks him fifty bucks a day.

Life is good.

John puts up with school, does his route, gets his fifty, goes back to the house, and slips into bed with girls who are now more often in their twenties than in their late teens and who are giving him an education he can't get in the classroom.

Yeah, life is good.

But it could be better.

47

"I want to deal my own shit," he tells Doc one day as they're sitting out in the lineup waiting for the next set.

"Why?" Doc asks. "You're making money."

"Handling *your* money," John answers. "I want to handle my *own* money."

"I don't know, man."

"I do," John says. "Look, if you won't supply me, I'll go to somebody else."

Doc figures that if the kid goes somewhere else he could get burned or ripped off or walk right into a police setup. At least if I sell to him, Doc thinks, I know the kid will be safe.

So now, in addition to his cash over his shoulder, John has fat joints taped to the bottom of his skateboard and sells them for five bucks each.

Now John is making money.

He doesn't spend it on albums, clothes, or taking girls out. He saves it. Not even sixteen, he hands Doc a pile of money and asks him to buy him a car.

A beautifully restored 1954 Plymouth station wagon.

48

Dig our brother John.

Seventeen years old, he rents not one but two houses in Dodge City.

One to live in, the other to store his dope in.

He makes more round-trips to Mexico than the Trailways bus, and he ain't skateboarding five-dollar fingers anymore. (He has three other grems doing that, and happy for the money.) He is wholesaling now, selling in volume to street dealers, making real money. He has so much grass stashed in that second domicile it becomes known as "The Shit Brick House."

He has a twenty-three-year-old girlfriend named Lacey living with him who has a sleek body, so flexible because it doesn't have a jealous bone in it. He can drive his own car now and has three of them, the Plymouth, a '65 Mustang convertible, and an old Chevy pickup he uses to put his surfboards in. He has a quiver of custom-made boards. He hangs out with the Dead when they roll through town. He gets high on trips with Doc to Maui.

He's still Doc's puppy, but now they say that he "runs with the big dogs."

John is a junior member of the Association.

49

Meanwhile, the country is going motherfucking insane.

While John is on the trajectory from taco-grubbing grem to successful young businessman, the United States goes McMurphy in the cuckoo's nest, aka the years 1968–1971.

Has anybody here seen my old friend Martin, has anybody here seen my old friend Bobby, Tet Offensive, riots in Cleveland, riots in Miami, *the* riot in Chicago, Mayor Daley, Hippies and Yippies, we go off the meds and elect Richard Nixon (the Nurse Ratchett of the American political psych ward), the *Heidi* game, the last prince of Camelot takes a girl to the terminal submarine races, the Chicago Eight, My Lai, I came across a Child of God he was walking along the road, Altamont, Janis dies, the Manson family, Cambodia, tin soldiers and Nixon coming, Angela Davis, *Everything You Always Wanted to Know About Sex*, *Apollo 13*, tie-dyed T-shirts, granny dresses, Attica.

With the exceptions of Woodstock and Janis dying, it pretty much all slides past John.

Come on, he's in Laguna.

Laguna Beach
2005

Don't let the Devil ride
I said don't let the Devil ride
'cuz if you let him ride
He will surely want to drive

—THE JORDANAIRES, "DON'T LET THE DEVIL RIDE"

50

The Gold Coast is silver.

Laguna's streetlights are shrouded in fog, and the lifeguard tower at Main Beach looks like it's floating on a cloud.

Ben likes the town this way.

Soft, mysterious, nighttime.

He just dropped O at her place and is now considering whether to go out, go home, or give Kari the waitress a call.

Uh-huh.

He gets on the phone. "Kari? It's Ben Leonard. From the Coyote?"

Just a short silence, then a warm answer.

"Hey, Ben."

"I wondered what you're doing."

Longer silence. "Ben, I shouldn't. I'm seeing somebody."

"Are you married?" Ben asks. "Engaged?"

She's neither.

"Then you're still single," Ben says. "A free agent."

But she'd feel so guilty.

"Makes the sex better," Ben says. "Trust me on this, I'm Jewish."

She's Catholic.

"In that case we have almost a *responsibility* to do this," Ben says. "We owe it to sex."

She laughs.

Ben drives past Brooks Street and keeps going toward Kari's place in South Lagoo.

Except—

51

Things you don't want to see in the rearview mirror:

(a) Your new cell phone crushed under your tire.

(b) Ditto your girlfriend's dead puppy.

(c) A goalie mask.

(d) Flashers.

Ben sees (d).

"Shit."

He pulls over on the PCH near the entrance to Aliso Creek Beach.

An empty stretch of road on a foggy night.

Looking in the mirror again, he sees that it's an unmarked car with a flasher attached to the roof.

But he doesn't have anything on him and the car is clean.

The plainclothes cop's face appears at the window. He shows his badge and Ben rolls the window down.

"License and registration, please."

"May I ask why you stopped me?"

"License and registration, please."

Ben takes his license from his wallet, hands it over, and then reaches toward the glove compartment for the registration.

"Keep your hands where I can see them," the cop says.

"Do you want the registration or not?" Ben asks.

"Step out of the car, sir."

"Oh, come on," Ben says. Because he just can't help himself— it's in his freaking DNA. "Why did you stop me? Do you have probable cause?"

"I saw marijuana smoke coming out of the driver side window," the cop says. "And I can smell it now."

Ben laughs. "You saw marijuana smoke from a moving car at night? And you don't smell anything—I never smoke in my car."

"Step out of the car, please, sir."

"This is bullshit."

The cop rips the door open, grabs Ben by the wrist, hauls him out, and arm-bars him to the ground.

Then the kicks start coming.

Ben tries to go fetal, but the kicks come into his ribs, his shins, his kidneys, his balls.

"You're resisting arrest!" the cop yells. "Stop resisting!"

"I'm not resisting."

Two more hard kicks, then the cop comes down with his knee on Ben's neck and Ben feels the gun barrel press against the base of his skull.

"*Now* who's the asshole?" the cop asks.

It's such a weird fucking thing to say, but Ben isn't focused on that.

Because he hears the hammer click back.

His breath catches in his throat.

Then the cop pulls the trigger.

52

O goes into her bathroom, turns on the exhaust fan, and lights a roach.

She'll make this small concession to her mother's sensibilities, but Paqu's hypocrisy on the subject of drugs is nothing short of epic, almost admirable in its bold two-facedness.

Paqu's medicine cabinet

behind the mirror mirror on the (bathroom) wall

is a pharmacopoeia of prescribed mood-altering drugs

a fact that O despises because it's such a cliché, and all the more so because she becomes a part of the stereotype (hence the "stereo" if you think about it) by consistently running to the shelter of her mother's little helper when the herb just won't do the trick.

"Can't you develop a blend," she has asked Ben, "called 'For Orange County Girls When Battlestar Galactica Isn't Enough'?"

"Working on it," Ben replied.

But so far to no result.

So O will occasionally raid CVS Paqu for

Valium

Oxy

Xanax or some other antidepressant

which makes Paqu's lectures about her marijuana-smoking more bearable, lectures that come with greater frequency in the weeks after Paqu returns from rehab with new material and a fresh flock of Twelve-Step buddies who hang around the patio and talk about their "programs" and before Paqu gets bored with the whole thing and decides that the real answer lies in yoga, bicycling, Jesus, or scrapbooking.

(The scrapbooking phase was especially excruciating, featuring as it did Paqu gluing endless pictures of herself taking pictures of O into volumes arranged by year.)

Actually, one of Paqu's lovers was a sad-looking guy from her "Friday meeting," whom a sixteen-year-old O asked, "Are you 'in recovery,' too?"

"I have thirty days," the guy said.

"Well, you ain't gonna have forty," O said.

Which proved prophetic on about day thirty-six, when O came out of her room to find Paqu and Sadly Sober Guy slinging (empty) Stoli bottles at each other across the living room before each departed to (separate) detox facilities, leaving O alone in the house to hold epic parties on the rationale that she was thoughtfully cleansing the house of alcohol in anticipation of her mother's return.

Anyway, like goaltenders and quarterbacks, Paqu is blessed with a short memory, so none of this history stops her from getting on O's case about her marijuana habit.

O's not in the mood tonight, so she sits on the toilet under the exhaust fan to get high and if Paqu comes nosing around she can just say she's constipated, which will engender a suggestion about an organic remedy rather than a ball-busting.

Because she feels like she's already had her balls, as it were, busted by Chon's utter rejection of her blatant (and admittedly clumsy) come-on.

"I'm sort of Bambi-esque"?

Jesus.

I wouldn't fuck me, either.

53

Ben hears the dry click.

His heart *slamming*.

The cop's laugh.

He feels something being pressed into his hand, then taken away, then the cop pulls his arms behind him and cuffs him.

"Look what I found," the cop says.

He shows Ben a brick of dope.

"That's not mine," Ben says.

"Yeah, I've never heard that before," the cop says. "I found it in the trunk of your car."

"Bullshit. You planted it."

The cop hauls him to his feet, pushes him into the backseat of the unmarked car.

And reads him his rights.

54

Like he has the right to remain silent.

No shit. Ben doesn't say *anything* except he wants his other right, the right to a lawyer.

Does Ben know a lawyer?

Are you fucking kidding? Ben sells the best dope in Orange County, ergo some of his best customers are lawyers.

(And doctors; as yet, no Indian chiefs.)

The fucked thing is that he doesn't know any criminal lawyers—

—but he calls an insurance lawyer who calls a buddy of his who hustles over in the middle of the night.

But not before the cops file charges against Ben under California 11359—possession with intent to sell—and resisting arrest (a "148," Ben learns), and throw in a 243(b) battery on a peace officer for good measure, and chuck him into central holding.

Forget the jail clichés.

No Mexican gang tries to turn him into a jerk-off sock. He doesn't have to fight Bubba for his bologna sandwich. Closest thing Ben has to an encounter in his OC jail cell is with a Rasta dude who asks him what he got busted for.

"Possession of marijuana with intent to sell, resisting arrest, and assaulting a police officer," Ben tells him.

"A 243(b), very cool," Rasta dude says.

Get up, stand up, stand up for your rights.

Mostly Ben just lies there—aching and angry.

At Detective Sergeant William Boland of the Orange County Sheriff's Office, Anti-Drug Task Force.

Who put a gun to his head and pulled a dry trigger.

Ben didn't see his life flash in front of his eyes—

He saw his *death* flash in front of his eyes.

"How bad can it get?" Ben asks.

"Bad," the lawyer answers. "You're looking at maybe twelve grand in fines and up to six years in the state pen."

"Six years?"

"Three on the dope," the lawyer explains, "one on the 148, maybe two more on the 243."

"*He* assaulted *me*."

"Your word against his," the lawyer says, "and in a drug case, the jury will go with the cop."

"Come on," Ben says. "You should get this whole thing thrown out. He had no probable cause, no reason to search my car, he planted the fucking dope—"

"It had your prints on it," the lawyer says.

"He pressed it into my hand!"

"Unless we can get a few Mexicans or blacks on the jury, you're fucked," the lawyer says. "My advice is to plead it out—I'll get them to drop the battery because Boland didn't seek medical attention, can probably get you probation on the resisting charge, you get three for the grass, serve a year."

"No fucking way," Ben says.

The lawyer shrugs. "You don't want to take this in front of an Orange County jury."

Mostly retirees and government workers (because they can get out of their jobs) who are going to hate Ben for being young and arrogant.

"I'm pleading not guilty."

"I have to advise you—"

"Plead me not guilty."

So Ben spends a long, sleepless night in jail, gets arraigned in the morning, pleads not guilty, and gets remanded for $25,000 in bail.

56

May Gray.

Local name for the "marine layer" of cloud and fog that drapes over the coast this time of year like a thin blanket, scaring the hell out of tourists who've plunked down big bucks to spend a week in sunny California and then find out that it isn't.

You look up at the sky at, say, nine AM, it's a steaming bowl of soup and you don't believe you're going to see the sun that day. Ye of little faith—by noon the carcinogenic rays are cutting through the fog like laser beams straight to your skin, by one it's the place you saw in Yahoo Images, by three you're in the drugstore looking for aloe lotion.

Ben has a different theory about May Gray.

A different name.

He calls it "transitional time."

"After the night before," Ben tells O on the subject, "people aren't ready for the harsh light of day first thing in the morning. In its benevolence, Southern California softens it for them. It's transitional time."

You get up in the morning and it's nice and soft and gray.

Like your brain.

You ease into the day.

It's like truth—better to come into it gradually.

Ben gently lowers himself into his usual seat at the Coyote—

his back hurts like crazy from Boland's shoe—and she comes over
with the coffee and the evil eye.

"I waited for you last night," she says. "You never showed up."

Yeah, Ben already knows this. It always amazes him how people
have to tell you things that you obviously already know. (You
never showed up. You're late. You have an attitude.)

"Something happened," Ben says.

"Something or somebody?"

Jesus Christ, Ben thinks, she's already jealous? That's getting a
head start on things. And by the way, isn't there another *guy*?

"Some*thing*."

"It better have been important."

"It was."

Someone showed me my mortality.

She softens a little. "The usual?"

"No, just coffee."

He feels too sick and tired to eat.

Kari pours his coffee, and the next thing he knows Old Guys
Rule shows up and sits down across from him.

57

INT. COYOTE GRILL - DAY

CROWE sits down across from BEN.

                    CROWE
    Look, you seem like a good kid. Nobody wants to
    hurt you.

Off Ben's incredulous look—

CROWE (CONT'D)

Okay, maybe someone got a little carried away. Adrenaline rush sort of thing. If it makes a difference,
he feels bad about it.

BEN

He put a gun to my head and pulled the trigger.

CROWE

And you didn't shit your pants. People were im-
pressed, by the way.

BEN

I'm thrilled.

CROWE

Lighten up—it's not like your hands are so clean.

BEN

What are you talking about?

CROWE
(smirking)

Yeah, okay.

BEN

So what do you want?

CROWE

You ready to listen now?

Ben doesn't say anything—he opens his hands—"I'm here."

CROWE (CONT'D)

Okay, here's what you do.

Ben packs a briefcase with $35K in cash and drives up to Newport Beach.

Chad Meldrun's office is on the seventh floor of a modern building overlooking the greenway, and his receptionist is so clearly fucking him that she can barely bother to look up from the magazine she's reading to tell Ben to take a seat, Chad is with another client and is running a little late.

Ten minutes later, Chad comes out of his office, his arm around a grim-looking Mexican guy, telling him to "chill out, it's going to be okay." Chad's in his late forties but looks younger, a result of swapping his services with a cosmetic surgeon in the next building who doles out Oxy along with the Botox.

So Chad has a virtually undetectable eye tuck and a total absence of worry lines, which is appropriate, as his nickname in the general drug defense industry is Chad "No Worries" Meldrun.

He ushers Ben into his office and into a chair, then sits behind his big desk and locks his fingers behind his head.

Ben sets the briefcase down by his own feet.

"You're lucky to get an appointment," Chad begins without small talk. "I'm overbooked. The War on Drugs should be called the Defense Attorney Full Employment Act."

"Thanks for seeing me," Ben says.

"No worries," Chad answers. He stands back up and says, "Let's go for a ride. Leave the briefcase."

They walk back out into the waiting room.

"I'll be back in twenty," Chad tells the receptionist.

She looks up from *People*. "Cool."

Ben follows Chad out onto the top floor of the parking structure and takes a seat in his Mercedes.

"Unless it's about the Lakers," Chad says as he turns the ignition, "don't say anything."

Ben doesn't have anything to say about the Lakers, so he keeps his mouth shut. Chad drives out of the structure onto MacArthur Boulevard, down to John Wayne Airport.

"We're just going to drive around for a few minutes," he says. "I know my car is clean, and if you're wearing a wire the signal is jammed at the airport. God bless John Wayne and Homeland Security."

"I'm not wearing a wire," Ben says.

"Probably not," Chad answers. "Okay, the thirty-five: Twenty-five of it goes to assure that the chain of evidence gets fucked up and you walk. Ten of it stays with me, call it a finder's fee. In addition, you pay my fee—three hundred a billable hour, plus expenses. I'm not just being greedy—you have to pay my fee to assure lawyer-client confidentiality and show that you're not just engaging me to deliver payoffs into the right hands."

"But that's what I'm doing, right?" Ben asks. "Engaging you to deliver payoffs to the OC Drug Task Force."

"Thirty-five K a month, kid," Chad says. "Call it the cost of doing business. Really you should be setting aside about twenty percent of your income for legal fees, anyway."

"Thanks for the advice."

"You're lucky this one is state and not federal," Chad says. "These federal guys these days? If you *can* touch them, they think they're first-round NFL draft choices. Now, don't even think what you're thinking—which is you could go to the state people directly, cut out the middleman, and save yourself my commission. You can't. First of all, you don't know the right people to approach, and if you touch up the wrong people you have bigger problems. Second, even if you did, I'm a frequent flyer, if you understand the concept, so they're not going to take your slice at the risk of the whole pie. Third, you're much better off having a long-term relationship with me, because if you ever really screw the pooch, I'm a stud monkey in court, and I also have jurors and judges in my inventory."

"I wasn't thinking it."

"No worries," Chad says, "I just like everything to be up front and out in the open from the start. That way, there are no misunderstandings later. Questions?"

"You guarantee the charges get dropped?"

"Locked in," Chad says. "You know who doesn't walk on cases like this? Poor people—*they're* fucked. It's a very bad business to go into undercapitalized."

Chad drives back to the office building.

"You park in the structure?" he asks Ben when they get there.

"I did."

"Bring the ticket back up to Rebecca," Chad says. "We validate."

Ben decides to just pay the fourteen bucks.

Cost of doing business.

60

Duane makes the call to his boss.

"Looks like he's playing ball."

"Okay. Good."
Duane's boss is a man of few words.

61

The phone rings in Ben's apartment.
"You went and saw Chad," Duane says.
"Did he give you your money already?"
"Piece of work, isn't he?"
"Piece of work."
"Don't sulk. Consider you got fined for bad behavior."

62

Here's the thing, though.
Ben doesn't consider it a "fine."
He looks at it as tuition.
For an education.
They took him to school.
Which is where they messed up.
They taught him how it works.

63

Every hero has a tragic flaw.

That one inner quality that will do him and everyone else around him in.

With Ben, it's simple.

You tell Ben to do one thing—

He can't help himself—

He's going to do exactly the opposite.

He's—

64

Subversive

(adj.) Likely to subvert or overthrow a government.

(n.) A person engaged in subversive activities.

Okay, that's Ben.

To wit: He pays the next month's "fee."

On the surface, he appears to obey, to be chastened, to have learned his lesson.

That's *apparent.*

(adj.) 1. Open to view: visible; 2. Clear or manifest to the understanding; 3. Appearing as such, but not necessarily so.

Ding.

Because Ben has a plan.

"*D-E-D-O*"
"Informer"
in beautiful cursive script
made up of men's intestines
laid out on the floor.

DEA Agent Dennis Cain stands in the Tijuana warehouse with his Mexican counterpart, a Baja state policeman named Miguel Arroyo—aka "Lado" ("Stone Cold")—and looks at the message from the Sanchez family that just as easily might have spelled out

"*C-H-I-N-G-A-T-E D-E-N-N-I-S*"

Translation: Fuck you, Dennis.

Because it gets very personal, this kind of long-term, close-range war. These guys all know each other. No, they don't actually know each other, but they *know* each other. The Sanchez family probably does as much intelligence on the DEA as the DEA does on them. They know where the others live, where they eat, who they see, who they fuck, how they work. They know their families, their friends, their enemies, their tastes, their quirks, their dreams, their fears—so leaving a message in human entrails is almost a grisly joke between rivals, but it's also a statement of relative power, like, look what we can do on our turf that you can't do on yours.

Dennis started his career as a uniformed cop in Buffalo. One morning in a frigid predawn, wind coming off the lake like the swing of a killing sword, he saw an old carpet leaning at an odd angle against an alley wall. The carpet turned out to contain the frozen corpse of a coke whore, and pressed against her cold chest was her frozen baby, blue in death.

He volunteered for the narco squad the next day.

Weeks later, he went on his first undercover and busted the

dealers. Took night classes, got his degree, and applied to DEA. Happiest day of his life when he got accepted, although he will say it was his wedding day, and later, the days his children were born.

(Undercovers are great liars—their lives depend on it.)

DEA threw him right back undercover—upstate New York, then Jersey, then the city. He was a star, a real stud monkey, making cases that the federal prosecutors loved. Then they jerked him up from under and sent him down to Colombia, then Mexico. Sandy-haired, boyish grin—Huck Finn with an East Coast mouth and a killer's heart—the targets loved him, fell all over themselves to sell him dope and put themselves in the shit.

(Undercovers are great con men—their jobs depend on it.)

A star now, he was moved to the Front Line of the War on Drugs, the two-thousand-mile border with Mexico.

They even gave him a choice of assignments—El Paso or San Diego.

Hmmm.

Lemme think—

El Paso or San Diego.

El Paso or . . . San Diego.

El Passhole or Sun Dog.

Sorry, Tex, no offense, pard, but—

—come on.

So Dennis Cain set up shop in the backyard of the Baja Cartel, just across the fence (literally) from the Sanchez Family Business, and no one's inviting the neighbors over for a cookout.

It's just war, day in, day out.

You wanna talk about the War on Drugs (of course, it should be the War *Against* Drugs, the ambiguity of the "on" having caused some spectacular HR problems at DEA, and Chon would tell you about a lot of guys who fought *their* war on drugs), this is

No Man's Land

All Unquiet on the Western Front.

Dennis and Cohorts bust a shipment, the Sanchezes kill a snitch. Dennis and Company find a tunnel under the border, the Sanchezes are already digging a new one. Dennis busts a cartel leader, another Sanchez steps into the gap to replace him.

The drugs and the money keep on turnin', Proud Mary Juana keeps on burnin'.

Now Dennis looks down at the eviscerated bodies of three men, one of whom was his snitch, and the calling card arranged with their intestines.

"What?" he says. "They ran out of spray paint?"

Lado shrugs.

66

O blurts out, "I want to meet my bio-father."

All Paqu would tell O—despite her persistent questioning when she was seven or eight—was that her father was a "loser" and, therefore, better out of her life.

O learned not to bring it up.

Now she does.

To Ben.

Ben's a little stunned. And more than a little distracted with converting his subversive plan into subversive action.

But Ben is Ben. "What do you hope to achieve?"

"By meeting the sperm donor?"

"That's what we're talking about, right?"

O lists the potential benefits:

1. Lay a guilt trip on someone else for a change.
2. Piss Paqu off.
3. Freak people out by performing hideously
   inappropriate PDA.
4. Piss Paqu off.
5. Pretend he's actually her Sugar Daddy.
6. Piss—

"Go back to five," Ben says. "You're on to something there."

"What do you mean?"

"Come on," Ben says. "Paqu is turning off the tap, so you're looking for a new . . . tap."

"That's deeply cynical, Ben."

"Okay."

"A poor little rich girl just wants some paternal love," she says, "and you attribute her motivations to a crass gold-digging campaign instead of the profound search for identity that—"

"Do you even know where he is?"

"I know his name."

67

She was looting (an absent) Paqu's dresser drawers for cash and found something even better.

A vibrator.

What she would refer to as

Paqu's Smartest Boyfriend

The Bestest Stepdad Ever.

Ubermann.

(With apologies to Chon's beloved Nietzsche.)

BNI

(Batteries Not Included).

No first dates, no awkward conversations, no futile fumbling, no messy human relationships. Just fire that bad boy up, find a suitable fantasy, and

The big O or

Os, plural, if you do it right.

However

Right next to the rabbit, she found something else.

Her birth certificate with the

Name of the father she'd never met.

Paul Patterson.

Her father's identity sitting next to a plastic phallus.

Three months in therapy right there.

68

"I mean, I could track him down, couldn't I?" O asks Ben.

"Maybe," Ben says, "but then what?"

He worries she has this fantasy—she's going to meet her dad, he's going to be great, they're going to have this relationship.

"I don't know, ask him questions."

Ben knows that she already has the answers in her head—her father always wanted to be with her, Paqu is the Evil (Step) Mother who forced him away.

"Like why he left before you were born?" Ben asks. "Like if he loves you? What's he going to say, O, that's going to make your life any better?"

She has the obvious riposte.

What's he going to say

To make my life any worse?

69

Dennis has a beautiful wife, two beautiful little daughters, and a beautiful if modest home in a nice suburb of San Diego where the neighbors grill steaks and salmon and invite each other over from across the fence. He goes to church on Sundays (one of those nice tame establishment churches that believes in God and Jesus but not so much that it's inconvenient) and comes home and catches the afternoon football game or maybe goes for a walk with the family on the beach.

He has the sweet life and knows it.

Career going great.

You get (good) headlines for the guys who sign your annual reviews, you put them between a bunch of cameras and bales of marijuana, you let them pose beside mug shots of Mexican cartel figures (autopsy photos even better), your life plan is looking pretty solid.

It's not cynical—

—this you must understand, you *have* to get this or none of it makes sense or has any meaning—

—Dennis does work that he loves and believes in, scrubbing the scourge of drugs from the American landscape.

He *believes.*

So where does it start?

You could say it starts that morning, as Dennis stands in front of the mirror shaving and feels that discomforting little tingle of undefined discontent. But *maybe* (the whole concept of "omniscient narration" is pretty fucked, anyway, right?) it doesn't.

Maybe it starts the night before with the discussion of the granite countertops. They're remodeling the kitchen and his wife really wants granite countertops, but when you look at the prices in the catalogs, it's like, holy shit.

Maybe it starts because his work is the kind of thing he wants to talk about at home on Thursday Pizza Night, when Domino's delivers and his oldest girl is already seriously into the *Idol* results show. When his wife asks the "How was your day" question he answers, "Fine," and that's it, and that wears him down, isolates him from the people he loves the most.

Maybe it's the cumulative effect of that, or—

Maybe it's a baby frozen blue in a dark gray dawn twentysomething years ago in a war that never seems to end.

70

Chon's face appears on the screen.

Via the miracle of Skype.

Ben angles the lappie so O can see him, too.

She breaks into a *huge* grin.

"Chonny, Chonny, Chonny, Chonny boy!"

"Hi, guys."

"How are you, bro?" Ben asks.

"Good. Yeah, fine. You?"

"Excellent," Ben lies.

Wants to tell him.

Can't.

Even when Chon asks, "How's business?"

"Business is good."

Because it seems cruel to tell someone about a problem he can't do anything about but sit and worry. And the last thing Ben wants to give Chon is a distraction. Take his mind off what he's doing.

And Chon looks tired, worn down.

So Ben commits a

Lie of omission.

So instead they make small talk, O assures Chon that she's taking good care of his plant, and then Chon's time is up and his face disappears from the screen.

71

Ben's lying.

Chon could see it on his face.

Something's wrong at home, something with the business, but he pushes the thought aside to focus on the mission.

The mission is simple.

He's done it a few dozen times now—night raids on a house.

Chon's team isn't involved with complicated counterinsurgency operations—gaining the trust of the people, setting up village security, building clinics, clean water systems, schools, winning hearts and minds.

Chon's team does "antiterrorist" ops.

"Degrade and disrupt" the enemy's command and control systems.

Put simply:

Find enemy leaders and kill them.

The theory being that dead people are probably degraded but definitely disrupted, death being more or less the maximum kink in someone's day.

The collateral theory being that if you kill enough leaders, it discourages middle management from applying for the job vacancy.

Nobody wants that promotion.

(More money

More responsibility

Corner office

Laser dot.)

Most Salafist leaders want to go to Paradise eventually, not immediately, generously yielding that privilege to lesser beings. Otherwise that cocksucker bin Laden would be standing on the top of the Sears Tower waving his arms like *Come and get me*, not hiding out.

Anyway, over the course of a couple of wars, Chon's unit morphed from counterinsurgency to antiterrorism because the latter is

Cheaper,

Faster,

And easier to tabulate.

Bodies (especially dead ones) being easier to count than hearts (fickle) and minds (transitory).

So he's used to missions like this.
There's just so goddamn many of them.
So many Bad Guys to kill.

72

Dennis has put Bad Guys away to see
      other Bad Guys take their places
Dennis has looked into
      the dead, tortured faces of his sources
Dennis has seen—
You've heard the expression "truckloads of cash"? And thought
it was a figure of speech?
    Dennis has seen, literally—
    —*truckloads of cash* headed south for Mexico to people who
have kitchens with granite countertops, and he turns those trucks
in to his bosses, who pose beside them while he dutifully puts a
little money away each month for his kids' college educations and
his wife clips coupons because while Paradise is Paradise, Paradise
is also expensive.
    Dennis sees his face get a little older, hair a little thinner, belly
no longer taut. Knows that his reflexes are a little slower, memory
not quite as acute, that there might be more calendar pages behind
than in front of him.
    So maybe that little nudge of discontent was fear. Maybe not.
Maybe it was just discontent, as in "the winter of" in a place that
knows no real winter.
    Anyway—

You need to know that Dennis hoards information. He feels justified in doing so because he's worked hard to develop sources—they're *his*—and he doesn't share them because he doesn't want to share the information they develop. This does not make Dennis particularly popular among his peers, but he doesn't give a shit—the life plan isn't to make friends among his peers, it's to rise above them, and then they're not going to like him, anyway.

So Dennis's modus operandi is to work his sources to develop information right up to the point of making a bust, then dole those busts out for the best possible political and promotion-creating effect.

That's why when one of his CIs—that's "Confidential Informants," and D has given a whole new meaning to the "Confidential"—tells him about this isolated little ranch house way the fuck out in East County near Jamul, he goes by himself.

The Lone Ranger

Or "the Lone Stranger," as he's known in the office.

(Undercovers are natural loners—they don't trust anybody—paranoia is a survival strategy.)

Sans Tonto, as Paqu might say, recalling that she's in her French phase.

To check it out.

Solo Surveillance.

Dennis has balls—big, clanging brass—so he drives out into the dark desert all by his lonesome, parks his vehicle on a ridge overlooking this ranch, and trains his nightscope on the house.

It's a cash dump.

(There's a phrase, huh?)

What's happening is that the dealers are bringing their cash there to be counted, sorted, and stacked for the relatively short dash down across the border. On any given night, there's going to be hundreds of thousands to millions of dollars in that house.

Dennis takes one look at this and knows it's the bust that could
Put Him Over.

Because what he also sees through that scope is

Filipo Sanchez.

Number Three in the Baja Cartel.

73

The night is eerie green.

Through Chon's night goggles.

Monster-movie green.

He rolls out of the APC

(Armored Personnel Carrier)

behind his team and rushes toward the compound of two-story
concrete buildings where the CIA boys said the AQ honchos are
holed up.

Pressing the butt of the M-14 rifle to his shoulder, he keeps it at
firing position as the C4 charges blow the gate off its hinges and
the team goes in.

Chon has a photo of the AQ asshole that is Target Number One
burned into his memory pan.

Mahmud el-Kassani.

Where are you, Mahmud?

74

Dennis knows Filipo—hells yes, he does, he has Filipo's picture pinned up on the bulletin board in his office. He knows the names of Filipo's wife and kids, knows what *fútbol* team he follows, knows that Filipo subscribes to the Padres games on satellite TV. This must be an important cash dump for Filipo to chance coming over the wire, so he must be up there checking up on things, making sure that all of the money goes south and none of it gets lost and wanders toward other points on the compass.

While Dennis would normally keep this house under surveillance for a couple of weeks and then turn it over to his superiors so they could get the credit, now he's thinking about playing leapfrog. The San Diego SAC is looking at retirement, and a pop like this could put Dennis's ass into his empty chair.

So this is totally a cowboy move, highly discouraged by the Powers That Be, but Dennis knows that he has a justification—he can always say that he had to take the chance—who knew when and if Filipo would ever come back, be on this side of the border, and there's a federal trafficking warrant on the guy, anyway, so—

He clips his badge onto his jacket, finds his DEA cap in the backseat, pulls his weapon, and goes in.

75

Chaos in the compound
(foxes in the henhouse)

as

women shriek, children scream, goats bleat.

No chaos for the team—they know exactly where they are and where they're going: up some stairs to the second floor.

Bullets zip past them as the AQ fight back.

Chon moves the rifle around smoothly—

Target, shoot

Target, shoot

Target, shoot

He makes it to the door and heads up the stairs.

One of the AQ shot out the lightbulbs at the sound of the explosion and it's black and tight in there.

Chon feels someone come out of a doorway beside him and he swings the rifle to take him out and sees—

it's a kid,

can't be twelve

in the traditional vest

the *waskath*

(from which Chon knows we got the word "waistcoat")

and skullcap

big black eyes

Shoot every male is the order but Chon isn't going to follow that order so he shoves the kid back in the room and moves up the stairs into a room that becomes

a charnel house

as the team shoots everyone inside and Chon sees

Mahmud.

Who doesn't want to become a martyr this night.

He puts his hands up to surrender.

Chon drills him twice through the chest because

Chon wants him to be a martyr.

(Paradise is Paradise, but it's also expensive.)

Yeah, they might try to slug it out with him.

In which case he's dead.

More likely they're just going to bolt

In which case most of them will make it

But it's Worth the Risk.

Nailing Filipo Sanchez? Come on.

So Dennis charges down there in his Jeep like a movie cowboy on his horse. There's no fence, no gate, because the narcos don't want to call attention to the house and Dennis just drives right up, slams the brakes, and jumps out, badge in one hand, pistol in the other, and announces, "DEA! This is a raid! Nobody fucking move!"

Dennis has balls.

Three gunmen are just standing there, open-mouthed, staring at him, clearly trying to figure out what to do. And this is the moment when, if they were going to shoot him, they would.

In the Jerry Bruckheimer version they do just that—they whip out the weaponry and let fly, missing almost every shot while Dennis guns them all down and—hit in the shoulder—bursts into the house and has a shoot-out with Filipo.

Roll credits, sweep up the popcorn.

Except a multi-billion-dollar poly-drug cartel doesn't get to be a multi-billion-dollar poly-drug cartel because they have a lot of stupid people working for them. And while this isn't your typical DEA raid with the typical cast of characters, it's still a DEA raid and these guys know that killing a federal agent on American soil—

—is going to cost a lot more money in the long run than is in the house

—subjects them to the needle instead of fifteen to thirty, and—
—even Filipo Sanchez is expendable.

That's just the truth, that's just life in the *vida narco*. Money is just money—they lose it all the time. Same with people—they go to jail, they come out—it's the chance you take. That even applies to Filipo—royal family or no royal family—it happens and the family goes on.

So what happens is they do freeze, and—

Dennis strides right past them into the house, where—

Filipo Sanchez looks up from a folding table stacked with cash and looks mildly surprised. And calmly says, "There's five hundred and fifty thousand dollars on this table for you if I go out that door."

77

Back down the stairs now.

Mission accomplished.

Everyone gets to go home, drink a beer, watch a DVD.

Women are already mourning, keening, ululating, but Chon no longer hears that.

White noise.

He's almost down the stairs when the kid steps out again.

Chon sees the kid's innocent black eyes and says,

"Oh, fuck"

as the kid reaches inside the *waskath* and detonates the bomb strapped to his body.

The green world goes red.

Few people ever have to find out
What they would do
       when their whole life has been based on one thing and
then they're offered
       the other.
Dennis knows that he can bust Filipo, and five other Filipos
will kill each other trying to take the job vacancy. Knows that
the job vacancy will be filled because the money is just too good.
Knows he should bust him, anyway, cuff him, and read him his
rights.

Filipo is showing no signs that he's going to resist or run.

Maybe if Filipo had been your Cineplex-stereotype Frito-
Bandito Mexi-cowboy in an embroidered black shirt and bright-
green lizard-skin boots it might have been a simple choice. But
Filipo wears a tailored gray sports coat over a white button-down
shirt, an expensive pair of jeans, and black loafers. Slightly tinted
bifocals, short-cut black hair with flecks of silver. Very understated,
muted, soft-spoken.

Not a trace of threat in his voice or smirk on his face.

Just business.

An exchange of value for value.

Money for freedom.

A lot of things go through Dennis's mind in a hurry. Things that
just the day before probably wouldn't have occurred to him, like—
$550K is
Granite countertops, is
His kids' education, is
Fuck the coupons.

He thinks about his pension down the road, how maybe it buys an RV that you stencil some name like "Buccaneer" on and drive across the country every other year. $550K invested wisely over those years buys you—

A place in Costa Rica, on the water.

Trips to Tuscany.

Granite countertops.

It would be

just this once, he thinks,

one time and one time only, and

never again.

Except Dennis knows that's not true, even as he's telling it to himself. He knows that a soul isn't for rent, only for sale. But, to save face, he says, "This doesn't change anything."

Filipo nods, but allows just the suggestion of a smile to show on his face because they both know this changes *everything*.

The river of time is tough that way.

Sometimes the current is so strong that you can never go back to who you used to be, even for a visit, but

Dennis just nods.

Filipo goes out the door, taking

A big chunk of Dennis with him.

Who knows

if

faith cracks or

erodes,

the river of time eating away at its banks until it just

crumbles.

Looks sudden.

Isn't.

80

Chon hears the ululations of mourning.

Lying on his back, he feels cold air rush over him.

Then nothing.

Laguna Beach
1976

Cocaine,
Runnin' all 'round my brain.

—RED ARNALL, "COCAINE"

81

Doc pulls a rabbit out of a hat.

Except it ain't no rabbit and it ain't no hat—Doc pulls a glassine envelope out of John's surfboard.

Magic.

John just got home from a surfing trip with Doc to Mexico.

It wasn't Third Reef Pipeline or anything like that, but it was fine and they had a couple of girls with them and everyone had a good time. Except now they're unloading their gear in John's driveway in Dodge City and Doc takes one of John's boards and busts it open and John is like, what the hey?

"It's the future," Doc answers.

John is pissed—for one thing, it's one of his favorite boards. Two, he's twenty-four now and eligible for adult felony time. If

Doc wants to take crazy chances, why doesn't he do it with his own board?

Except Doc is like a god to him.

And now God speaks.

"You think there's money in grass?" Doc says. "Grass is Junior Achievement. Coke is Wall Street. The hippie thing is over—peace, love, stick it up your ass. Jimi—dead. Janis—dead. It's Sympathy for the Devil now."

The future is in money and the money is in coke. Stockbrokers do coke—movie producers, music executives, doctors, lawyers, Indian chiefs—they do coke, not grass.

Grass is a house in Dodge City—coke is a place on the beach.

Grass is a new van—coke is a leased Porsche.

Grass is hippie chicks and patchouli oil—coke is models and Chanel.

John gets it.

John goes with it.

It's 1976, it's the—

BuyCentennial.

82

She stares into the mirror and slowly, meticulously draws the eyeliner pencil under her eye.

The eyeliner is perfect, the mascara is perfect, the subtle blue eye shadow is perfect, the slight blush that highlights her porcelain cheekbones is perfect. She brushes her straight, lush blonde hair to a perfect shine.

Coldly, objectively, critically, Kim decides that she is
perfect.

Getting up from the stool, she steps over to the full-length mirror attached to the door of her tiny room in the double-wide down in the flats of San Juan Capistrano near the strawberry fields.

Kim straightens the classic little black dress and checks that it shows enough—but not too much—thigh, and enough—but not too much—cleavage. The dress represents months of waiting tables at the Harbor Grill in Dana Point for shitty tips and sidelong glances because Kim is a looker who doesn't look
seventeen.

She decides that the dress is perfect.

So is the black bra that pushes her breasts into the perfect globes she sees in *Vogue, Cosmo,* and even *Playboy,* which she studies to discover what men think a woman should be, and *Penthouse* to learn what men think a woman should
do.

Kim doesn't otherwise know because she's never had a boyfriend, never gone out on a date—she isn't going to get into the backseat, she isn't even going to get into the car.

She is Kim the Ice Maiden, Kim the Frigidaire, and she doesn't care what they say about her—she isn't going to waste herself on high school boys who can't do anything to make her life better or give her what she wants, which is

Something better—much better—than the series of crappy apartments and mobile homes that her mother has worked her ass off to provide, better than the series of bedmates that her mother brings home and urges to leave early before her daughter wakes up.

Kim has been saving herself, keeping herself *to* herself.

Watching, watching

Waiting, waiting for
her body to grow into her soul, for it to be
Perfect, and
Perfectly irresistible
Because you use what you have.
The world didn't give her money, or family, or position, but it
gave her
                              beauty
And now she sees that she's ready to go looking—*hunting,*
really
                    for a better life.
                    Kim has a plan.

83

She's been working on it for months.
Okay, all her life, but this particular plan came to her months
ago as she scanned the social pages of the *Orange County Regis-*
ter that customers at the diner left on the table with their spare
change.
An annual fund-raiser for cancer at the Ritz-Carlton Hotel.
She studies the photographs of the rich—their happy, perfect
smiles, their coiffed hair, beautiful, stylish clothes, confident tilts of
the head away from the camera. She sees their names, the Mr. and
Mrs., Dr. and Mrs., and thinks—
I am one of them.
They just can't see it because

They can't see me.

Kim takes the society pages home, clips the photos, and pins them to the cork bulletin board above the small desk in her room. Studies them harder than she studies algebra or chemistry or English, because those subjects will get her

nowhere

and one day on her way home from work—her pink uniform dress smudged with grease stains and coffee spots—she stops at a fabric store and buys a dress pattern. Three weeks later, she buys black fabric.

There's a problem, though—

She doesn't know how to sew and anyway they don't have a sewing machine, so the next morning she gets up, takes the pattern and the fabric, walks across the gravel "lawn," knocks on the door of Mrs. Silva's trailer, and asks,

"Can you help me?"

Mrs. Silva is in her early sixties. Her husband goes back and forth to Mexico and is often gone for weeks at a time, and Kim can hear her sewing machine from inside her room.

Mrs. Silva smiles at the pretty *guera*.

"Are you going to the prom?" she asks.

"No. Can you help me?" Kim shows Mrs. Silva one of the society page photos. "It needs to look like this."

"*Sonrisa,* that's a thousand-dollar dress."

"Except I want the neckline to be more like—"

She draws her index finger from left to right in a diagonal line across the chest.

"Come in. We'll see what we can do."

For the next two months, Kim spends every spare moment beside Mrs. Silva at the sewing table. Her new *tía* shows her how to cut, how to sew. It's difficult, complicated, but Mrs. Silva is a good seamstress and a wonderful teacher, and Kim learns.

"You have an eye for fashion," Mrs. Silva tells her.

"I love fashion," Kim confesses.

She knows that she'll need more than the dress.

There's a newsstand at the corner of Ocean and the PCH where the owner likes to look at her legs so he'll let her stand there and browse and not buy anything while she goes through *Vogue* and *Cosmo* and *WWD* and takes notes.

The makeup she sees is expensive, but she saves as much of her pay as she can (what doesn't go to help her mother with rent and food) and all her tips, and she is so careful, so careful, about her selections, so when she takes the bus to the mall and goes to Nordstrom she knows exactly what to buy—and nothing more—for the effect she wants to achieve.

The calendar is not her friend.

As Kim crosses off the days to the fund-raising event she does the unforgiving mathematics of time, her income, and what she still needs to buy.

$2.30 per hour.

Times twenty hours.

Plus $15–$20 a shift in tips

Times five . . .

Minus $60 a week to her mother for household expenses . . .

It's going to be tight.

At one of the (many) dress fittings with Mrs. Silva—

Tía Ana, now—

Tía Ana says, "The dress is coming along, but the dress without the proper foundation is nothing."

Kim doesn't know what she means.

Tía Ana is frank. "You have beautiful breasts, but they need the proper bra to make the dress look just so. An expensive dress with cheap undergarments? It is a beautiful house with a cracked foundation."

And then there are shoes.

"Men look at you from the top down," Ana says, "women from the bottom up. The first thing those *brujas* will do is look at your shoes, and then they will know who you are."

So Kim starts looking at shoes—in the newspaper, the magazines, in shop windows. She sees the perfect pair in the window of a snooty shop on Forest Avenue.

Charles Jourdan.

$150.

Out of her reach, and while she can make a dress, she knows she can't make shoes.

It's a problem.

Then there's jewelry.

Obviously she can't have the real thing—diamonds are as beyond her reach as the stars—but she finds that she has a flair with costume jewelry, and Tía Ana helps her pick out a few pieces—a bracelet, a necklace—that set off the dress.

But the shoes.

Kim goes home and looks at the waning days of the calendar—there are more X's than blank squares—does the math, and realizes that she's not going to make it.

Her mother might have told her so.

In the few hours between (scant) sleep and cleaning other people's houses, the former Freaky Frederica, now just Freddie (her hippie days long behind her), sees her daughter's activity—the photos on the bulletin board, the pattern bag, the comings-and-goings from Mrs. Silva's trailer. Like Mrs. Silva, she misinterprets it as something to do with a prom or a dance or even (finally!) a boy, but she worries that her daughter is headed for

heartbreak

because she seems to be overreaching for a social strata in snobby Orange County that she can't achieve.

Most of the girls at Dana Hills High have money, have access, have, above all, attitude and will quickly sniff out that Kim lives in a trailer and that her mother cleans houses for a living.

She doesn't want her daughter to feel

ashamed

and, besides, she's proud of who they are, who *she* is, an independent woman making it (just, but making it) on her own.

Kim is smart, Kim could go to community college, maybe even a four-year school on a scholarship if she'd study, but Kim is too interested in the fashion magazines and the

mirror.

Freddie tries to tell her so, but Kim doesn't listen.

What she could tell her mother is that you don't start your journey of Upward Mobility on the stairs; you take the elevator.

But either way, you need the right

shoes.

84

Stan accepts the rolled-up dollar bill from Diane's hand—

—oh, Eve—

—leans over the counter at the Bread and Marigolds Bookstore, and snorts the line of cocaine.

Doc grins at him. "And?"

"Wow."

Diane is already grinning because Doc, chivalrous gentleman that he is, offered her the first line. Her brain buzzes and the little bees quickly work their way down to her pussy, industrious ("busy as") and lascivious (flower-to-flower) creatures that they are.

Doc has a sense of reciprocity—Stan and Diane turned him on to acid; now he's returning the favor with coke. He and John have come over to the store with a sample.

Fair being fair.

Friendship being friendship.

And business being business.

(Not to mention alliteration being alliteration.)

It's good business to turn the owners of the Bread and Marigolds Bookstore on to a free sample of your new product, because while the bookstore ain't what it used to be, it's still a nerve center of the counterculture (read "drug") community, such as it is anymore.

(The community, not the drug.)

It's timely.

Stan's looking for something new, anyway.

He's tired of selling the hippie stuff, worried he's trapped in a fading culture, and, truth be told, he's a little bored with Diane, too.

And she with him.

And the political scene?

The revolution?

That they thought they won when Nixon

—the Über Villain

—the Evil Stepmother

—be honest, the Scapegoat

—(They are both conversant enough with their ancestral religion to know that the goat was loaded with all of society's evils and driven from the town)

fell from power

and The War ended

It's come to Jimmy Carter.

Jimmy Carter.

Jimmuh Cahtuh.

With his lust in his heart.

Diane doesn't want lust in her heart, she wants lust in her puss, in her yoni, if you must, and it's been a while since she's felt it with Stan. It's all right . . . it's pleasant . . . but . . .

pleasant?

Funny thing is, even in the free love days—when people were twisted around each other like worms in a coffee can in the bookstore's back room—she didn't participate. Neither did Stan. She out of reticence and he, she suspected, more from a fear of disease.

Now they both wonder if they missed out on something.

The other thing they wonder about is money.

It used to be something you weren't supposed to care about— bourgeois—

but now people seem to

want it and people seem to

have it.

Like Doc, for instance

Taco Jesus has more than taco money, now, and he isn't throwing it around or away. He's buying things—clothes, cars, homes—and it looks good on him, and Diane can't help but wonder—

are they missing out on something, or worse

have they missed out on something

like they're standing on the banks of a river watching the future flow away from them, and now

Stan is looking at her as if he's thinking the same thing, but she ponders if he is standing on the bank with her or floating away, and she also wonders if she cares.

She turns and watches John "do a line"—in this new vernacular. All traces of his adolescent cuteness are gone. He's lean, muscular, and powerful, and suddenly she realizes that she is ten years—a *decade*—older than she was. This boy, this child who used to sell joints from the bottom of his skateboard, is now a young man. And rich, if you believe the gossip.

Gossip, hell, she thinks—certainly John owns the house two doors down from the one they still rent. And the parade of sleek young women going in and out screams of money, and one morning she saw Stan, his fucking teacup in hand, looking out the window watching one of John's girls getting into her car, admiring—lusting after?—her long legs, her high breasts, her *Charlie's Angels* blonde hair. (Who is the actress—the one with the fake, silly name?) And then he pretended he wasn't staring, and she wished he had the honesty—okay, the balls—to come out and say, yes, he thought the girl was sexy, because she could see him chubbed up against his faded jeans, the ridiculous bell-bottoms, and if he'd been that honest she might have given him some relief, gone down on her knees and sucked his dick and let him shoot shiksa fantasy into her willing mouth, but instead he said some mealy-mouthed thing about the "superficiality" of it all so she decided to leave him hanging, as it were.

Now John hands her the rolled-up bill—it's her turn again. Feeling a little silly, Diane pushes a finger against one nostril and inhales with the other and feels the coke blast her brain and then the acrid drip down her throat.

They each do another line, then, far too restless to stay in the store, decide to go for a ride.

Stan insists on driving and they all pile into their clunky old Westfalia van and she finds herself in the back with John as they cruise south on the PCH with her head and puss buzz-buzzing and she hears Doc talking to Stan about a "distributorship" like it's Amway or something.

"Even if you just buy for yourself," Doc is saying, "we'll give it to you wholesale, so you're already ahead. Then if you decide you want to make a business of it . . ."

Buzz buzz.

". . . serious money . . ."

Buzz buzz.

". . . can't be a lot of profit in leather bracelets . . ."

Suddenly she watches herself turn to John and hears herself say, "Kiss me."

John looks startled. "What?"

She repeats herself with some urgency, with some heat, with her husband two feet away, she offers her mouth, her full lips, and John takes them and she sucks his tongue into her mouth and sucks on it like a dick and she feels moist, wonderfully wet, and then Stan pulls off the road into the Harbor Grill because apparently the men are hungry and as he turns off the engine he turns and looks at her and she knows that he saw.

85

The waitress hands them menus.

"I know that girl," Doc says, watching her walk away. He turns to John, sitting in the booth beside him. "We know that girl."

John shrugs. They know lots of girls, and he's still a little blown away by Diane kissing him with her husband right there.

But if Stan is pissed, he's not showing it.

Not showing it at all, because his hand is under the table, stroking his wife's thigh, and she's looking across the table straight at John, her lips curled into a smile that wants to become a laugh.

"I know that girl," Doc repeats, then gives it up and asks Stan, "So what do you think?"

Stan strokes his beard.

Black and bushy.

"I don't know," he says, studying the menu. "I don't know."

"Don't know what?" Diane asks, as if she hadn't overheard the conversation in the van.

"Doc has a business proposition," Stan says.

"You know," Doc says. "Business."

"Oh," says Diane. "*Business.*"

"Should we be talking about this here?" Stan asks.

Diane is surprised that she feels contempt for him.

The waitress comes back for their orders.

She's pretty, Diane thinks.

A cheerleader.

They all order omelets.

Diane sees Stan (sneakily) look at the girl's tits.

"Do we know each other?" Doc asks the girl.

"I don't know," she says. "I don't think so."

You couldn't describe the girl as bubbly, Diane thinks, but you wouldn't call her cold, either.

She's reserved.

Older than her age.

"I just think I know you from somewhere," Doc says.

Kim thinks, maybe it's because you used to sleep with my mother with me there, but she doesn't say anything. If Doc doesn't remember her, good. If no one remembers her, good.

"Jesus, will you let it go?" John mutters at Doc.

Kim remembers him, too.

The boy who lived in the cave and ignored her.

Stan watches her ass as she walks away, then says to Doc, "I don't think we have the money to buy in."

"That's the beauty of it," Doc says. "You don't have to. You just go down to Mexico, bring some back with you, and keep a piece for yourself. Sell that piece and you're in business."

"I don't know . . ."

Doc leans over the table and says to Stan, "You could sell right out of the store. I'm telling you, this is *money.*"

"I don't know," Stan answers. "We'll have to think about it."

"Don't think about it too long," Doc says.

Cocaine doesn't make you exactly patient.

Diane looks at John.

86

As they're undressing for bed Stan asks, "So what do you think?"

"About the cocaine?"

"Yeah."

Or about me kissing another man, Diane thinks. Nothing about that? We're just going to let it slide? She tosses it back at him. "I don't know, what do you think?"

"Do we want to be drug dealers?" he asks.

She knows that they can go on for hours like this, answering questions with questions with questions.

"We dealt grass," she says; "is it so different?"

Stan unbuttons his denim shirt and hangs it up in the closet. Shucks off his jeans and hangs them on a hook on the back of the door. "Isn't it? I mean, grass is natural—this is a powder."

"That comes from a plant," she says.

"So does heroin," Stan counters. "Would we deal that?"

"No," she says, impatient now, naked now, sliding into bed. "But is cocaine addictive?"

"I don't know." He gets in beside her. "It would be nice to have some money."

"We could buy the house," she says, thinking that if he says anything about "feminine nesting instincts" she'll punch him in the face.

"But it's *drug dealing*," Stan says. "Is that what we started out to be?"

"What did we start out to be, Stan?"

To his credit, he laughs at his own pretension. "Revolution-aries."

Volunteers of America.

"The revolution is over," Diane says.

"Who won?" Stan asks.

Diane laughs and then takes him in her arms, pulls him close. His body is warm and familiar, and he gets hard quickly. She knows that he wants to slide into her, but she rolls over and straddles him.

He looks up at her, his eyes shining, and she can see him thinking.

"You saw me kissing him," she says.

He nods.

"Did it turn you on?"

He doesn't answer.

She hovers, supports herself on her thin, strong—surprisingly strong—arms, her cunt just on the head of his cock. "You can't have it until you tell me. Tell me it turned you on, watching your wife kiss another man."

"Yes."

"Yes what?"

"Yes, it turned me on. Watching you."

She lowers herself down on him and he moans. She rises and then drops again, and then she says, "I'll fuck him and you fuck her."

"Who?"

" 'Who?' " she mocks. "The Hitler Youth waitress you were ogling."

She leans over, rocks on him, and whispers, "I'm fucking him and you're fucking her. You're fucking her sweet little blonde cunt, you're feeling her tits, her ass . . ."

Stan grabs her by the waist and turns her over. Pulls her up onto her knees and plunges into her. Uncharacteristically, ungently, he pounds her, bruises her ass and the back of her thighs.

"That's right," she says. "Take her. She wants you to just take her. That's right, that's right, that's right, that's right . . ."

Then she feels him go soft.

"I just . . ." he says. "I just want *you*."

Like the sex narcs are watching you, she thinks.

Later, he says, "I'll talk to Doc in the morning."

87

Diane sips her coffee and looks out the window.

At John's house.

She pretends to vacillate, but she already knows what she's going to do. Diane's too honest to fool herself for long. Too honest not to acknowledge that she now feels justified by jealousy over Stan's easy acquiescence to her manipulation, fantasy-fucking the teenage waitress, then unable to carry it all the way through.

Setting the cup on the counter, she walks out the door.

Warm spring morning.

Knocks on John's door.

It seems like forever before he answers, but then he opens the door. His hair is sleep-tousled, his denim shirt unbuttoned.

Barefoot.

A cup of coffee in his hand.

"Hi," he says.

88

Stan and Doc meet at the Harbor Grill.

Kim is their waitress.

"Do you ever go home?" Doc asks her.

"I wanted extra shifts."

Charles Jourdans.

$150.00.

Money she isn't going to make no matter how many extra shifts she works. She takes their order and goes to the kitchen.

"Have you thought it over?" Doc asks.

"Diane and I talked about it," Stan says.

"And?"

Stan hesitates.

He's more than aware of Diane's (irrational, unfair) contempt for him. She despises him for not wanting to have sex with another woman? Not even a woman, but a teenage girl?

It's crazy, but he does feel emasculated.

He knows that money would make it better, money would give him his balls back, the kind of money Doc is talking about . . .

"We're going to say no," Stan says.

"That's cool," Doc says.

Stan can see he thinks it's anything but cool.

He thinks it's pussy.

But Stan has weighed the pros and cons. The money would be great, but you have to weigh it against the risk of getting busted, spending years in prison, maybe a *Mexican* prison, and then there are the ethical issues . . .

"Not that we don't appreciate the offer," Stan says.

"Sure," Doc says.

The waitress brings their food and they eat pretty much in silence, with forced, desultory conversation.

Doc is relieved when Stan gets up and says he has to open the store.

"I've got the check," Doc says.

"No, let me—"

"Nah, I got it."

Stan thanks him and leaves.

The waitress comes over with the check, lays it on the table, and says, "*I'll* do it."

"I'm sorry—what?"

"*I'll* do it," Kim says. Just one time, but—

I'll do it.

89

"She's a fucking kid," John says.

"You were a fucking kid."

"It's different."

"How?"

"That was grass," John says. "This is coke. That's hard time."

Doc shakes his head. "It's juvenile time. Worst that can happen is that she does a few months in juvie."

Doc knows this, for chrissakes—he did time in the juvenile system. He also knows that she may go in a kid, but she won't come out one. Between the girl gangs and the dykes, she'll be just a piece of white meat.

"She asked me," Doc says defensively. "I didn't ask her. Anyway, I remember who she is."

"That's great," John says. He doesn't ask, he doesn't care.

"You remember Freaky Frederica?" Doc asks.

"No."

"When you were living in a fucking cave, hotshot?" Doc prompts. "That was her little girl."

John doesn't remember her.

"She'll look just like any other teenager with a fake ID," Doc says. "She'll bat those blue eyes and walk right through."

"Yeah?" John asks. "What if she doesn't, Doc? What if she gets popped? You think she's going to keep her mouth shut and do her time? She'll give us up in a heartbeat."

Worse, he thinks, is that we won't know it. They'll tape that coke back up to her and let her bring it right to us.

With an escort of narcs.

Doc's ahead of him. "Our Mexican suppliers will clock her through the border check. If she doesn't go right through, we go straight to the airport, cool out in Tahiti for a while."

And the girl, John thinks, what's her name . . .

Kim?

. . . can cool out in juvie.

Nice.

Kim walks toward the border check

like any number of American teenagers who go to Tijuana for a day of drinking and then come back to San Diego over the pedestrian bridge at the San Ysidro crossing.

Medical tape is wrapped around her rib cage, holding the bags of cocaine firmly under her breasts. Slimmer, smaller packets—still valuable—are taped to the insides of her thighs.

She had stood, humiliated, in her bra and panties inside a house while the Mexican *abuelas* taped the packets to her body. Mentally, she removed herself from the scene, trying not to feel their hands on her, or the eyes of the drug trafficker who stared at her with undisguised lust.

I am a princess, she told herself, being prepared for a ball

No

I'm a high-fashion model and they are fussing over last-minute details before I go out on the runway, and the man is

A photographer, studying how he can best capture my beauty, my

essence for his camera, and *finally*

they were done and she pulled the loose-fitting peasant blouse over her head and slipped back into the jeans and the women stroked and patted her until they were satisfied that the packets could not be seen or even easily felt, and then she put on her tennis shoes and hefted the cheap canvas bag over her shoulder.

Doc told her that most kids might slip a couple of joints or a bag of cheap ditch weed into the bottom of their bags, and that's what the customs guys will be looking for.

"If they search anything, they'll search the bag," Doc said. "When they see that it's clean, they won't do a body search."

Say what you will about Doc, he makes the kids go to school.

The leering drug trafficker drove her out near the border crossing, and now she walks toward the checkpoint and tries to control her fear.

The truth is she's terrified.

Despite Doc's reassurances.

"You won't get caught," he said, "but if you do, you'll spend a few weeks—maybe—in juvenile hall."

Now in the pedestrian line at the checkpoint she balances a few weeks in juvenile hall against the pair of Charles Jourdans and tells herself that she made the right choice, but she's still frightened and knows that's a bad thing.

"They look for signs of nerves," Doc told her. "Sweating, fidgeting. Whatever you do, don't touch yourself, like, to make sure the packets are still in place. They will be. Keep your hands away from your body. Just act natural."

(Doc doesn't know

Kim doesn't know

that she's spent her entire life so far

trying not to act

natural.

Nature is a cave

Nature is dirty.)

Now there are only two people in front of her. She shifts her weight onto one hip, posturing a teenager's impatience.

"If you get caught," Doc said, "which you won't, they'll ask you who gave you the drugs. Just say that some Mexican guys approached you on the street and offered you money and you couldn't resist the temptation."

"How much money?" Kim, always pragmatic, asked.

"Five hundred dollars," Doc said.

They were going to meet you at the trolley stop at the main

train station in San Diego. You were going to go into the ladies' room stall, give the dope to a woman there, and get paid.

Now she rehearses the story in her head.

Some Mexican men came up to me on Avenida Revolución. One of them was named Miguel. He offered me five hundred dollars. That's so much money—I'm a waitress. I went into the bathroom of a restaurant with his girlfriend—I think she said her name was Rita—and she taped the drugs to me. I'm sorry, I'm so sorry. I've never done anything like this. I'll never do it again, I swear. Ever.

Only one person ahead of her now.

She feels her heart race.

She thinks about turning around, going back.

Then the customs agent waves her forward.

91

Doc hangs up the receiver of the pay phone on Ocean Avenue and walks back into the Marine Room.

John sits at the bar, nursing a beer and idly watching the base-ball game on television.

"She's in line," Doc says.

His tone is cool, but John can tell that Doc is nervous.

92

Stan and Diane sit in their small living room.
Reading.
He Updike, she Cheever.
She looks up from her book and says,
"I fucked John McAlister."

93

The customs officer tells Kim to set her bag on the table and open it.
He watches her, not the bag, as she does.
And sees
Nothing.
The girl is totally calm
unconcerned.
Aloof, detached.
He looks into the bag and sees
the strand of Kotex that Doc provided her with, told her to put on top.
Kim looks at the customs officer coolly, as if to say
Hey, *you* told me to open it.
He hands her the bag and welcomes her back to the United States.
She crosses the bridge.

94

Kim walks into the shop and asks to try on the Charles Jourdans.

The clerk looks at her in her pink waitress uniform with that "You're wasting my time" look, but something in Kim's eyes makes her go find a pair of 5½s and bring them out.

Kim makes her bring out 5s and 6s, too, just to be sure, but the 5½s fit

perfectly

and Kim says she'll take them.

The clerk takes the shoes to the counter and asks for a credit card.

Kim pays cash.

God as my witness, I'll never be hungry again.

95

Tía Ana dresses her.
For she knows not what
But
the girl is beautiful.
No, not beautiful—
Exquisite.

For a week, Stan says nothing about Diane's announcement.

He's sly enough to know that this seeming indifference is the best revenge, the harshest way to punish her, to inflict retaliatory pain, to pretend that her infidelity

isn't important enough to merit discussion, and besides,

he doesn't know what to say, having already confessed that her kissing John turned him on, and also, the truth of it is—

he's afraid to talk about it

Afraid of the confrontation igniting a

conflagration

that might end in his having to demand a divorce

(What if she doesn't apologize? What if she says she's going to do it again? With John? With other men? What if she demands an "open marriage"?)

which he doesn't want.

So Stan pretends that his silence is a punishment and Diane pretends to believe the same, although she's pretty sure that—

He's actually afraid, and it deepens her

Contempt, which tempers her

shame

Not so much that she cheated on her husband, but the fact that she bestowed herself on John, who didn't seem to think it was such a

Big deal.

They did it, and it was nice, it was good, but it was nothing special, and afterward he got up and got a beer and offered her one (she declined) and he didn't ask "What now" or "What next" and she just went home and washed him out of herself and couldn't avoid the truth that she betrayed Stan for nothing

and then Stan decided to punish her with silence, which was so stupid because couldn't he see that she'd done it largely to give them

something to *talk about?*

But they settled into silence

an unspoken agreement to pretend and

Diane begins to think that maybe it's the necessity of marriage to let scar tissue form over the wounds so that you both become, literally,

callous.

They settled into silence until

tonight

Stan sets his Updike down, gets up, and says that he's going to the store to

take inventory.

97

Kim pauses in the lobby outside the fund-raiser cocktail party and experiences

A moment of self-doubt.

The women are so elegant, so beautifully turned out, so confident in their wealth and elegance. The men are so casual and handsome, so well dressed. Their laughter comes out of the room like a challenge to her, saying—

You don't belong here

Trailer-park trash

Waitress
Your mother cleans our houses and
You lived in a cave.
She stops and stands there.
Thinks, as she did at the border check, of simply turning around and going home to the trailer, where she belongs.
It's her eighteenth birthday.

98

Stan gets a gun.
Freudian, sure, but there it is.
Finding a gun in Dodge City is like finding sand on the beach.
All he does is walk over to John's house and let himself in.
The pistol is under John's bed.

99

She turns heads.
She's that beautiful.
Exquisite, Kim walks into the cocktail party uninvited
    with her head high
        you might call her bearing
           regal

and no one stops her at the door, no one has the nerve to tell this lovely creature that she can't come in.

Even the women, although jealous, are intrigued. They want to see what's going to happen, they want to test their husbands and boyfriends and their own attractiveness against this newcomer.

Kim walks through the crowd, seemingly unconscious of their stares—certainly not self-conscious—walks to the bar, asks for a glass of Chablis, and gets it

She looks twenty-three, at least

No one asks for an ID or an invitation—

And then, glass at her lips, she coolly turns to survey the crowd as if to determine whether they're

worthy of her interest.

It's a stunning debut.

Kim is certainly not a debutante, there was no money for even a Sweet Sixteen, but this is her

Coming-Out Party.

100

John's at a different kind of party.

What would come to be known as the Great Laguna Blizzard of 1976.

It snowed like hell inside Doc's house that night.

Cocaine *everywhere,* and most of the Association boys nose-deep in it. Cocaine on mirrors, cocaine on tabletops, cocaine on magazine covers—Doc hosting like some kind of surfer-dude Mad Hatter at the tea party.

John sits back and watches the circus.

He doesn't do coke.

Well, he did when they brought it up from Mexico. John took a couple of snorts the way a winemaker might take a couple of sips, pronounced it "okay," and then forgot about it.

Coke is too crazy for him.

People get too jacked up.

But this is a coming-out party for coke, in Laguna at least, a sort of motivational seminar for the sales force—

You can only sell what you love. Is everybody excited?!

—so John could give a shit. He smokes a j, sips a little Scotch, and lets it snow, snow, snow.

And scopes the women.

Shit, Doc has really stocked the pond on this one. Sleek, long-legged women are everywhere, and they're digging the coke. He doesn't even have to get up from the couch and—bingo, bango—an incredibly gorgeous auburn-haired chick in a miniskirt comes up and sits down next to him.

"I'm Taylor," she says.

"John."

The white smudge under her nose looks cute, but John leans over and wipes it off.

"Don't waste that," she says. She holds his wrist and licks the coke off his fingers, then says, "Taste of what's to come."

Except he hears

"You slept with my wife."

John looks up and Stan is standing over him, looking stupid in his denim jacket and jeans, stupider with this look of rage on his face.

"You slept with my wife," he repeats.

Taylor giggles.

John tries to go the chivalric route. "Stan, I don't know what you're—"

"She told me."

John says, "Okay, I slept with your wife."

Like, now what?

Stan doesn't know.

He stands there looking confused and uncertain and stupid and John just wishes he would go away so that he can get back to Taylor and things to come and is about to tell him so when

Stan pulls a pistol from his pocket.

101

Kim is a triumph at the cocktail party.

Think Cinderella (if you haven't already), think Sabrina (see above); point is, she kills.

Even the Orange County bitches, who normally would have sliced her up like a gang of Benzedrine-crazed chefs at Benihana, can't touch her. It's not a matter of kindness, God knows, but of cowardice. Not one of them is brave enough to be the first shark to draw blood and start the feeding frenzy, and by the time they work themselves into a sufficiently collective indignation at this parvenu to socially gang-rape her, it's

too late

because one of the Young Men recognizes himself as a cultural trope and obediently plays

Prince Charming.

Brad Donnelly is a scion of OC nobility. Twenty-five, UCLA

alum, doing great things in Dad's real estate business, looks to match.

"I'm Brad," he says. "I don't think we've met."

"I'm Kim," she says.

It's working

just the way she

imagined it a million times

just the way she

planned it.

He smiles and walks her onto the broad deck, with its stunning view of the beach and the ocean, the sun setting like it knows it's in her movie.

"Who *are* you?" Brad asks. "Why haven't I seen you before?"

"I guess you haven't been looking."

"I'm looking now."

"So I see."

He juts his chin back toward the party inside. "They're all talking about us, you know."

"I know. Do you mind?"

"I don't care," Brad answers. They make inconsequential chit-chat for a few minutes, then Brad asks, "You want to get out of here and go to a really cool party?"

"I would love to."

102

Here's how fucked-up coke is—
This is *funny*

Guy pulls a gun and points it in somebody's face and most of the partygoers think it's a hoot. It's even funnier if you know Stan, because it's so totally un-Stan-like.

Winnie-the-Pooh packing heat.

Pretty much John's reaction—

He doesn't say—

Stan, don't.

Or

Please, don't kill me. He says, "Stan, where did you *get* that?"

"Never mind," Stan says, realizing it sounds dumb. "I should kill you."

The "should" is the giveaway.

He "should"; he's not going to.

John says, "I didn't *rape* her, Stan."

Doc, ever the good host, comes over and says, "Come on, put that away, Stan. It's a *party.*"

"He had sex with Diane," Stan says.

Doc ponders this for a moment, and then delivers a response that becomes Laguna *legend.*

"Well," Doc says, "so have *you.*"

Cocaine logic.

Irrefutable.

"Come on, man," Doc says, putting his arm around Stan's shoulder, "join the party, do a few lines."

Stan sets the pistol down on the coffee table and starts to cry.

"My man," Doc says.

"Have you ever done coke before?" Brad asks her.

"No," Kim says truthfully, neglecting to mention that the cocaine on the glass table in front of them had once been taped to her torso.

Brad does a line, then Kim does a line, and it isn't long before she lets him maneuver her into one of the bedrooms as if it were his idea. When they shut the door, he starts to undress her, but she pushes him away.

And then undresses herself.

She peels off the black dress and stands in front of him in her black bra and panties, knowing that she's a vision. She lets him look for a few seconds, then reaches behind her and unsnaps her bra.

Brad smiles, kicks off his shoes, and hurries out of his slacks and Jockey shorts. He picks her up and then drops her onto the bed. Then he nudges her legs apart, kneels between them, and reaches for her panties.

Her hand blocks him.

She looks into his eyes, smiles, and says, "No, Brad. If you want *this,* you'll have to marry it."

No one comes into Kim's room.

Without paying.

104

Coked out of his skull
Stan takes inventory.

Takes a long look at the Bread and Marigolds store and the merchandise they're trying to sell to a diminishing customer base and decides that it's over.

Sees himself in his shabby denim and feels stupid.

Less than.

Who?

John?

Doc?

Diane?

Bread and marigolds, he thinks.

Jesus.

The place is a fire trap, anyway

It only takes a little kerosene and a match.

The fire this time.

105

"Your boyfriend is pretty ripped," Doc says to Kim.

She looks over and sees Brad slumped on a sofa, his eyes glassy from coke and booze. He'll be out cold any second.

"My fiancé," she corrects.

"You're going to marry that stiff?" Doc asks.

"For a while," she answers.

"Come on," Doc says, taking her hands.

"Where are we going?"

"You know."

In his bedroom he says, "Take them off, Kim."

"Take what off?"

"The pretty clothes."

She does and stands in front of him.

Pirouettes.

"My God," Doc says.

He admires her perfect body for several seconds and then lays her down on the bed.

"Look at *that*," he says.

She puts her hand over herself and says, "No, Doc, if you want this, you'll have to—"

He laughs.

Long time coming, this rendezvous.

She wraps her arms around his broad back.

Remembers lying in a cave hearing him with her mother.

Soon it's like she's tumbling over a waterfall, and she holds him tighter.

Turns her head and sees the Charles Jourdans.

Her pretty shoes.

John pulls on his slacks and walks back into the living room.

He's fucked out.

Taylor wasn't a ride, she was the whole amusement park.

Six Flags.

Magic Mountain.

Knott's Pussy Farm.

That girl Kim, the mule, is on the couch next to a life-size Ken doll who looks like he just had his head handed to him.

She's sitting there like there isn't a drug-crazed orgy going on all around her, like there's not a pistol on the coffee table at her demure knees. Like she's about to answer questions from Miss America judges and then twirl fire batons while singing a medley from *Oklahoma!,* but whatever, because

speaking of fire

there is one.

Outside, the sky is on fire.

107

The Bread and Marigolds Bookstore is, as they say, engulfed in flame.

They all stand across the street and watch as the fire department pretty much lets it go, trying only to contain the fire and keep it from spreading to buildings they *don't* consider a public nuisance.

Their faces red in the reflection of flame, they stand and watch—

Doc

Kim

John

Stan and Diane, arms around each other's shoulders

Doc asks, "Anyone have marshmallows?"
They laugh, even Stan.
They are
Stardust
Golden
Caught in the devil's bargain.

Laguna Beach
2005

108

The sun comes red over the Laguna hills.
Ben strides to Chon's apartment.
Knocks on the door.
Waits.
A sleepy O, clad in one of Chon's T-shirts, opens the door, sees the look on Ben's face, and screams
Nooooooooooooo!

109

He's all right, Ben tells her as he walks her to the bed and makes her sit down.

He's wounded, some shrapnel, they got most of it out, he's in the hospital, he's going to be okay.

"God."

Ben allows himself a slight smile. "He called—classic Chon—and said—"

110

"I fucked up."

111

"Is he coming home?" O asks.

"No," Ben says. "Also classic Chon. He's hoping they can 'put him back together' enough so he can go back to his team."

"Jerk," O says. When Chon calls her a couple of hours later she asks, "They didn't shoot your dick off, did they?"

"No, it's still there."

She feels good hearing him laugh. She says, "Okay, I'm going out and buying a nurse's uniform . . ."

He laughs again. "*A Farewell to Arms.*"

"Is that some kind of sick joke?"

"No, it's a book."

"Yeah, I don't do books," she says. "Okay, 'Navy Nurse' or 'Candy Striper'?"

"Candy Striper. Definitely."

112

Ben walks back to his place.

He was going to tell Chon about being shaken down, but now he can't.

No way he piles on with this.

So he needs to handle it himself.

He needs a plan.

That leaves Chon out of it.

113

Chon hangs up and relishes the thought of O for a few minutes, and then moves off it because a real nurse comes with his meds.

Sanitized word for drugs

Which there's a war on. And there's also a War on Terrorism and they're connected, Chon contemplates as the meds take hold— the politicians either are on drugs or should be.

A bunch of religious fanatics mostly from Saudi Arabia fly planes into buildings and we invade . . .

Iraq.

It's a generational thing, Chon muses.

Bush Sr. goes to war against Saddam Hussein and puts troops in Saudi Arabia (which was bin Laden's reason for going to "war" against America), and Hussein tries to kill Bush Sr., and then Bush Jr.—faithful son, loyal son—uses bin Laden's attack as an excuse to get payback for Hussein's attempted hit on his dad.

41 as Brando

43 as Pacino

and featuring Saddam Hussein as Virgil "The Turk" (near miss there) Sollozzo. And the U.S.A. as a collective, credulous Diane Keaton

Just this once, Kay, I'm going to let you ask me about my business

Shut the fucking door in her face and get on with it, lock yourself up with the Cabinet and the Congress and

Guzzle the Kool-Aid.

No, Chon decides, the problem with the politicians is not that they're on drugs, it's that they're not.

The drugs they have for bipolar, schizophrenic paranoid delusions are so good now.

They work.

Problem is, they work so well that the patients think they're cured and stop taking them and get sick again and do crazy shit like invade Iraq in the delusional belief it's going to make their fathers love them.

So please, Mr. President

Chon thinks as he floats into a drug cloud of his own

Please

Don't go off the meds.

114

Drug Warrior Dennis Cain

Gets up in the morning feeling no different, which is almost a disappointment after making a Faustian deal for his soul.

I mean, you think you'd notice, right? *Something* different.

Yeah, not so much.

He makes his coffee, drinks his orange juice, kisses his wife on the cheek, makes two scrambled eggs and eats them while exchanging sleepy early-morning talk with his girls, says to his wife,

"Those countertops? I've been thinking. We can afford them."

"Really? You sure?"

"Yeah, why not? You only live once."

He finishes his breakfast, says goodbye, gets into his car, says hi to the neighbor who is getting into *his* car, and joins the other pilgrims in the commuter-hour snarl on I-15 South.

It's a pisser.

You sell your soul and no one even notices.

Not even you.

115

Judas took the thirty pieces of silver, but

Would Jesus?

If he'd been made the offer?

And if Judas was worth thirty, Jesus had to be worth, what—

Three hundred, easy.

Just sayin'.
Anyway, history shows that
They bought the wrong Jew.

116

Ben is not going to make the same mistake.

Ben is a careful consumer—O can tell you stories about Ben driving her crazy spending *weeks* trying to decide which flat-screen TV to buy, debating the relative merits of Samsung and Sony—but there is no *Consumer Reports* on Drug Cops.

He knows he has to trump the county level. The next obvious choice would be a state cop, but Ben takes the long view—if he comes up with a state cop he leaves room on the board for OGR to jump him.

("King me.")

So what he needs is a fed.

Not easy, not easy.

For one thing, the feds are notoriously honest.

(Chon would object to the pairing of "notoriously" with "honest," but he's in Afghanistan, so fuck him.)

Two, the feds are also notoriously paranoid—

(clears with Chon)

always checking on each other, and

Three, Ben has no clue how to approach a fed, or

Four

Which fed to try.

He's walking on the beach pondering this dilemma when he

sees a fisherman jam a small fish on his hook and then cast it deep in the water.

117

You can Google anything.
You can even Google a federal drug agent.
What Ben does is he goes on Google and enters
"Federal Drug Busts+California"
and gets
three million twenty thousand hits.
Your tax dollars at work.
He scrolls through, rejects most of them, and then he hits
"Massive Marijuana Seizure in Jamul."

Sees a photo of triumphant narcs standing beside bales of ditch weed and a story about this being a massive blow against the Sanchez-Lauter Cartel, the "massive blow" quote coming from a DEA agent named Dennis Cain, who has a particular look of triumphalism ("Mission accomplished") on his grille.

Dennis, Ben decides, looks like a candidate.

Ambiguity intentional.

So—

Ben gets on a pay phone and waits for Special Agent Dennis Cain to answer. When he does, Ben says simply, "5782 Terra Vista in Modjeska Canyon. Grow house. Premium hydro."

"Who is this?"

"You want it or not?"

"Can you repeat the information?"

"Come on. The call is recorded."

Ben clicks out.

Then he calls his grower at 5782 Terra Vista in Modjeska Canyon.

"Bail."

"What?"

"Bail," Ben repeats. "Take as much of the good shit as you can get into your car and leave the rest. Do it *now,* Kev."

Dennis listens to the recording, doesn't recognize the voice.

He's not big on anonymous sources.

Usually it's a practical joke, someone trying to harass an ex-girlfriend or wife, or it's a new player. Tracking the call, he finds out it came from a pay phone at John Wayne Airport. He thinks about giving it to the OC Task Force, let them waste *their* time, but it's a slow day so he decides it's worth a ride up to Orange County to check it out. Always a nice drive along the ocean up through

Camp Pendleton, and he feels like getting out of the office, so what the hell.

The anonymous source proves to be pure gold.

Well, pure marijuana.

120

Ben waits for ten days and then hits him again, this time from the Amtrak station in downtown San Diego.

"Who are you?" Dennis asks.

"The guy who's going to get you your next promotion," Ben answers. "Unless you keep asking me who I am."

"Let's meet."

"Let's not."

"I can guarantee your security," Dennis says. "No surveillance, no wires."

"Trust you?"

"You absolutely can."

"You want this tip or you don't?"

Dennis does.

121

Ben mixes it up next time.

Sends Dennis a typed letter with a fake return address—

"Orange County Register—Classified Ads—Houses for Rent— You'll figure it out."

Dennis figures it out—there aren't that many houses for rent, and only two that have the potential to be grow houses. One turns out to contain a retired couple, the other turns out to be a grow house.

Dennis is falling in love.

But who with?

It's kind of fun having a Secret Admirer; at the same time he's a little sick of the flirtation. So far the guy has given him product, but no people.

Confiscations, not arrests.

He's getting dope off the street, but no dealers.

He tells this to Ben the next time he calls.

122

INT. DENNIS'S OFFICE - DAY

DENNIS is on the phone with BEN.

                    DENNIS

Look, I know you're getting your rocks off moving a
federal agent around like your personal sock puppet,
but that game is over. I'm not your right hand—go
jerk yourself off.

                    BEN

Hold on—I have to set the phone down.

                    DENNIS

It's that little skinny thing in your shorts. I'll
wait.

                     BEN

Jesus, what has your panties in a wad?

                    DENNIS

Let me lay this out for you, you can tell me if I've
got it right. You have some beef against a dope operation. I don't know—they're not paying you enough,
they canned you, the boss fucked your girlfriend in
the ass and she never let you, who cares. Doesn't
matter. You decide to get even, you want to fuck the
man, but you don't want to hurt your old friends and
coworkers. So you give me the grow houses and then
phone in a warning. How am I doing?

                     BEN

Not even close.

                    DENNIS

Yeah? Then how come every time I pop one of your tips,
it's a neutron bomb? The stuff is there, but all the
people are gone.

                     BEN

I don't know. Maybe you make a lot of noise going in.

                    DENNIS

You know what else makes a lot of noise going in? A
hollow-point into your brain. Which is what you're
going to get when these people figure out it's you,
which they probably already have. You need protection, which I can't offer you unless you give me a

```
meet. You need to put these people behind bars. I'm
trying to save your life here.
```

BEN

```
You're trying to make cases.
```

DENNIS

```
So call it a symbiotic relationship.
```

123

symbiosis (n.) A close and often long-term relationship between different biological species.

For example—narcs and drug dealers.

Truth is, neither can live without the other.

Ben agrees to meet Dennis.

124

O comes through the door; Paqu is in the kitchen.

"Have you been out looking for a job?" Paqu asks.

"I want to meet my father."

125

Ben sets a lot of conditions—

He's not coming into the freaking DEA office in Dago. They'll meet at a place of Ben's choosing.

Dennis comes alone—no partners, no surveillance.

It's off the books—Dennis doesn't open a CI (Confidential Informant) file.

Ben will never testify, never appear in court.

Dennis agrees to all of it, because—

Why not?

End of the day, he'll do what he wants and the CI can't do shit about it.

126

Dennis drives slowly back and forth across the Cabrillo Bridge in San Diego's Balboa Park.

On his third pass, a young man opens the passenger door and gets in.

"This is where gays meet," Dennis says by way of introduction, "to suck cock."

"I'm disturbed you know that," Ben says. "Drive down to the airport."

Dennis takes Laurel Street down through Little Italy to Lindbergh Field, where Ben has him park in the cell phone lot.

"So talk," Ben says.

He isn't who Dennis was expecting. Most marijuana types are scruffy retro-hippies—this guy looks like he could have stepped out of an Up with People rehearsal.

"Right up top," Dennis says, "if you won't testify, I can't offer you immunity."

"This isn't *Survivor,*" Ben answers. "I'm not asking for immunity."

"Got it. I'm just obligated to tell you."

"You need me to sign a release form?"

"Maybe down the road," Dennis answers. "You have a name?"

"Ben."

"I need arrests, Ben."

Ben shakes his head. "That's not your problem."

"What is my problem?"

"Self-absorption," Ben answers. "You haven't asked me what *I* need, Dennis."

"That's fair, Ben. What do you need?"

Ben tells him.

Symbiosis.

127

Wounded.

Chon hates the word.

wounded: Simple past tense and past participle of "wound."

1. Suffering from a wound, especially one acquired in battle.
2. Suffering from an emotional injury.

I am wounded (2) that I am wounded (1), Chon thinks.

He is of course aware that the word comes from the Old English "wund," from the Saxon "wunda," the Norse "und."

The Norse.

The Vikings, who believed that if you died with your sword in your hand you went straight to Valhalla to join your fallen brothers in perpetual feasting, drinking, and fucking.

(Which is clearly why they slaughtered the Christians so easily.

Come on—grubbing, guzzling, and boinking versus playing the harp?)

But if you didn't die with your sword in your hand you were basically fucked.

So Chon is a rehab *animal*.

The rehab techs have to force him to slow down, back off, but it's a challenge because Chon is determined not to be one of the wounded. He has a medical board coming up.

He's going out with his sword in his hand.

Speaking of which, he got a card from O.

Her (sort of) wearing (parts of) a Candy Striper uniform.

Sword, meet hand.

128

INT. PAQU'S HOUSE - LIVING ROOM - DAY

O and PAQU stare at each other.

<u>O</u>
I'm going to find him.

DON WINSLOW

         PAQU
I don't want you doing that.

         O
I don't care. I'm going to.

Paqu's jaws tighten.

         PAQU
Don't do it, Ophelia.

         O
Why not? Just tell me. Why not?

                129

He left when I was pregnant with you
Paqu tells her.
That's the kind of man he is.
That's the man you want to meet.

                130

Ben goes to Chad's office and leaves a briefcase.
$35K.
In Monopoly money.

160

131

"Cock*sucker*."
Duane says when he gets the word from Chad.
Decides it's time to go see
The Powers That Be.

132

The Powers That Be
Are powers because they've figured it out.
Specifically—
You don't want to be in the drug business, you want to be in
the turf business.

You get cops, judges, lawyers, muscle and charge a fee for people to sell drugs on your turf. You don't own a stall in the market,
you own the market and take a percentage of everybody else's stall.

The marijuana stall, the cocaine stall, the heroin stall, the meth-
amphetamine stall, the whatever-the-fuck-as-long-as-it's-illegal-to-
sell stall, you get your piece.

And it's not just the dealers—you get a referral fee from the
lawyers and money launderers you send them to.

In the great movie franchise that is the illicit drug trade, you
aren't actors or writers or even directors or producers.

You're CAA.

Look at it this way: if you take 15 percent of the top ten dealers
in your area, you *are* the biggest dealer in the area.

Without ever touching a drug.

Low profile, high profit.

You can't be busted.

The actual drug dealers take all the risks and bring in money every day.

If they don't—

And at some point you hope they don't, because then you

Lend them the money to make the payments.

Of course, this requires no monetary outlay on your part; you simply extend their payments while charging interest in the form of late fees.

Dig it—now you're your own credit card company.

They can never catch up—at some point you own their entire business and they become your employees—and you let them make enough money to eke out a living until you bust them out and then—

Somebody else volunteers to take their place. The suckers stand in line to take a number and get fucked because even owning 85 percent of themselves they can make a lot of money if they don't fuck it up.

It's a beautiful thing, being

The Powers That Be.

133

So Crowe goes to report that one more idiot is trying to jump off the conveyor belt.

Get him in line is the answer.

Because if one clown thinks he can dance solo, they'll all think it.

Then you don't have a business anymore.

134

Crowe finds Ben in his usual spot, usual time, sipping a latte and reading the *New York Times* online.

Duane pulls out the chair across from him and sits down.

Ben looks over the computer top. "Good morning."

"No, it isn't," Duane answers. "It's going to be a very bad morning. Monopoly money?"

Ben smiles.

"If you didn't have the money this month," Duane says, "you should have just said so. We could have worked out a payment plan."

"I have a payment plan," Ben says. "My plan is not to make any more payments."

"What are you saying?"

"I'm saying," Ben says, "I'm not paying anymore."

"Then you're out of business."

Ben shrugs.

"We'll put you *under* the jail," Crowe says. "All those charges can be reinstated. And we'll just bust you over and over and over again."

Ben says nothing.

His version of passive resistance.

He calls it "Verbal Gandhism."

("The other guy can't play tennis," Ben explained to Chon one time, "if you don't hit the ball back."

"He can't play tennis," Chon answered, "if you shoot him in the head, either.")

Duane stares at Ben for a second, then gets up and walks out.

Verbal Gandhism works.

135

So do symbiotic relationships.

Dennis walks into the Orange County Task Force office, flashes his fed-creds, and demands to see the boss.

Commander Roselli looks like he just swallowed hot piss, that's how happy he is to have a fed on his turf, trodding on the flowers, making the dogs bark. But he summons Boland upstairs and makes the introductions.

"Deputy Boland, Special Agent Dennis Cain, DEA."

Boland nods at the fed. "To what do we owe the pleasure?"

"You have an op going against a Benjamin Leonard?" Dennis asks.

Boland hesitates, looks at Roselli.

Roselli says, "Go ahead."

"Boss—"

"I said go ahead."

Boland turns back to Dennis. "Yeah, I do."

"No, you don't," Dennis says. "Whatever you had going, shit-can it. Now."

"You can't just walk in here and—"

"Yeah, I can," Dennis said. "I did."

"Leonard is dealing marijuana in our jurisdiction," Boland argues.

"He could be selling enriched uranium to Osama bin Laden outside the teacup ride at Disneyland," Dennis says, "and you will stay the fuck away from it."

"What," Boland asks, "you want the bust for yourselves?"

"He's a federal CI, idiot," Dennis snaps. "You keep fucking around, you're going to jeopardize an operation that is so far above you, you'd need a ladder to sniff its asshole. You burn this guy, you're going to be on the phone to the AG—that's the attorney general—of the *United States,* dipshit—explaining why."

Roselli says, "You're running an op on our turf, you should have let us know."

"So it could leak to our target?" Dennis asks.

"Fuck you," Roselli says.

"Okay, fuck me," Dennis answers. "Who you *don't* fuck is Leonard. Dicks out, hands off. Him, his friends, his family, his dog if he has one. There is a force field around him that you don't get near unless you want to get zapped. Do we understand each other?"

They do.

They don't like it, but they understand.

Ben Leonard is untouchable.

136

No one is untouchable.
What Duane gets told.
For example—

137

What do the following have in common?

(a) Sonny Corleone
(b) Bonnie and Clyde
(c) Filipo Sanchez

The answer is:
They should stay the fuck out of cars.

138

Nevertheless, Filipo Sanchez sits in the back of the black Humvee, the seat piled high with presents for his daughter's birthday.

Elena is going to be angry, he thinks. She believes he spoils Magda, but what's a daughter for if her papa can't spoil her? Elena says they have already spent more than enough on the party itself—and threatened to flay him alive if he was even ten minutes late—and that Magda doesn't need more things, but a girl can never have too many pretty things.

He's looking forward to the party, to seeing his daughter's face light up.

Filipo lives for these moments.

He glances down at the ridiculous blue lizard boots that his bodyguard insists on wearing. Filipo keeps trying to tell Jilberto that they live in the city now, in the very best *colonia* in Tijuana, not out on some Sinaloan backwater, but he won't listen.

They come to a traffic signal.

The light is about to turn yellow.

"Run it," he tells his driver.

He must not be late for this party and risk Elena's wrath.

But the Humvee stops.

"I said—"

Jilberto opens the door and gets out.

The driver flattens onto the seat.

Dios mío.

Three men appear in front of the car, AK-47s in their hands.

Filipo reaches for his gun as he starts to get out, but Jilberto kicks him in the chest, sending him back into the car.

Then Jilberto raises his Uzi and lets loose.

The three men open fire through the windshield.

The bullets shred Filipo and, with him, all the presents in their pretty wrappings.

Duane Crowe cracks an egg on the side of the cast iron skillet and carefully squeezes it into the hot canola oil.

He used to cook his eggs in bacon but his doctor busted his balls about his body-fat percentage, so it was either the beer or the bacon and Crowe chose the beer.

He tried turkey bacon, but . . . it's turkey bacon.

Crowe has one of those one-cup coffeemakers that even he sees the sad symbolism of. A one-cup coffeemaker is what you get when you've had two marriages go south, and now even if you have a woman stay the night, it's easier to take her out for breakfast because that way she's, well . . . out.

Last thing in the world he needs is another divorce settlement taking half of what the last two wives left him, not to mention child support.

Two kids he rarely sees, and Brittany is already applying for college (shit, where does it go?) and she's a really bright kid—a *great* kid—with good grades.

Last time she called she was looking at Notre Dame.

Crowe gets a percentage from Chad Meldrun for every client he sends through the door. It sounds like a lot of money, but he has to kick 20 percent up to the Powers That Be, so every dollar coming in means something, and every dollar lost means more.

He scoops the eggs onto a plate, shakes pepper and salt (fuck the doctor) on them, sits down at the breakfast counter, and turns on the news.

The talking head is chirping about "drug violence in Mexico" (This is news? Crowe wonders), and then a still photo of Filipo Sanchez comes on the screen.

Apparently, he's now the *late* Filipo Sanchez.

Crowe is surprised, but not *surprised.*

Filipo has developed a nasty habit of not paying his fees. Maybe it was him trying to prove his chops to the Lauter family, trying to show them that he could do more than just marry Elena, but Filipo was on a campaign to cut the Powers That Be out of the payment loop. Always bitching about the money, trying to negotiate the rate downward, missing payments, a real pain in the *culo.*

Crowe didn't blame him—you do what you can do—but Filipo's rebellion was unwise given the Lauters' ongoing war with the Berrajanos. He just became too much of a pain in the ass, and the Powers That Be decided to switch sides. It's not that they whacked Filipo, they just signed off on the Berrajanos' doing it.

Filipo didn't want to pay the fees, the Berrajanos did.

That simple.

Crowe hopes that this Ben Leonard also saw the news and took a lesson from it.

He finishes his breakfast and heads out.

Should be an interesting day today.

A real popcorn movie.

The Empire Strikes Back.

140

Ben walks back to his place—

Dennis Cain is out front waiting for him.

"Uhhh, what the *fuck,* Dennis?"

In front of my apartment? Where I live? (Where my wife sleeps and my children play with their toys?)

"It's time for your monthly contribution to the Dennis Cain Promotion Campaign," Dennis says.

Ben already knows this.

"But you don't want to be seen with me," Dennis says. "Most of my snitches like to meet on neutral ground, but every once in a while I like to show up in their native habitat so they don't get to feeling too secure."

"Let's go inside," Ben says.

They go inside.

"You want anything?" Ben asks.

"You got Diet Coke?"

"No."

"Then I don't want anything."

Dennis sits down on the sofa. "So what have you got for me? And before you answer, don't even start with a grow house or a van full of dope."

Ben looks at him—that's exactly where he was going to start.

"I know who you are and I know what you've been doing," Dennis says. "You grow top-grade hydro and you've been giving me your own factory seconds. I look like the outlet mall to you, bunkie? You pull off the freeway and sell Dennis a shirt with one sleeve longer than the other?"

"I have a lead on some high-grade—"

"You read the papers, watch the news?"

"Sure."

"Then you should know I'm a rock star," Dennis says, "and I don't want any green M&Ms in my dressing room. My last hit on the Baja Cartel went platinum, and the last thing I need is any more boo. I get any more marijuana I'll have to lay it off on eBay."

Ben is stretched out between the rock and the hard place and he has nowhere else to go.

Dennis likes the situation.

Arrogant Ben Leonard has his head caught in a vise, and Filipo Sanchez is never going to be in a position where he can testify about making a payoff to a certain federal agent.

Someone El Norte gave the nod to Filipo's assassination and is forming a new partnership with the Berrajanos. If it's true, the Sanchez-Lauters are in big trouble. Not only are the American partners changing sides, but Filipo was the last male in the royal line—there's no one to head up the family.

Dennis wonders if Filipo's guts spelled anything as they spilled out of him.

Narco Sesame Street.

Today is brought to you by the letter "F."

Fuck you, Filipo. And fuck you, Ben Leonard.

"So what do you want?" Ben asks.

"We've been over this," Dennis says. "Arrests of human beings. Growers—better yet, buyers—wholesalers, preferably. It's time for you to name names, Benny boy."

"That's not going to happen," Ben says.

"Look," Dennis answers, "I pulled you out of the shit, I can drop you right back in. It takes one phone call, and I can have an assistant make it. 'You want Ben Leonard? Take his ass. He isn't *producing* anymore.' "

"Nice."

"You want 'nice,' get into another business," Dennis says. "Sell teddy bears, Candygrams. Puppies, kittens, they're 'nice.' I'm in the arrest business—and you're in that business with me."

You're going to name names, you're going to wear a wire, you're going to help make cases, Dennis tells him.

"You want me to keep the heat off you," Dennis concludes, "you'd better wake up every morning asking yourself the following question: What can I do today to make Dennis happy?"

Dennis ain't gonna be happy.

Because Ben isn't going to name names.

He comes from a family for which the McCarthy hearings were living history. Discussed around the dinner table as if they were in that day's news. And the worst of his parents' scorn was reserved for those witnesses who

named names.

They're worse than the freaking Mafia in that regard, Stan and Diane, with their leftie *omertá,* and Stan still refuses to watch *On the Waterfront* because Kazan

named names.

You were blacklisted back in the day, and do the math, Stan and Diane were *infants*; it was a badge of honor. You were one of the Hollywood Ten, you were a hero, I'm telling you—

John Gotti is going to

name names

before Ben does.

He doesn't know the solution to Cain's demand, he just knows what he's not going to do.

He also knows that he's caught between the grinding wheels of two machines—the Orange County machine and the federal machine.

Big Government and Bigger Government.

It's enough, Ben thinks, to make a Republican out of you.

O goes to the library.

First she has to find it, and is pleasantly surprised to discover that they keep the thing right downtown and she's walked past it, like, five hundred and fifty-seven thousand times.

She could get on her computer at home, but Paqu is on the warpath, in "high dudgeon"—

O heard that phrase in a movie and always liked it, even though she doesn't know what a dudgeon is and Chon isn't around to enlighten her—

and not talking to her, which usually comes as an intense relief to O, except this time Paqu isn't talking to her while coming around every five seconds to glare at her, and she also suspects that Paqu has implanted spyware on her laptop in the completely justified paranoia that O uses her credit card to access online porn.

The last thing she wants is Paqu tripping over the words "Paul Patterson" on her computer and going bat-shit crazier.

So O goes to the library.

To do what most people who go to the library do—use the computers.

She seriously doubts that her Paul Patterson will be on Facebook but gives it a try anyway, only to find there are a few zillion Paul Pattersons on Facebook. Then she Googles Paul Patterson, only to get a few hundred zillion hits. She thinks of narrowing the search to

Paul Patterson+404 Father

But doubts that the search engine has her piquant sense of humor. So she hits

Paul Patterson+Laguna Beach

And there are some, but none who meet the demographic of her
potential daddy, so she tries
Paul Patterson+Dana Point
No luck.
She decides to go literally in the other direction with
Paul Patterson+Newport Beach.
This is what it's come to, she thinks as she scans the results—
We search for our parents on Google.

143

Crowe swings by Brian Hennessy's place and honks the horn.
Hennessy comes out a second later and gets in the car.
"You ready to do this thing?" Crowe asks him.
Brian looks down at the cast on his arm. What Ben Leonard's
attack dog did to him.
Yeah, he's ready to do this thing.

144

Scylla and Charibdis.
The rock and the hard place.
Either Ben cooperates with Cain or Cain throws him back to
OGR and Boland, who are going to be, shall we say, vindictive.

Ben needs a move and he doesn't have one.

He wishes Chon were here to help him think it through, but as they say in football, there is no play in the book for fourth and twenty-three.

It's all so fucking stupid, Ben thinks in his frustration.

Nixon declared the War on Drugs in 1973.

Thirty-plus years later, billions of dollars, thousands of lives, and the war goes on, and for what?

Nothing.

Well, not nothing, Ben thinks; it makes money.

The antidrug establishment rakes in billions of dollars—DEA, Customs, Border Patrol, ICE, thousands of state and local antidrug units, not to mention prisons. Seventy-something percent of convicts are behind bars for a drug-related crime, at an average cost of $50K a year, not to mention that most of their families are on welfare, and about the only growth industry in America right now is prison construction.

Billions on prisons, billions more trying to keep drugs from coming across the border while schools have to hold bake sales to buy books and paper and pencils, so I guess the idea is to keep our kids safe from drugs by making them as stupid as the politicians who perpetuate this insanity.

Follow the money.

The War on Drugs?

The Whore on Drugs.

He's in the middle of this happy thought when the doorbell rings.

145

O breezes past him into the apartment.

Talking the whole way.

"Paul Patterson," she says. "Newport Beach. Stockbroker. Appropriate age. More money than God. *Exactly* the kind of man Paqu would fix her bull's-eye on."

She lies down on the sofa like she's in some old-fashioned shrink's office. Ben, recognizing his role, sits down in a chair and asks, "Are you going to contact him?"

"I dunno," she moans. "Should I?"

The doorbell rings again.

"Hold that thought," Ben says.

He gets up and opens the door.

146

It's Chon.

Laguna Beach
1981

It may be the Devil or
It may be the Lord
But you're gonna have to serve somebody.

—BOB DYLAN, "SERVE SOMEBODY"

147

John watches the wave roll toward him.

First of a set.

Thick, bottom-heavy.

He starts to paddle into it, then changes his mind—like fuck it, it's too much work—and duck-dives through the lip of the wave.

Bobby Z sits on the other side.

Bobby Zacharias, like John, one of the younger members of the Association. Ultra laid-back, ultra cool, moves literally tons of Maui Wowi from the Best Coast to the Least Coast, lighting up Times Square like it ain't never been lit up before.

John slides down the backface.

"Didn't want it?" Bobby asks him.

"I guess not."

They didn't come out here to surf, they came out to talk away from the eyes and ears of too-cozy Laguna, away from the binocs and microphones of the DEA and the local heat, and, let's face it—

—hard to keep a wire dry in the water.

Not because they don't trust each other, but because they don't trust *anybody*.

Sign o' the times.

The seventies are cooked.

The silly season is *over*.

You don't think so, ask Jimmy Carter. You don't believe Jimmy, ask Ronald Reagan.

Ronald Reagan.

Say it again—

Ronald Reagan.

President Ronald Reagan, and that cowboy was ready to scrub Iran off his map like it was mustard on his tie, and ayatollahs couldn't wait to give back those hostages when Ronnie got the news to them that either the hostages go to Germany or Germany comes to Tehran in the form of the 101st Airborne armed with nuclear-tipped .44 Magnums.

Make my day.

Do you feel lucky, Khomeini?

Apparently not—

444 and out.

Like, we ain't fuckin' around anymore

We *like* dusting people off.

We don't *drink* the Kool-Aid, we put our boot on your chest and pour the Kool-Aid down your fucking throat.

Reagan, like all American trends, came out of California. The country migrated out to the West Coast, got closed out by the shore break, and now it's all backwash. Dig it, it has nowhere else to *go* but back.

It's business now, baby, it's the eighties, it's you do not fuck with the money, you don't lust in your heart—you lust in your portfolio, Gordon Gecko ain't quite there yet but he's on his way, he ain't heavy he's my brother—bull*shit*, that fat lazy chucking-down-the-Quarter-Pounders-like-they're-Necco-Wafers-motherfucker is *heavy*, he's *obese*, and you ain't carrying him anywhere, he can drag his own lard-ass into the gym, or not, whatever, he's OHO

—On His Own—

Didn't he listen? What did he have, cotton in his ears? Didn't he hear the Great Communicator communicate that we're back to the good old mythical days of

Rugged Individualism?

You drive your *own* Forty-Mule Team (not to be mistaken for forty acres and a mule—that's for, you know, *them*) of Borax across the economic desert, you stand tall on your *own* two feet.

Commune?

Commune with my ass.

And trust?

I got your trust for you right here, motherfucker.

Unless you're talking trust *fund,* keep trust out of your mouth, baby. "Trust"—the verb—is mostly for the past tense, as in

"I trusted him"

—ex-wife

"I trusted her"

—ex-husband

"I trusted him"

—guy sitting in the hole after selling dope to a trusted friend who had a mike taped to his shaven chest

hence—

John and Bobby meet out in the ocean, where neither one of

them can wear a wire. They let the next wave roll under them, then Bobby says, "I heard that Doc got busted."

"Bullshit," John says.

If Doc got popped, he'd tell me.

Wouldn't he?

"I hear it's federal," Bobby says. "Serious weight, serious time."

John knows that Bobby's concern isn't for Doc's welfare.

"Doc wouldn't flip," John says. Even if he would, John can't help thinking, Doc can't trade up. He's on the top of the pyramid, and the feds don't trade down.

Bobby's ahead of him. "Maybe the cops would go for quantity over quality. How many guys could Doc give up?"

The answer is a lot, but John doesn't care how many, he cares who.

Like him.

"If Doc's looking at fifteen years," Bobby says, "maybe he gives us all up instead. Maybe he gives them the whole Association."

"That's not Doc."

"That's not the *old* Doc," Bobby answers. "The *new* Doc . . ."

He leaves it hanging.

Doesn't need to finish. John knows what he means.

Doc has changed.

Okay, who hasn't, but Doc has *changed*. He isn't the Doc you knew in the old days, springing for tacos. He isn't the "this pie is big enough for everybody" Doc—he's the "this pie is big enough for Doc" Doc.

It's coke.

Coke isn't grass.

Grass makes you mellow, coke makes you paranoid.

Grass inhibits your ambition, coke makes you want to be—

King of Everything.

Which is what Doc seems to want. More and more John hears

Doc using the first-person possessive pronoun—singular—more and more he hears him use "my" instead of "our." It's Woodstock to Altamont—this ain't *our* stage, asshole, it's *my* stage. And you don't come on *my* stage.

And Doc is starting to treat the Association like it's his stage.

To be fair, other guys are getting weird, too. Mike, Glen, Duane, Ron, Bobby—all the Association guys are getting hinky with each other, starting to quarrel over territory, customers, suppliers. Guys who used to share the same wave can't share the coke business.

And narcs love that. They *exist* on the divide-and-conquer, it's their bread and butter. And now they've busted Doc?

"We don't know if it's true," John says.

"Can we take the chance?" Bobby asks. "Look, even if it isn't true this time, it's going to be true the next. The way Doc's going, it's not if, it's when. And you know that, John."

John doesn't answer.

The last wave of the set rolls through.

148

Being a shrink in Laguna is like being a fisherman at SeaWorld.

(What Chon would later come to call a Target-Rich Environment.)

You dip your line in *those* waters, your net is going to be full of thrashing, flopping, gasping creatures faster than you can say, "And how does that make you feel?"

Which is what Diane now asks the woman sitting (not lying) on the sofa across from her.

After the Viking funeral of the Bread and Marigolds Bookstore, Stan and Diane decided that society's ills were more likely to be cured by Reich and Lowen than by Marx and Chomsky.

So they went back to school (UC Irvine, and if that ain't irony for you, you haven't been to Irvine) and became

Psychotherapists.

Stan and Diane soon developed a clientele of sixties refugees, acid casualties, strident feminists, confused men, manic-depressives (not "bipolar" yet), drug addicts (see "sixties casualties," supra), alcoholics, and people whose mothers really *didn't* love them.

It's easy to make fun, but Stan and Diane turn out to be really good at what they do, and they help people. Except maybe not so much the young woman in Diane's office right now, working through her (let's face it, probably *first*) divorce.

"I don't know if you *can* help her," Stan said over dinner last night. "That kind of narcissistic personality disorder is almost impossible to treat. There is no pharmacological protocol, and schema therapy has its own problems."

"I've been working more with cognitive techniques," Diane answered, sipping the excellent red that Stan brought home.

They've built a nice, tidy life since she went a little crazy with John McAlister and Stan responded by burning down the store. They made enough money from the insurance settlement to buy the house in what was formerly known as Dodge City and use it as both a home and an office. They've made new "couple" friends, exchange gourmet dinner parties, and now Stan has become quite the oenophile with a small but sophisticated cellar.

If this life lacks excitement, it also lacks chaos.

"Have your cognitive techniques had any effect?" Stan asked drily, in regard to her difficult client.

"Not yet," she answered.

Now she sits and tries to focus on Kim's umpteenth and constantly changing repetition of her story—her upbringing in a wealthy albeit emotionally unavailable family, which provoked her young marriage to a "white knight" savior who was just another version of her remote father and who doesn't understand or appreciate her and how she cannot seem to relate sexually no matter how hard she tries, and what Diane is thinking is—

I want a baby.

149

John takes a carpet cutter and methodically slashes the tires of the BMW.

Then he turns to Taylor and says, "*Now* go."

"That's *my car*," she says.

A new silver 528i.

"I bought it for you," John answers.

"That doesn't mean you can just *mutilate* it."

John shrugs—apparently it does. He bought the Beamer, he bought the Porsche 911 that sits next to it, bought the three-car garage that also holds the '54 Plymouth wagon, bought the house on Moss Bay.

Cocaine been bery bery good to me.

"Now you're just going to have to pay for new tires," Taylor says.

Which means she isn't leaving, John thinks with mixed feelings. She says she's going to leave, she threatens to leave, she even *starts* to leave, but

she doesn't leave.

The coke is too good, the sex is too good, the house is too good. She's not about to move back into some efficiency apartment in West Hollywood and blow producers for one-line roles on shitty TV shows.

John loves her in his own way, which is sort of

detached.

She's so fucking beautiful, will do anything in bed, looks good on his arm when they go out, and can actually be pretty nice when she doesn't want to fight.

But the girl does like to fight.

John doesn't know how this latest one started. He doesn't even know what it's about because she hasn't told him yet. All he knows is that he came home from "surfing" with Bobby and she was waiting with a head of steam worked up.

"I have enough problems today," John said, hoping to hold it off.

Nah—

"I want to talk about the 'c' word," she snapped.

" 'Cunt'?" he asked.

Because he's not a big believer in argument foreplay. Might as well just get into the fucking fight.

Yeah—

Next thing John knew, shit was flying around the kitchen like *The Amityville Horror*. When she figured she'd broken enough expensive glassware she went upstairs to pack. John stood in their bedroom doorway and watched her jam things into suitcases.

Dresses he bought her, shoes he bought her, jewelry he bought her.

Suitcases he bought her.

"This time you're really leaving, right?" he asked.

"That's right."

She stormed down into the garage, and that's when he slashed the tires.

Now she stands there looking at him.

God, she is fucking gorgeous, John thinks. He grabs her by the waist and sets her on the hood of the car. Spreads her legs, tears off her panties, and does her right there. Only thing that could have made it better is if he could have started the engine first.

He pulls out, tucks himself in, looks at her, and says, "Now I'll have to get it detailed, too."

She says, "I'm pregnant."

150

Kim thanks God that among the long list of things at which Brad did not succeed, one of them was knocking her up.

He didn't succeed at taking over his father's car dealership, didn't succeed at investments, didn't succeed at the club, didn't succeed in the bedroom. He did succeed at getting blow jobs from his receptionist, that was one thing. (My God, if he had failed at *that*.)

He did succeed at being her Starter Husband, providing her with a good divorce settlement and enough income to live, as they say, the life to which she had become accustomed.

And on which she wants an

upgrade.

She thinks now of quitting therapy, it doesn't seem to be doing her

any good

and she sniffs a scent of condescension in Diane's tone these days, as if Kim's problems are not sufficiently compelling to warrant her full attention.

No, she decides, the money would be better spent on improving her nose, which, let's be honest, is somewhat less than
                    perfect
Twenty-three now, the body requires maintenance, as it will soon be reentering a very competitive market. The next husband will have to be a
                    Stockbroker
                    Real estate developer
Better yet
                    Old money.
And for that, the nose must be perfect, the boobs perfect, the stomach flat and taut, and, thank God, again—
                    No stretch marks.
Sometimes terror strikes her like a blow to the chest.
She feels like she can't breathe.
This existential fear.
Of the nothingness of herself.

151

John arranges to meet Doc down at Dana Point Marina.

Doc shows up in a bloodred Lamborghini Countach and pulls up beside John's Porsche.

It bothers John because cops hate this kind of flash. The straight cops think you're rubbing it in their noses and go after you all the harder; the guys on the arm don't like you flaunting it, because the honest citizens see what they think are drug dealers tooling around openly and wonder why, if they can see it, the cops can't.

Plus, the cops on your payroll see you riding a $300,000 sled and think maybe you're not paying them enough.

It's just a bad idea.

Doc sees the look of disapproval on John's puss and says, "Hey, we take the risks, we should enjoy the rewards, right? Otherwise we might as well be selling insurance."

"There are limits, Doc."

"That's not exactly a Toyota," Doc answers, pointing at the Porsche.

John sees that there's no point in arguing—Doc is tooted up. It's becoming a problem, Doc hoovering his own product. It makes him irrational, unpredictable, prone to mistakes. Maybe one of those mistakes got him popped, John thinks. Maybe it's true.

It's a problem. John and Doc aren't just in the dope business together—they have a restaurant together, a bar, a couple of apartment buildings. John gets popped and the feds could take it all.

They walk through the marina, then across the bridge out toward the long, narrow jetty.

"Taylor's pregnant," John says.

Doc says, "They know what causes that now, you know."

"She was on the Pill."

"That's what she told you."

"You're saying she got knocked up intentionally?"

"You saying she didn't?" Doc says. "Come on."

"What?"

"Grow up."

John gets what he's saying. Another word for "baby" is "income." A fat check once a month for the next eighteen years. Taylor wouldn't be the first woman to palm the Pill for a payday.

"No," John says, "she's getting an abortion."

"She wants you to stop her," Doc says.

"You don't know Taylor."

("I have my career to think about," Taylor said. "I can't audition if I'm all fat and blotchy and shit."

John wanted to answer, "What fucking career? Six seconds on *Mannix* and you haven't been to an audition in a year." But he didn't need another fight.

Quit while you're ahead, right?

Anyway, she already called the clinic and made an appointment. She only told him because [a] she needed the money to pay for it, and [b] it would be nice if he took her and brought her home.

Which he's not real keen about doing, but will.)

"Okay." Doc smiles.

They walk onto the jetty. It gives them a long view—they can see anyone following them, and the cops would need a hell of a microphone to pick up anything at this distance.

"So what's really up?" Doc asks. "It isn't just your girlfriend getting knocked up."

John's surprised he feels nervous. Has to suck it up to ask, "You have something you want to tell me, Doc?"

"Like what?"

"Like you got busted?"

"The fuck you talking about?" Doc laughs.

Suddenly he looks sneaky to John. Say what you will about Doc, he was never that. He was always straight up, out there, who he was.

John hates it. Says, "If you have a problem, let's talk about it. We can work it out."

Doc laughs.

"That's big of you, junior," he says. "But save the Beatles songs for somebody else. I'm fine."

"Yeah?"

"Where are you getting this shit?" Doc asks. "Who you been talking to? Ron? Bobby?"

John doesn't answer, but Doc knows the answer.

"Look," he says, "those assholes wouldn't have known coke from Coca-Cola if it wasn't for me. I was first at the party. Shit, I *started* the party. Now the guests want my house."

It makes some sense, John thinks. If the other guys contaminate Doc, he goes into the dope version of quarantine—people won't deal with him—and they can move in on his market share.

"They're working you, J," Doc says. "Trying to drive a wedge between you and me."

That also makes sense. Doc and John are fucking Batman and Robin. You can't fight them together, but split them up . . .

"I'll deal with Bobby," John says.

"No, don't," Doc says. Then he does a terrible *Godfather* imitation. " 'Keep your friends close, your enemies closer.' Stay close to them. Get the lay of the land. Feel them out, find out who's with me, who's against me. Can you do that, Johnny, can you do that for me?"

"Sure."

"You and me," Doc says. "It's always been you and me. Always will be. Nobody can get between us, right?"

No, that's right, John thinks. They go too far back, and Doc's been

Like a father to me.

"Anyway, look," Doc says. "I'm working on some shit. I didn't want to bring it to you until it was more, you know, fully formed, let's say, but now . . ."

They drive down to Dago.

You haven't done a buck and change down the 5 through Pendleton in a bloodred Lamborghini, you haven't had the full California experience.

It's a . . . rush.

Especially with Doc steering with one hand and snorting coke off the dashboard with the other. Nevertheless, they make it to San Diego alive and pull off on India Street in Little Italy.

"You develop a sudden craving for meatballs?" John asks.

They walk into a sandwich shop—a few booths and a long counter with red stools. Doc sits down on one of the stools, orders two *sausiche* sandwiches with peppers and onions, and asks, "Is Chris around?"

"Yeah, somewhere."

"Do me a favor? Tell him Doc's here?"

" 'Doc'?"

"That's me." Doc grins.

"What are we doing?" John asks.

"Keep your shirt on."

A few minutes later, a thirtyish guy in a black suit, no tie, comes in and shakes hands with Doc.

"Chris, this is my partner, John."

Chris offers his hand. "Nice to meet you, John."

"You, too."

"Chris, you have a few minutes?" Doc asks.

"Sure," Chris says. "Let's take this somewhere else."

Doc goes to pay for the sandwiches but Chris waves it off. "I got it."

"A tip?" Doc asks.

"No."

They walk out onto Laurel Street. The planes coming in to land make a lot of noise. Doc says, "Chris, I wanted John to hear what we've been talking about."

Yeah, John wants to hear what the fuck they've been talking about.

Chris says, "I talked with my people, and they're eager to get in. We'll take as much product as you can give us, offer national distribution, a certain level of protection."

"Who are your 'people'?" John asks.

He realizes that he sounds a little rude.

Chris looks at Doc, like, who's your little friend?

Doc says, "Chris, give us a minute?"

Chris nods. "I'll go get a coffee. Just give me a wave when you're ready."

When he's out of earshot, John says, "What the fuck, Doc? The Mafia?"

"The amateur hour is over," Doc says. "These people can give us national distribution—Chicago, Detroit, Vegas—"

"I thought they worked with the Mexicans."

"Chris says they'd rather work with white people," Doc says. The truth is that the Mexicans are bypassing them, dealing directly with L.A., and the San Diego mob wants its own source.

"Jesus Christ, Doc," John says. "Once you let these people in, you never get them out."

"That's all the movies," Doc says. "They're businessmen, same as us."

"I don't know."

"What do you want to do?" Doc asks, "just stand around with our thumbs up our asses, let Bobby and them steamroll us? Fuck that. Fuck 'the Association.' That shit's over. We gotta look out for ourselves."

He waves to Chris.

Chris comes back out on the sidewalk. "We all on the same page now?"

"Totally."

Chris looks at John. "Yeah?"

"Yeah."

They get down to details—price per ounce based on volume, delivery methods, who talks to whom when and how—the nitty-gritty logistics of the dope trade.

Then Doc says, "Chris, I have one other thing."

"Tell me."

"Some people aren't going to be happy about this," Doc says. "They might try to do something about it."

Chris says, "No problem."

"No?"

"Your turn to get coffee," Chris says. "Let me make a phone call."

Twenty minutes later Chris and another guy walk into the coffee shop.

The guy is middle-aged, professionally dressed, built like a refrigerator.

"Doc, John," Chris says, "this is Frank Machianno. He's going to move up to Laguna for a while, keep an eye on things."

Frank offers his hand to each of them.

"It's a pleasure to meet you," he says.

Very quiet voice.

Competent.

John doesn't miss it—

Frank's a stone killer.

John's coming out of Papa's Tacos in South Lagoo when Bobby Z rolls up on him in his pickup.

"Hop in," Bobby says. "We need to talk."

John's not so sure they need to talk, but then he remembers Doc's request to stay close, feel Bobby out, so he gets in.

"You give any thought to what we talked about?" Bobby asks.

"I don't believe that Doc would flip on us."

Bobby says, "Someone I want you to meet."

They drive back north, up into the canyon, and pull over in the parking lot where hikers leave their cars. A white Ford Falcon's sitting there with a guy in it, and both the car and the man have narc written all over them.

The cop rolls down the window when the truck pulls up. Bobby doesn't waste any time.

"Tell this guy what you told us," he says.

"Halliday's under indictment in the San Diego Federal District," the cop says. "I don't have details because it's sealed, but I know it's a Class A felony, fifteen to thirty. They've had him under surveillance for two years."

"Tell him the rest," Bobby says.

"They've got him out there proving 'good intent,'" the cop says. "Man's a walking sound studio."

"Will he testify?" Bobby asks.

"He better," the cop says. "No testimony, no deal. Anything else?"

"Anything else?" Bobby asks John.

John shakes his head.

The narc rolls up his window and pulls out.

"Horse's mouth," Bobby says. "He's Dago DEA."

"I get it."

"Do you?" Bobby asks. "I mean, the rest of the guys are going to want to know where you come out on this thing."

"What thing?"

"We're not just going to sit back and let Doc give us up one by one," Bobby says.

John's reeling.

First, proof that Doc is ratting them out. Shit, he could have been wearing a wire while they were talking in Dana Point, while they were meeting with the people down in Dago. Then there's what Bobby seems to be saying—

"Are you talking about what I think you're talking about?" John asks.

"You wearing a wire, too?"

"Come on."

"Open your shirt."

"Fuck you."

"Open your fucking shirt!"

John opens his shirt and shows Bobby his chest. "Happy?"

Yeah, John thinks, ain't nobody happy about anything these days. But Bobby seems satisfied that John's not miked up.

"So where are you at with this thing?" Bobby asks.

"I'm neutral."

"No such gear on this bus," Bobby says. "Not to traffic in clichés, but you're either with us or against us."

John gets it.

Like the man said—

You're gonna have to serve somebody.

Sitting back in his chair, Stan puts his fingers together in a prayerful gesture in front of his chin and asks, "How can I help you?"

This man slept with my wife, Stan thinks, and now he's coming to me for help? It will be a pleasure to turn him down, cite ethical reasons, and refer him elsewhere.

"It's Doc," John says.

"What about him?"

"He's out of control," John says.

"I don't think that Doc would agree to come in and—"

"I'm not asking you to 'treat' him," John says in a tone that makes it clear what he thinks about psychotherapy. Then he tells him about the possibility that Doc has been arrested and might be making a deal with the feds.

"I don't see how that's my business," Stan says.

"You *don't?*"

"No."

"Let me explain it to you," John answers. "If Doc talks, he's not just going to give them dealers and customers—he's going to name investors."

Stan goes a little pale, and they both know why. He and Diane had taken some of the insurance money from the Bread and Marigolds Bookstore settlement and invested it in the Association.

Stan figured he'd missed the big coke train once, he wasn't going to let it pull out of the station without him again. The money from the coke paid for the house, the nice little life, the modest wine cellar.

He and Diane are shareholders. They're not involved in the day-to-day, even the year-to-year, but on major decisions, they have to be consulted.

And killing the king is kind of a major decision.

"What are you asking me to do?" Stan asks.

"Sign off."

"On?"

John just stares at him.

"Oh," Stan says, getting it.

John mocks him. "Oh."

Stan sits there, staring at the neat row of books on the shelves. Books that are supposed to have the answers.

"No one's asking you to do anything," John says. "Just give your okay."

"And if I don't?"

"You take your chances," John says.

Stan looks stricken. "I never thought . . ."

"What?"

Stan fumbles. "I never thought I'd ever have to be involved in something like *this*."

"Who did, Stan?" John asks. "If you want to talk to Diane about it—"

"No," Stan says quickly. "We don't need to bring her into this."

John shrugs. Then, "So."

"Do what you need to do, John."

John nods and gets up.

Love and peace, he thinks.

He's in the doorway when he hears Stan say, "When you had sex with my wife, did she like it?"

"I had sex with Diane?" John asks.

Must have been stoned.

It was the seventies, Stan.

Kim is surprised to see him.

"John," she says, "what a delightful surprise."

In a voice to make sure he knows that it is a surprise, but by no means a delight.

That she isn't the girl he knew from the cave.

Or the drug mule with cocaine strapped to her body.

Or the wannabe debutante performing fellatio at a party.

She's a wealthy young divorcée, long separated and well insulated from that life. The fact that she has invested some of her divorce settlement into a common business does not make them peers.

He is a dope dealer.

She is a businessperson.

"I won't keep you long," John says.

It made him laugh, he had to go through a security kiosk to get to her house on Emerald Bay. Now she stands outside her front door, looking cool, blonde, and beautiful in a summer dress and jewelry.

Princess fucking Grace.

Come off it, he thinks.

I sold coke to buy my place.

You sold your gash.

In the words of Lenny Bruce—"we're all the same cat."

"What can I do for you?" she asks.

"It's about Doc."

"Doc?"

You remember Doc—he used to fuck your mother in a cave while you lay there humming? He strapped cocaine next to your precious twat and then boosted you onto the first step of the social ladder? He turned your little investment into a small fortune?

That Doc?

"Is he unwell?" she asks, apparently recovering her memory.

"I guess you could say that," John answers.

He runs through the whole thing again.

Kim's quicker on the uptake than Stan.

And more decisive.

"I don't owe Doc anything," she says, bending over to inspect the job that the Mexican gardeners did on the flower bed. "In fact, I barely remember him."

But, like Stan, she has to get in a parting shot as he walks away—

"John?"

"Yeah?"

"Don't ever come here again," she says. "And if we should ever run into each other in public . . ."

"Got it," John says.

It's the eighties.

156

Yeah, okay, so he has the sign-offs, but
So what?
Getting permission is one thing, doing it another.
They're Surfers Slash Dope Dealers
Not Killers
Not Gangbangers

Not one of them—not Ron, not Bobby—*none* of them has ever walked up to another human being and pulled the trigger. One thing to see it in the movies, something else to do it, and none of them can even contemplate it.

So they'll have to sub it out.

Yeah, but to who?

Again, it seems to be an automatic in the movies—everyone seems to know someone who kills people—but in real life?

Laguna?

(To the extent it replicates real life.)

You have, what, respectably married middle-aged gay guys who run art galleries and do hits on the side? Murder followed by Brie, wine spritzers, and a soak in the tub?

You have some gangs up in the northern part of the county.

Mexicans in Santa Ana

Vietnamese in Garden Grove

But how do you approach them?

How do you go to them and say we want you to kill this guy

Our old friend Doc?

It doesn't matter—

John explains to BZ

Out behind the break at Brooks Street.

"He's mobbed up now," John says. "They sent a guard dog named Frankie Machine. Even if we could find someone to . . . you can't get near him."

Hire this job out to some gangbanger, all you're going to get is a dead gangbanger.

Only one who can get next to Doc these days is a close

trusted

friend.

157

John drives back down to Dago.

Has a need for *sausiche*.

158

"My appointment's tomorrow," Taylor reminds John.

"Okay."

"You're still taking me, right?"

"Right."

"And bringing me back."

"Round-trip, Taylor."

"Where are you going?"

John's slipping into a light jacket.

"Out."

"It's two in the morning!"

"Yeah, I know what time it is, Taylor."

159

The lights are pretty down in the harbor, bobbing gently with the boats moored in their slips. John eases the pistol from his jacket pocket and holds it low beside the seat.

Doc pulls a vial of coke out of his pocket and pours two lines out on the dash. Leans down and snorts them right into his nose.

John pulls the hammer back.

Doc shakes his head to knock the coke down, looks at John, and says, "I did all right, huh? Snorting blow from a Lamborghini Countach? Doesn't get much better than that, does it?"

"Hey, Doc," John says, "remember when you used to buy me tacos?"

"Yeah, I remember," Doc says. "Seems like a long time ago now."

He looks out the window, down at the pretty lights.

"Goodbye, Doc."

Guys out fishing on the stone jetty will later say that they saw the muzzle flash.

They didn't see John get out of the car and get into a black Lincoln that pulled up.

160

"The job get done?" Frankie Machine asks him.

"Yeah," John answers.

The job got done.

Frankie drops him a block from the house.

"I want the baby."

"What?" Taylor asks.

She's sleepy. It's three o'clock in the morning and John woke her up.

"I want the baby," John says.

"It's not a baby," she says, "it's a fetus."

"It's a human being."

"What are you, like, Catholic all of a sudden?" she asks. "We can't have a baby, John—we *are* babies."

You have to hand it to Taylor, John thinks.

She ain't honest often, she ain't real often, but when she is—

Bang.

She gets the job done.

"That's what I mean," he says. "If we had a kid, we'd *have* to grow up, right?"

"I don't know," she says. "I mean, I've never pictured myself as a, you know, *mother.* Can you really see yourself as a father?"

Funny fucking thing is, all of a sudden he can.

With Doc gone . . .

He's not the kid anymore; maybe he's ready to be the father.

"Let's get married," he says.

"What?"

"It's what real people do, isn't it?" John asks. "They grow up, they get married, they start families?"

It's what they do.

Isn't always what they should.

But it's what they do.

162

Stan can't sleep.

(Macbeth hath murdered sleep.)

The guilt is ferocious and yet he has to admit that he feels a little titillated.

Powerful.

Giving, if not the order, the permission.

He rolls to his side and pushes against Diane's warm ass. Reaches around and strokes her until she stirs and wiggles back into him.

She's wet enough and he pushes into her.

Into it now, she cooperates and rolls her hips.

He's harder than usual and she feels it.

"Baby," she says.

It's the best sex they've had in years. She arches her neck and pushes her ass back against his hips.

"You're so deep," she murmurs.

"I know."

She comes before he does. Reaches back and touches his face when he comes, deep inside her.

A seminal fuck.

163

John paddles out with what's left of Doc's friends at Brooks Street, paddles out and joins the circle they form with their boards. The guys look at each other guiltily, not wanting to read each other's eyes because they know what they're going to see there.

Relief.

Pretty much the same emotion that permeated the funeral.

Everyone sat there on wooden folding chairs and stared at a closed casket with this smiling photo of Doc staring back at them while some minister intoned some bullshit that Doc didn't believe in and felt guilty relief that

(a) they didn't have to deal with Doc anymore, and
(b) they didn't have to do what they were thinking about doing because
(c) Doc did it for them.

"I just can't believe that Doc killed himself," Diane said at one point.

Hard not to believe, though—the cops found Doc in his car with a pistol in his hand and most of his brains on the window.

"Did he leave a note?" Diane asked. "Give a reason?"

"Cocaine is its own reason," Stan said.

But as they were leaving he pulled John aside and asked, "Did he really kill himself?"

"Don't ask questions you don't want to know the answers to," John said. "He killed himself. Leave it at that."

Everyone will feel better if we—

—leave it at that.

Especially me.

Same thing at the paddle-out.

Some surfer-cum-minister says some lame shit and then they each float wreaths out onto the tide.

Aloha, Doc.

Surf on, dude.

John looks back to the shore and there's cops standing on the stairway.

Cops

taking pictures like it's the *Godfather* wedding or something.

An Association family portrait.

Thanks, Doc.

Time to shut it down for a while, John thinks. Let the cops get bored and move on to the next thing. He has enough money stored up, enough investments to go into hibernation for a while, manage the rental properties, sell the restaurant.

Live the life of a quiet, successful young businessman. Let the rest of these boys figure out who's going to be the next King.

The crown is a cop magnet.

Three weeks after the paddle-out John and Taylor have a small service at the gazebo overlooking Divers Cove. A few friends—most of them Taylor's—come, and they have a reception back at the house before flying off to honeymoon in Tahiti.

They stay for a month, and when they come back John sells the house on Moss Bay and moves to more modest but still comfortable digs up in Bluebird Canyon. He keeps the Porsches in the garage and drives a BMW instead.

Good thing he does.

It takes the cops about six months before they roll up the Association like an old carpet. Turns out Doc gave them a lot of names before he couldn't take the guilt and "killed himself."

Bobby, always the smartest one, took off and vanished, leaving behind only a legend.

But Mike, Duane, Ron—one by one they go off to double-digit sentences in federal lockups.

Not Stan, not Diane.

Not Kim.

John and Taylor clean up their act. Taylor gets off the blow and their baby is born healthy.

They name him John.

He's three months old when the feds indict John for drug trafficking.

Laguna Beach
2005

I watched the world float to the dark side of the moon,
After all I knew it had to be something to do with you.

—3 DOORS DOWN, "KRYPTONITE"

164

Chon stands in the doorway, leaning on a cane.

O does her happy dance and then throws her arms around him.

"Chon's home," she chants. "Chonny's home, Chonny's home, yay, yay, yay, Chonny's home!"

"Easy," he says, just maintaining balance on the cane.

"What are you doing here?" Ben asks.

"I'm a civilian now," Chon says. He walks O back over to the couch and sets her down. "Honorably discharged. Physically unfit for duty."

"Morally unfit," Ben says. "Ethically unfit, psychologically unfit, but physically unfit, no."

"What I told them, but . . ."

Ben peels O off him and hugs him.

"Welcome home, bro."

"Good to be back."

"What do you need?"

"Cold beer," Chon answers. "Hot shower. In-N-Out."

O trots to the fridge and gets him a Dos Equis.

"I'll take it into the shower," Chon says. "I'm going to be in there awhile."

Chon lets the hot water pound him and the cold beer slide down his throat and can't decide which is better.

Then he remembers he doesn't have to choose.

Doesn't have to watch his back.

Doesn't have to listen for the sound of an IED going off or the whistling of a mortar round coming in.

Doesn't have to wash a buddy's blood off his hands.

Doesn't have to kill anyone tonight.

Tonight he can close his eyes.

There's no war here.

165

Scott Munson drives to the pull-off on the Ortega Highway that winds through the hills east of San Juan Capistrano.

The customer's already there.

For three pounds of Ben and Chon's best boo.

He's a new customer, and delivering this kind of weight to a newbie is a violation of Ben and Chon's rules, but three pounds is $12,000—a profit of $2,400—and if the newbie turns into a regular—which he will once his customers get a taste of this shit—Scott is looking at a new income stream.

Which he needs because he wants to give Traci a ring for her birthday—speaking of violations of Ben and Chon's rules, Traci is a ride-along on this delivery—

Strictly verboten.

("Another word for 'passenger,' " Chon has lectured the sales force, "is 'witness.' Another synonym is 'snitch.'

"You don't want to put your friends and loved ones in a morally impossible situation," Ben added, "in which they have to choose between their loyalty to you and their freedom. Just don't do it.")

Yeah, fair enough, but you try to tell Traci she isn't coming for a ride.

Shoulder-length auburn hair, tight rack, almond eyes, and the sweetest personality in South Orange County. Let Chon tell her she has to sit at home while you drive out to East Jesus—

More B&C Rules:

> Your customers *never* come to your house, you go to
>   them
> You make your meets in remote areas
> between nine PM and six AM, because cops don't like to
>   work those hours.

three out of four ain't bad, and what B&C don't know won't hurt them, so you let her come along because it's a long drive and you like to smell her hair.

"Just wait in the car," Scott tells her as he pulls over. "This will only take a minute."

"Cool."

He leaves the battery on so she can listen to the radio and gets out.

166

"There's a chick in the car," Brian says.
"Bad luck," answers Duane.
"Maybe we should call it off."
"You got twelve grand on you?"
He opens the car door and gets out.

167

Scott bends over to take the bags from the trunk.

Duane pulls the pistol from the back of his jeans and shoots him in the back of the head.

The muzzle flashes light up the car.

Duane walks around and opens the passenger door.

The pretty girl's hands grip the dashboard, she stares straight ahead, her mouth wide open in terror.

"I'm not going to hurt you," Duane whispers in her ear. Her hair smells nice, like she just washed it with some expensive shampoo. "Just close your eyes while we get back into the car. Don't open them until you've heard us drive away, okay?"

She nods, unable to speak.

Then she closes her eyes tight, like a child trying not to remember a bad dream.

Duane strokes her hair with the back of his hand.

Then he steps back and shoots her.

168

"I want to do it," Chon says.

"Go for it," Ben says, smiling.

Chon leans out the window and talks into the speaker.

"Two double-doubles," he says, "with everything, and a choco-
late shake."

He's been waiting a long time to say that.

Good to be home.

In California.

169

"The name *California* is most commonly believed to have derived from a fictional paradise." —Wikipedia

170

"Too bad about the chick," Brian says.

"You'd rather, what," Duane answers as they drive away, "she
flashes those beautiful browns to a jury while she points at you?"

Not that there's much chance of that.

They'll chuck the gun into the ocean and the car they boosted down in Dago, so if the cops do the CSI tire-tread thing they'll come up with some clueless beaner gangbangers.

Still, you don't leave witnesses.

Not even ones you'd like to fuck.

"I'm just saying," Brian mutters.

I'm just saying.

171

Chon finishes his burgers and smiles.

"Better than sex?" O asks.

"No," Chon says.

But close.

172

But as the saying goes, close only counts in horseshoes, hand grenades, and certain presidential elections.

Chon lies in bed in his apartment—fighting jet lag and residual pain—when the door opens and O comes in.

He watches her slip out of her clothes.

Her body pale in the moonlight that comes through the window.

She gets onto the bed and carefully straddles him.

"Don't think I've missed you or I love you," she says, "or that I'm not pissed at you for turning me down the last time. This is just a mercy fuck for a wounded vet."

"Got it."

"A patriotic gesture," she says, bending down, amazingly supple for a girl for whom exercise is anathema. "Like tying a yellow ribbon around something."

She takes him in her mouth, makes him hard(er), then straightens up and hovers over him.

"Just lie there and let me do all the work," she says.

"O?"

"Chon?"

"Don't hurt me."

173

But she does.

Small as she is, slight as she is, she hurts him as she rocks on him, tries to be gentle, tries to be soft, but it feels so fucking good she can't stop and she sees he'll trade the pain for the pleasure as he grabs her hips and starts to move not slower but faster not softer but harder and she thinks Chon is in me and she grips him tighter and sinks into it with a poem and a prayer—

Your skin is my skin, your scars mine, your hurts mine
I'll heal them with my cunt
Silvery, slippery warm
Take you inside where there is no
pain or fear

you can
cry when you come
come in me
a chalice
for you
my friend
my lover
my magic boy.

174

"Holy fuck," Chon says.
She runs a finger up and down his chest.
"Who knew?" he asks.
I did, she thinks.
Always have.
Since the night you rescued me.
The night that started all this—

175

That night
She was fourteen and
The quarterback was really agg.

Aggressive.

And he wanted to fuck O.

Not even subtle about it—the boy's idea of technique, of charm, was to get her down the beach away from the party and say "I want to fuck you."

"Yeah, no."

O would come to a time in her life when she was pro-fucking—her friend Ash would say that O handled more packages than UPS—but not with this jerk, not, like, ten minutes after he handed her a beer and thought that was his ticket to the show, and plus—

She was fourteen years old.

"I'm going back," she said. Meaning back to the beach party they walked away from, the party Paqu didn't want her to go to.

"After," Quarterback insisted. He was seventeen and next year's starting quarterback, and they were already talking USC and the NFL draft so he was getting used to getting what he wanted.

He grabbed her by the wrist.

O was, like, small. Petite, her mother called her, gamine. Whatever the fuck that meant, because Paqu was in a French phase, probably because she was doing this wine importer from Newport Beach and kept yapping about moving to Lyon because Paris would be cliché, *n'est-ce pas*?

Yeah, right, O thought—Paqu is going to leave Orange County about the time Michelle Kwan or some other anal-retentive anorexics do their triple axels in hell. Paqu is never going to get more than a ten-minute drive from her gyms, her spas, her plastic surgeons, shrinks, gardeners, or her OC (that's Orange County, but yes, Obsessive Compulsive works, too) pals, not even for Marcel or Michel or whatever the hell he *appelles* himself, it just ain't gonna happen, but what really had O angry about the situation she was currently in is that it was *exactly* the situation Paqu warned her about if she went to parties with boys she didn't know.

"Do you know what happens to girls who go to parties with boys they don't know?" Paqu asked.

"They get knocked up and have daughters like me," O answered, "who go to parties with boys they don't know and get knocked up and have daughters like me. It's *le circle de la vie*."

Paqu was nonplussed.

Then again, it is very hard to pluss Paqu.

"I married your father," she said.

Briefly, O thought.

"Anyway," she argued, "I know him. He's a junior and he's going to be the starting quarterback next year."

Paqu heard that—she understood status. Still, Ophelia was only a freshman, and the boy was a junior. She forbade O to go to the party, but then went to a party of her own and O simply left the house and went down to the beach, where she found the party around a bonfire and also found Quarterback, who soon took her away from the party and down the beach where they could be alone.

Anyway, O was small and Quarterback was big and all weight room, protein powder, supplements, maybe testosterone the way he was acting—anyway, he was strong and wouldn't let go and she couldn't rip her wrist away so she was thinking—

Fuck me.

Not, like, wanting him to.

Like, wanting him not to.

Quarterback offered her an alternative. "At least blow me."

He started to push her down to her knees.

176

Your nuts can't lift weights.

Okay, maybe they can, maybe you're that guru who nut-lifts five-pound stones from the Ganges, or you're that guy who wins the Darwin Award on YouTube and becomes an eRoom *legend*, but as a rule there are no reps you can do to strengthen your junk against a well-placed knee delivered with bad intent.

Which O had.

Which O did.

She just cocked that knee back and let fly and then Quarterback was on the sand on *his* knees and O should have walked away right there, but she paused to admire her handiwork and Quarterback lunged and cracked her one in the side of the face.

O was stunned.

He grabbed her by the front of her shirt, took her down, and fell on top of her. His junk was hurting way too much for him to focus on his original intent, but now he was in a rage—all he wanted to do was hurt her, and he pressed her down into the sand and pummeled her ribs. She could hardly breathe, her head was still whirling, and she knew she was in big trouble.

Except not.

Because suddenly she felt the weight literally being lifted off her and this one guy had QB by the neck and another was pulling her to her feet.

Ben asked, "Are you okay?"

"Do I look okay?" O answered.

Ben said that she didn't.

"Did this guy hit you?" Chon asked.

They didn't recognize each other. It had been years since the school in the canyon. O just vaguely recognized them as seniors.

"Yeah."

Chon shook his head at QB and said, "Not cool."

QB was jacked up and a little overconfident from the gym and the fact that five of his boys rolled in just now to back him up so he actually said, "Mind your own fucking business, asshole."

Then he grabbed O by the front of her shirt like he was going to haul his property away.

Chon's kick came up and snapped QB's elbow like a Popsicle stick.

QB went down screaming.

None of his boys wanted any piece of Chon after that, so they picked QB up and carried him down the beach.

Chon stood there, breathing, coming down from the adrenaline.

"Do you have a name?" Ben asked the girl.

"O."

"O."

"It's really Ophelia," O admitted.

"I'm Ben. This is Chon."

Yes, O thought.

Yes it is.

My magic boy.

177

Yeah, except the magic boy was *fucked*.

Not enough voodoo in the world to pull him out of this shit.

The starting quarterback wasn't gonna start—not next season, maybe not ever with that broken wing—and his family had considerable swag in Orange County. You put that up against the son of a dope dealer with a bad track record of his own and—

Chon was going to jail.

Maybe prison, because he'd just turned eighteen.

O wanted to stick up for him. Said she'd press charges against QB—for sexual assault, battery, her mom knew lawyers who would help him, but—

Chon told her not to.

A survivor of the high school experience, he knew what she couldn't—as a freshman, her high school life was already going to be miserable. If she took his side in this thing the whole school was going to make her into the slut, the cocktease who got the star QB injured, who ruined the season. It was going to be bad enough as it was; there was no sense in making it worse.

He told her to let it go as just a fight on the beach.

Ben talked him into going to see his dad.

Here's why this was maybe not Ben's best idea—

178

Here's a story about Chon and his dad:

Chon's mom took off the day John came home from prison, but she came back a few days later on the pretext of picking up her juicer but really just to bust balls.

Bad timing, because John was coked up and pissed off and the two of them got into a fight. Not an argument—a *fight*—and John pushed her up against the wall and raised his hand.

Fourteen-year-old Chon stepped in.

Shoved his dad aside and yelled, "Leave my mom alone!"

John smirked. "What? You a man now? You the man?"

Chon stood his ground.

Which was a mistake because John hit him with a closed fist, right in the face. Chon's head snapped back with the impact. Chon put his hands up and rushed forward, but, as Taylor screamed, John beat the uncouth piss out of his kid. Pushed him backward over the arm of the sofa and punched him in the face, the head, and the body. Rolled him onto the floor and kicked him a few times. And when Taylor tried to pull him off he turned on her.

Chon tried to get up off the floor but couldn't, and finally his mom ran out the door. John came back, loomed over Chon, and said, "Don't you *ever* raise your hand to me again. You give me *respect*."

Chon didn't call the cops or Child Protective Services. What he did was, he waited for his old man to pass out that night, then quietly opened his father's bureau drawer, found his .38, and pressed the barrel into John's temple.

Big John's eyes opened.

"You touch me again," Chon said, "I'll wait until you're asleep and splatter your brains all over the wall."

Big John blinked.

Chon pulled back the hammer.

"Unless you want me to do it right now," he offered.

Big John slowly shook his head.

Chon eased the hammer down, put the gun back in the drawer, and went to his room.

His father never laid a hand on him again.

So John smirked when he heard Chon's story about snapping the quarterback's arm.

"Still defending damsels in distress," he said. "So what do you want from me?"

"You have lawyers."

"I do?" John asked, smiling. "Why would you think I have lawyers?"

Chon looked him straight in the eyes. "Because you're a drug dealer."

"Was," John corrected. "I *was* a drug dealer. I paid my debt to society, as they say. Now I put roofs on people's houses."

"Right."

John got himself a beer and offered one to Chon, who refused. John shrugged and said, "If you're man enough to get yourself in this kind of trouble, *Chon*, you're man enough to get yourself out. You want some advice about how to get by in the joint, I can give you that: never accept a favor or a gift because you'll end up paying with your ass."

"Personal experience?" Chon asked.

John said, "Here's what you do, kid—you go join the navy, get your ass out of town. There, I helped you."

Chon left and found Ben.

Ben drove him down to San Diego.

180

Now, in bed, O tells Chon all about her plan to find her father.

Chon listens to the whole thing, then asks, "What good will it do?"

"What do you mean?"

Chon shrugs. "I know *my* father, and I wish I didn't."

181

The call comes in the morning.

Ben detaches his arm from beneath Kari's brown shoulder and picks up the phone.

Hears.

"You reading the *New York Times*?"

Ben, sleepy: "Not yet."

"Well, try the *Orange County Register* instead, Mr. Untouchable."

182

Ben doesn't get the *Register*
(too Republican).

Runs down the street to a news rack, inserts his quarters, and pulls out a paper.

Front page, above the fold:

TWO FOUND DEAD IN MISSION VIEJO

There's a photo of a blood-stained car.

A Volvo.

Frantically, Ben reads—"Names are being withheld pending notification . . ."

But he thinks he recognizes the car.

He gets his phone out and hits Scott Munson's number. It rings six times, then Scott's voice comes on. "You know the drill. Leave a message. Later. Scott."

For the first time in his life, Ben feels absolutely terrified. Worse, he feels helpless. He doesn't leave a message, just clicks off.

His phone rings again.

"Scott?" Ben asks.

"That's sweet."

"What did you do?!"

"No," OGR says. "What you should be asking your*self* is— what did *you* do?"

Good question.

Then OGR posits an even better question to him.

What are you *going* to do?

"Why didn't you tell me about this before?" Chon asks after Ben has laid it all out for him.

"What were you supposed to do about it from Afghanistan?" Ben asks. "Then from a hospital bed?"

"We've always told each other everything," Chon says. "That was the deal."

"I know. I'm sorry."

"Yeah, well, I'm guilty, too." He tells Ben about Brian and the Boys. "That guy was testing us, seeing how we'd react. The second I left, he moved in on you."

Ben is *worked*. Two people dead because of him. It's wrong, Ben says, just flat-out fucking wrong to let them *literally* get away with murder.

Ben just can't let it happen.

And won't let it happen.

184

"Glad to hear you say it," Chon says.

"You're not going to be glad to hear me say this," Ben answers. "We're not going 'drug war.' No 'eye for an eye.' "

"So what do you suggest?"

"I'm going to the cops."

"Which cops?" Chon asks. "Theirs?"

"Not every cop is dirty."

What Ben can't seem to get through his head, Chon thinks, is that the justice system is set up for the system, not the justice. The drug laws make us *out*laws. Outside the protection of the law. The only protection we have is *self*-protection, and you cannot go Gandhi on that, you just can't lie down in the street, because the other side will be happy to run you over and then throw it in reverse and do it again.

"I'm not asking you to do it," Chon says, "I'm just asking you to step aside and let me do it."

Ben says—

185

No.

186

The power of no is absolute
Ben has always believed.
A refusal to participate
In wrong,
In evil
In injustice.
You don't have to do it.
You just say no.

INT. BEN'S APARTMENT - DAY

BEN and CHON glare at each other.

                    CHON
     The fuck you mean, "no"?

                    BEN
     I mean, no. I mean I won't step aside and "let" you
     murder people.

                    CHON
     You think you have choices here?

                    BEN
     I think there are always choices, yes.

                    CHON
     Such as?

                    BEN
     I have a plan.

                    CHON
     Your last plan got two people killed. If we'd taken
     out these guys the first time they made threats—

                    BEN
     Like you did?

                    CHON
     You're right—my mistake, leaving them alive.

                    BEN
     Always your answer, isn't it?

CHON

There are bad people in the world, Ben. You're not going to change them, or persuade them, or make them listen to reason. You get rid of them—they're toxic waste.

BEN

Nice world.

CHON

I didn't create it, I just live in it.

BEN

No, you just kill in it.

CHON

You're just like the rest of this fucking country, B—you don't want to know what it takes to keep any more buildings from falling on your head. You want to sit here and talk about "peace" and watch *Entertainment Tonight* and let other people do your killing for you.

BEN

I didn't ask you to kill for me—

CHON

Too late, Ben.

BEN

And I'm telling you not to kill for me now. I'll deal with this in my own way.

CHON

Which is what, exactly?

188

Ben gets on the phone and says,
"You win."

189

Perhaps Elena's greatest sorrow is that Magda will always associate her birthday with her father's death.

A harsh fact for a girl who loved her papa so much.

Elena sits and looks at the closed casket, white, draped in flowers.

Armed men stand in the back of the room and at the doors, waiting for an attack that could very well come.

She had to tell Magda that she could not attend her own father's funeral tomorrow.

Too dangerous.

In a world bereft of decency.

Are the armed men sentries or vultures, she wonders, ready to pounce on the carcass of the Sanchez-Lauter family? They are all wondering what she is going to do.

Still beautiful, still relatively young, she could go away to Europe, find a new husband, a new life. Certainly the option is attractive—she has enough money to live well forever, and raise her children in peace and comfort.

Or will she step into her dead brothers' and husband's shoes and take charge of the family?

A woman.

There is already grumbling about it; she has heard it. How they will not serve under a woman.

Do you have a choice? she thinks.

A woman is all that's left.

She lifts a black-gloved hand and Lado appears at her side.

Lado, the policeman now openly in her employ.

A killer—his black eyes as cold as the obsidian blades the Aztec priests used to disembowel their sacrificial victims.

"Lado," she says. "I have a job for you."

"*Sí, madrone.*"

She's decided.

190

Chon tosses his cane on the sand and limps toward the water.

Swimming is the best exercise to get him back in shape. Stretches his muscles, breaks up his scar tissue, improves his cardio, but puts no weight on the wounds.

The water is cold, but he doesn't wear a wetsuit.

Not sure he could even pull one on, and anyway, he likes the pain of the sharp cold.

He starts swimming with easy overhead strokes, not pushing it.

Rhythmic, strong.

Peace lasted exactly one night.

Now it's back to war.

EXT. STAIRCASE - TABLE ROCK BEACH - DAY

BEN and DUANE stand on a landing halfway down the long set
of stairs. Waves smash against Table Rock.

Duane pats Ben down to make sure he's not wearing a wire.
Satisfied—

> ### DUANE
> What do we have to talk about?

> ### BEN
> I need to have a going-out-of-business sale.

> ### DUANE
> You just don't fucking learn, do you?

> ### BEN
> Look, I have all this inventory—

> ### DUANE
> Your problems are your problems.

> ### BEN
> My problems are your opportunity.

> ### DUANE
> Speak.

> ### BEN
> I'll sell cheap. Fifty cents on the dollar. To you.

> ### DUANE
> Why the fuck would you do that?

                    <u>BEN</u>

I wouldn't, except what choice do I have? I can't find
a fucking buyer, they're all too scared they're going
to end up dead in their cars.

                  <u>DUANE</u>
                 (smiling)
I wouldn't know anything about that.

                    <u>BEN</u>

Yeah, okay. Look, the point is—you win. Just give me
a chance to get some of my money out.

Ben watches anxiously as Duane considers this.

                  <u>DUANE</u>
Let me think about it.

                    <u>BEN</u>
Think quick. I'm dying here.

                    192

Chon follows Old Guys Rule away from the meeting.

OGR gets into his four-door Dodge Charger and heads north
on the PCH, back up toward Laguna, turns south onto Arroyo and
then onto Lewis up into Canyon Acres. Eventually he pulls into a
driveway.

I could do him now, Chon thinks.

The VSS Vintorez sniper rifle—with a scope he doesn't need and a sound suppressor he does—rests under a blanket on the passenger seat. It would be a simple matter of rolling down the window, waiting until OGR gets out of the car, and putting two in his head.

Yeah, except it doesn't necessarily solve anything, Chon thinks. It does get justice for the murders, and it definitely sends a message that we're not to be fucked with, but OGR is more the gofer type, not the boss.

OGR gets out of the car and goes in.

It's a nice house—California bungalow—small and well maintained. But nothing about it says "kingpin." Nothing about it says the owner is taking a "licensing fee" from every successful dope dealer in the OC and San Diego.

Unless, Ben thinks, OGR is just a guy who has a cop buddy and they thought they'd do a shakedown on a gullible pot grower.

The other possibility is that OGR is a big player who's smart enough to lie low. Live under the radar until he has enough stowed away to pull out and go to some island paradise.

Don't get ahead of yourself, he thinks.

Just take the next step, like get OGR's name.

He puts in a call to an old buddy from the Stan.

· 193

Ben answers his phone.

Hears OGR say, "We'll take your shit off your hands, but at thirty cents on the dollar."

"You sure you don't want to fuck me in the ass, too," Ben asks, "while you're at it?"

"You say one more word, it's twenty-five."

"Thirty-five," Ben says. "Come on, don't be a dick—you're making huge money on this."

"What kind of weight we talking?" OGR asks.

"Jesus, on the phone?"

"I'm clean," OGR says. "Hey, if you're not . . ."

"One twenty, give or take."

"*Pounds?!*"

"No, *gallons,* dickwad."

"Watch your fucking mouth."

"We on, or not?"

"I'll get back to you with a time and place," OGR says.

"Bring cash," Ben says.

194

Chon's buddy—late of the SEALs, now with the Oceanside PD—calls him back.

"I ran the address."

His name is Duane Alan Crowe, forty-eight years old, occupation: roofing contractor.

"You want me to ask around?" Chon's buddy asks. "See if he's on anyone's radar?"

Chon tells him no thanks. Last thing he wants is to let anyone in OC know there's interest in Crowe.

"Hey, I owe you."

Chon pulled him out of the shit in Helmand one time.

"You owe me nothing."

Friends look out for friends.
Way it is.

195

Chon watches Crowe come out of his house, a big briefcase in his hand, and get into his car.
11:30 at night
About fucking time.
Chon is used to sitting still waiting to spring ambushes, but that doesn't mean he enjoys it.
He follows Crowe as he drives off.

196

Guy is standing out front, waiting for OGR to pick him up.
Brian Hennessy is wearing a short jacket, and Chon can see the gun bulge underneath.
Sloppy prick, he thinks.
Brian gets into Crowe's car.
Chon follows them out to the 405.

197

Californians can have entire conversations using mostly numbers.

"The 133 to the 405 to the 5 to the 74" being fairly typical.

Crowe turns east on the 74 and drives up into the range of hills that flank the coastal plain.

No-man's-land.

Surprisingly rural for this part of the world. Lots of switchbacks, dirt roads, little meadows hidden in oak groves.

That's where Crowe's headed now, and it freaks Chon out.

If he's going to meet Ben, which is a real possibility—

—to do whatever the fuck it is that Ben thinks he's doing.

Chon thinks he knows the place they're headed—a little picnic area they've used to make exchanges before.

He pulls his car over, grabs the rifle, gets out, and starts trotting through the oak trees, hoping he can get there in time.

198

Miguel Arroyo, also known as Lado, leads a caravan of Suburbans through the streets of Tijuana and pulls up outside of the nightclub. His black-clad men pour out of the trucks, their M16s carried at high port, and surround the concrete block building, a hangout of the Sanchez-Lauter faction that went over to the Berrajanos.

Then Lado leads a squad through the front door.

"Police!" Lado yells.

There are about a dozen men in the club, with their girlfriends or their *segunderas.*

"Police!" Lado yells again. A few of the men start for their weapons but quickly realize they're outgunned and raise their hands.

Lado's men relieve them of their weapons and line them up against the wall.

Then they step back and, at Lado's curt nod, open fire.

199

Ben pulls the van into the picnic area and waits. The back of the van holds one hundred and twenty pounds of his best hydro, plastic-wrapped into quarter-pound packages in twenty-pound bales.

$120K at normal street value, but this is a

fire sale

at

$42K.

Cocksuckers.

He also has a couple of little surprises wrapped up in two of the bales.

Finally a car pulls into the parking lot. After a few seconds OGR and another guy get out.

Ben does the same.

OGR shines a big flashlight onto the van.

"You come alone?" he asks.

"Like you said."

"Open the back."

Ben opens the sliding door. As he does, the guy with OGR reaches to his waist.

200

Chon sees it and switches his aim from Crowe to Brian, sci-fi green in the nightscope.

Fifty yards away in the trees, prone position, rifle on a bipod.

If Brian goes for the gun, it's over:

Two shots into him, swing back, two shots into Crowe.

Chon puts pressure on the trigger.

201

"It's okay," OGR says.

Brian's hand relaxes.

(Chon's doesn't.)

"Take your clothes off."

"What?"

"I want to make sure we're not podcasting on the DEA network," OGR says. "You and your little buddy, Agent Cain."

"Fuck him."

"Take them off."

"You take yours off."

"I'm not the one who wants the deal."

"Bullshit—you're here."

"Off."

Ben takes his shoes off, then his shirt and his jeans. Holds his hands up, like, you satisfied?

"All of it."

"Come *on.*"

"You could have a wire taped to your dick or under your balls," OGR says. "I've seen it done."

"I could have it up my ass," Ben says. "You want to check that, too?"

"I might, you keep talking."

Ben steps out of his shorts.

202

Chon doesn't like it.

On several counts.

First, it's humiliating, and he hates to see Ben humiliated.

Second, they might want to shoot him like that, really send a message, like the Mexican cartels do.

His finger tightens.

So does his head

Saying

Do it now

Do them both

Get it over with

Sooner rather than

Later.

Remembering what an officer in the Stan once told him—

I've never regretted killing a terrorist—I've only regretted not killing him sooner.

You let the villager go one day, next day he comes back with a bomb.

Do it now

Do them both.

203

"Check the van," OGR tells Brian. "Mikes, wires, what the fuck."

Brian gets into the van.

"Can I get dressed?" Ben asks.

"Please. Not that you're not a good-looking guy."

Ben gets dressed.

Hears Brian digging around in the van with all the subtlety of an orangutan on crank. Then Brian comes out of the van, says, "It looks clean."

"It *looks* clean?" OGR asks. "I don't care what it looks like, I care what it is."

"It's clean," Brian says.

"Better be," OGR says.

"Can we *do* this now?" Ben says. "Did you bring the money?"

"First things first," OGR says.

He pulls a knife from his waistband.

204

Lado bends over, slices the dead man's stomach open, pulls out his intestines, and carefully forms them into the letter "S."

The last letter in the word

"*T-R-A-I-D-O-R-E-S*"

Traitors.

205

Crowe doesn't know how close he is to dying as he slices one of the bales.

Chon eases off the trigger.

Heart rate drops.

206

Crowe takes out a QP package, cuts it open, and smells the dope.

Turns to Ben, smiles, says, "Jesus Christ."

"To coin a phrase."

Crowe shines his flashlight on the dope—sees red hairs and

crystals. Runs some through his fingers, nice and dry, no excess moisture weight. "Very nice."

Ben shrugs—what did you expect? "You want to smoke up, go for it."

"No need," Crowe says. "You want to be a grower for us, maybe we can talk."

"Pass."

Crowe tosses the bale to the ground, then another one, and grabs the next bale. He slices into it and pulls out another handful of dope. Smells it and nods approvingly.

"Just wanted to make sure the rest wasn't ditch weed."

"Your trust in me is touching."

"Ain't nothing about this business that has anything to do with trust," Crowe says. He turns to Brian. "Load it up."

"Whoa," Ben says. "My money?"

"I almost forgot."

"Good thing I'm here, then."

"Get the money," Crowe tells Brian.

Brian goes to the car, comes back with a briefcase, and hands it to Crowe.

207

Chon shrugs his shoulders to make sure they're relaxed, and recalibrates his aim.

If this is a rip, this is when it goes down.

The briefcase is empty or

Crowe pulls a gun from it or

They pop Ben while he's counting except

They won't because they'll both be dead before they can point their guns at him.

208

OGR hands Ben the case.

"Count it if you want."

"Yeah, I will."

Turning his back on them

(Oh, Ben, Chon thinks.)

he sets the case down on a bale of dope and counts the wrapped stacks of bills. It's all there, $42K. He closes the case back up and nods at the dope. "Go for it."

Brian starts to load the packages into the trunk of their car.

"How about the equipment, you want that?" Ben asks.

"Hold a yard sale," OGR says.

Brian finishes loading the dope.

"I guess this is goodbye," Ben says.

"It better be," OGR says. "We hear anything more about you— you sell as much as a nickel bag to a college kid—you end up with *your* head on a steering wheel. You got that?"

"Got it."

"Good."

OGR takes a second to fix him with one more bad-guy glare and then gets into the car.

Ben watches them drive away, thinking

209

Fuck you.

210

Dennis watches the little GPS light blink red on the monitor.

"When do you want to take them?" the other agent asks.

This is when Dennis has a flash of inspiration. He looks at the map with the little red dot, pushes a couple of buttons, points to the screen, and says, "Let's wait until they're by that high school."

Genius.

Vicious.

211

Duane and Brian are cruising past Laguna High when the world explodes. Flashing lights, sirens, cop cars coming from all compass points.

Duane thinks about trying to run for it but sees it's futile so he says, "Quick, throw the gun out."

"What?"

"Throw the fucking gun out the window!" Duane yells.

The presence of a gun on a drug charge doubles the sentence, and he also doesn't want to give the cops an excuse to vaporize them.

Brian throws the gun out and Duane pulls over.

The cops do the whole dramatic get-out-of-the-car-and-walk-backward-toward-the-sound-of-my-voice thing and then the put-your-hands-behind-your-back thing and Duane gets to stand there handcuffed while

Dennis opens the trunk and does the whole well-what-have-we-here thing and then

walks over to Duane and does the whole you-have-the-right-to-remain-silent-anything-you-say-can-and-will thing while another cop works on Brian with the whole we-saw-you-throw-something-out-the-window-if-it's-a-gun-do-the-right-thing-and-tell-us-so-some-schoolkid-doesn't-find-it-and-get-hurt thing.

Then Dennis gets cute with it. He says, "SB 420 allows you eight ounces of dried, processed cannabis. I'm guessing you're about a hundred and nineteen pounds over the limit here, chief."

Duane says nothing.

Then Dennis slices open one of the packages and pulls out a bag of

Heroin.

212

"Uh-oh," Dennis says.
To which Duane responds

213

"Tell Leonard he's a dead man."

214

Leonard knows.

Ben sits in his apartment and thinks.

It isn't exactly justice for the murders, but it will do.

Part of the deal was that Dennis promised federal instead of state prosecution, which he can do because of the quantity involved.

So—

Ten to twenty years on that quantity of marijuana. A twenty-year minimum on the heroin, proximity to a school, possession of a firearm. And there's no "good time" on a federal sentence. You serve the full sentence.

The likelihood is that Crowe dies in prison.

Brian comes out an old man.

And they'll try to kill me.

But the trade-off is worth it.

For a little justice.

Thing is, Dennis isn't so interested in justice.

More in promotion.

It's like a TV game show.

You work your way up the pyramid to the big prize.

He explains this concept to Crowe, but starts off in biblical terms:

"I am the way, the truth, and the life," he says to Crowe, who sits on the other side of the metal table. "No one comes to the Father—in this case Uncle Sam—except through me."

"What the fuck are you talking about?"

"In my Father's house are many rooms," Dennis says, "and you can occupy one of them for many, many years, or—"

"What?"

"Let me put this in profane terms," Dennis says. "You are totally, completely, utterly fucked. You are more fucked than two teenage virgins on their wedding night. You are more fucked than the volunteer subject at a Viagra test. You are more fucked than—"

"Okay, okay."

"Duane," Dennis says. "This is a win-win for me. I can get out of the game now and win, or I can stay in the game and win. If I get out of the game now, you lose big, but if you can persuade me to stay in the game a little longer, you might lose less. Are you following along here?"

"No."

Now Dennis gets into the pyramid bit.

"It's a pyramid," Dennis says. "In my game, we try to go to the top of the pyramid. Right now, I have you somewhere about middle-high pyramid. Now, we can stop there, collect our money, and you go to federal prison for the next thirty or forty years, or you can give me the people at the top of the pyramid and then we have a new game, i.e., Let's Make a Deal."

"They'll kill me," Duane says.

"We can work on that," Dennis says, "depending on what you can give me. We can talk sending you to a very safe facility, we can talk about the Witness Protection Program—note the key word 'witness,' Duane—we might even be able to talk about you walking away from all of this, but first I need names, and I need to hear you say you're willing to wear a wire."

"I want a lawyer," Duane says.

"I'm going to pretend I didn't hear that," Dennis says, "for your sake. Think about it. You call that lawyer you're thinking about, the first thing he does when he leaves here is he goes to the guys at the top of the pyramid and tells them that you've been busted. Then your options are severely limited because those guys aren't going to talk to you anymore, and I can't reward you for conversations you can't have. But you have the right to an attorney, and by all means you can—"

"I'll hold off a little bit," Duane says.

"To *think*," Dennis says. "Exactly. So while you're thinking, think about this—"

216

"One, you're not the only player in the game," Dennis says. "I'm going to talk to Mr. Hennessy now, and if he rings the bell first . . . fuck you. So don't take too long to think, but do think about . . .

"Two—a question, to wit . . .

"Are the guys you want to be loyal to going to be loyal to you?" Dennis asks. "Or, if and when they do find out you're looking at thirty to life, are they going to decide it's not worth the risk and have you clipped anyway? In which case, your loyalty to them is moot. And so I return to my original theme . . .

"I am the way, the truth, and the life. No one comes to the Father except through me."

Dennis 4:16.

217

"I don't want to go to jail for the rest of my life," Brian says.

Dennis laughs at him. "Who gives a flying fuck about what *you* want? This is only about what *I* want. And you'd better start thinking real hard about what it is that *I* want. One, two, three, go."

It's painful watching Brian try to string his thoughts together to form one line of cause and effect.

Dennis runs out of patience.

"Let me be the local news," he says, "and tell you what's happening in your world. You think you don't want to spend the rest of your life behind bars? Your buddy Crowe *really* doesn't. In fact, I just left him because I needed to get a new box of Kleenex, he's been crying and snuffling and sniffling so much in there. Are you ready for this? He's trying to give me you for the Munson murders."

Because, for all his corruption, Dennis is a man of his word.

He promised Ben Leonard that he'd try. And one look at Brian's eyes, Dennis knows it's true. He and Crowe killed the Munson kid and the girl.

"What?!" Brian yelps.

"Yup," Dennis pushes. "He says you pulled the trigger. He's got the needle pointed right at your fucking arm."

"No way. He—"

Brian stops short.

"We know it was one of you," Dennis says. "The question is, which?"

Neglecting to mention that it doesn't fucking matter who actually pulled the trigger. But if Brian doesn't know that, tough shit. Ignorance has its costs. If you're going to be a criminal—know the fucking law, asshole.

"I don't think it was you," Dennis says. "You don't strike me as the type who'd kill a girl. You just don't. I think it was Duane, but he's in there sobbing that he watched you do it . . . he has nightmares . . . 'Brian just blew her brains out. He was laughing as he did it.' Juries love that shit, Brian."

Brian gets this look of feral cunning on his face.

"Wouldn't I be guilty anyway, though?" he asks. "Even if I was just there? Which I wasn't, but if I was?"

Goddamn it, Dennis thinks. If there's anything he hates it's a half-intelligent skell with a little information. *Law & Order* has totally fucked up the interview room.

"True," Dennis says. "But there are distinctions in terms of sentencing. One of you gets life, the other gets the cocktail. Which you're not going to think is a big distinction until they strap you down, and then you're going to think it is, because Duane will still be eating meals and taking shits and jerking off, and you . . . well, they say it's painless, but they say a lot of things, don't they?"

Brian toughens up. "I don't know anything about those killings."

"That's too bad," Dennis says, "because now you can't give me what I want."

He starts out the door, then stops and turns.

"If you haven't already figured this out," Dennis says, "Duane and the boys can't risk keeping you around."

"You're saying they're going to kill me?"

"No, they're going to give you a pony," Dennis says. "What the fuck you think they're gonna do?"

Dipshit.

218

Lado has kept one of them alive.

To watch the dissection of his friends and learn.

The man is naked and chained to a wall, and now Lado takes the point of the bloody knife and presses it into the man's stomach, just enough to draw blood.

"Tell me now," Lado says.

"Anything," the man sobs.

"Which *guero*?"

"What?"

Lado presses the knife a little harder. "Which American agreed to the assassination of Filipo Sanchez?"

The man gives it up.

Raised in the slums of Tijuana, Lado found many of his childhood meals in the garbage dumps that rose in his barrio like Mayan temples. When his father had work, it was as a *carnicero*, a butcher, and when the family got meat, it was usually a *cabra*, a goat.

So he knows the sound of a goat when you slash its belly, and that's what the man sounds like as Lado lifts the knife through his guts.

219

INT. HOLDING CELL - NIGHT

CROWE sits at the table as DENNIS comes in.

>   DUANE
> I want a lawyer.

>   DENNIS
> Bad call, but yours to make.

>   DUANE
> Right.

>   DENNIS
> I know who you're going to call—I think I have him on
> speed dial—but before you do, you need to know that
> evidence isn't going to disappear, the chain of cus-
> tody isn't going to get fucked up. Maybe this guy can
> get ten years chopped off, but so what?

>   DUANE
> I want a lawyer.

>   DENNIS
> Then let's get you a phone, loser.

"What did you give them?" Chad Meldrun asks, sitting across the table.

"Nothing," Crowe says.

"Don't jerk me," Chad says. "I need to know."

Yeah—Duane knows who needs to know.

It's been the deal forever. You get busted with serious weight, you're allowed to play certain cards—you can give up locations of stashes, safe houses. You just tell the lawyer, who tells the boys so they can move the stuff.

What you can't use to trade your way out are people. You do that, it's a—

problem.

"I gave them shit," Duane says.

"Go ahead and give them something," Chad says.

Duane shakes his head. "They don't want it. They just want the guys."

"And you didn't do that."

"How many times you need to hear it?"

"Okay, we're good," Chad says.

"No, *you're* good," Duane says. "I'm fucked. This was a setup. The fucking fed is in bed with Leonard. Leonard set us up."

"If you knew that, why did you do the deal?"

"I fucked up," Duane says. "I thought he was, you know, cowed. And thirty-five cents on the dollar . . . shit."

"Okay, okay," Chad says. "What about Hennessy? Will he hold up?"

Duane shrugs.

"We have another lawyer coming for him," Chad says. "He'll get Hennessy out on bail."

"Fuck him," Crowe says. "Get *me* the fuck out of here."

"I'm going to do my best, cowboy."

"I'm not a cowboy," Duane says irritably. "You see boots and a dumbass hat?"

Cowboy . . .

Fuck.

221

"Your Honor, given the potential severity of the likely sentence," Assistant DA Kelsey Ryan says, "the defendant is most definitely a flight risk. We ask that bail not be set."

The DA is a looker.

Pretty, blonde, blue-eyed.

And a killer.

Verrrry ambitious.

Dennis would like some of that.

Chad Meldrun stands up.

Very interesting that Chad showed up, Dennis thinks. Either Duane's bosses are backing him up big-time, or they want him out of lockup where they can kill him.

"Your Honor," Chad says, smiling like he's about to say that night tends to be darker than day, "Mr. Crowe has no prior drug arrests, never mind convictions, he has ties to the community, and he owns a business. You and I both know that this case doesn't even belong in federal court—this is the government throwing its weight around—and, in fact, I'm preparing a motion to have the case removed to the jurisdiction of the State of California, where it belongs. As we both know, that motion has an excellent chance of success. I'm going to request that you do grant bail, and set it at a reasonable amount, so that my client can continue to make a living and also fully participate in his own defense."

"And he's going to do that from where, Costa Rica?" Ryan snaps.

"That will be enough of that," Judge Giannini says.

"He's a flight risk, Your Honor," Ryan repeats. "And may I remind the court that these charges include possession of a firearm while in the commission of a drug felony. Mr. Crowe is a danger to the public."

"The gun was not in Mr. Crowe's possession," Chad argues. "It was found in the vicinity of Mr. Crowe's vehicle."

"And had Mr. Hennessy's fingerprints on it."

"Mr. Hennessy is not Mr. Crowe," Meldrun says.

Ryan says, "May I also remind the court—"

"The court does not have Alzheimer's," Giannini snaps.

She's in a pissy mood, Dennis thinks.

Good.

Ryan keeps pressing. "This is not only a marijuana charge. Heroin—a Schedule Two narcotic—is involved, and in the vicinity of a school."

"At one in the morning," Chad says, throwing his arms in the air. "No jury is going to believe that Mr. Crowe was attempting to sell to schoolchildren."

"The law does not specify intent," Ryan answers. "Proximity is sufficient."

Chad turns and looks directly at Dennis. "We have seen these shenanigans from Agent Cain before. This is an old dog doing old tricks. It's an outrageous abuse of authority."

Dennis smiles at him.

"Your Honor," Ryan says, "Agent Cain is not on trial here."

"He should be," Chad snaps. "This whole case is a setup from jump street, Your Honor, and I will argue entrapment. The government has used a so-far-unidentified CI to lure an otherwise innocent—"

"We'll produce the witness at trial," Ryan says.

Giannini says, "Let's get back to the point here. I tend to agree that the weapons allegation will probably not survive judicial scrutiny as to Mr. Crowe. I also tend to agree that while the severity of possible penalties is an inducement toward flight, Mr. Crowe's standing in the community and the fact that he owns a business are mitigating factors. Therefore I'm inclined to grant bail. Would the government like to suggest a figure, Ms. Ryan?"

"Ten million dollars."

"Look at my face," Giannini says. "Do I look like I'm in the mood for jokes, Ms. Ryan?"

"May I suggest OR?" Chad asks.

"Same answer, Chad, but nice try," Giannini says. "I'm certainly not inclined to release Mr. Crowe on his own recognizance, but I do see a need for a serious deterrent toward flight. You want to come down on your bid, Ms. Ryan?"

"One million."

"Bail is set at five hundred thousand dollars," Giannini says, "with Mr. Crowe's residence and business as security. Can you post the ten percent today, Mr. Crowe?"

"He can, Your Honor," Chad says.

I'll bet he can, Dennis thinks.

The boys want him out, no question.

Question is

Who are the boys?

222

"You cut them loose?" Ben asks.

They're sitting in Dennis's car in the parking lot of Albertsons in Laguna.

"We can't hold them on the murder," Dennis explains. "Unless one flips on the other, we have nothing."

"I'll go in," Ben says. "If that's the problem, I'll—"

"It won't do any good," Dennis says. "You can't put them on the scene, and they have alibis."

"If I go in and swear out a complaint against Crowe for extortion—"

"The most you have on him is making a threat," Dennis answers. "You can't even tie him to the beating Boland gave you, never mind the murders."

"So now what?"

"Run."

"What?"

"Run, Ben."

Because these guys are out, and they're going to kill you.

223

Because, as Chon points out, the justice system is more about the system than the justice.

Maybe Crowe and Hennessy jump bail, maybe they roll the

dice with a trial on the drug charges, maybe they take a chance on each other's holding firm, but the point is—

They have problems of their own now.

And so do the higher-ups.

Someone paid a lot of money to spring Crowe and Hennessy for fear they might flip in the interview room. But Duane and Brian still have good reason—double-digit prison sentences—to trade up, so the question is—

"Did they get them out to get them out," Chon asks Ben, "or to get them out of the way?"

The latter of which leaves two options—

Crowe and Hennessy jump bail and disappear, or—

Someone disappears them.

In either case, the plan worked—drop Crowe into the shit and see who throws a line.

But how do we track the line back?

One of Ben and Chon's favorite movies is *All the President's Men*. They can practically quote it. Well, not "practically." Actually. Driving back from Ben's meet with Dennis, they go into the routine:

Hunt's come in from the cold. Supposedly he's got a lawyer with $25,000 in a brown paper bag.

The prices have gone up, Bob.

Follow the money.

"Follow the lawyer who brought the money," Ben says. "Somebody sent Chad to bail Crowe out. He's going to report back to that somebody. And he isn't going to do it over the phone."

"Can you do it, bro?" Chon asks. "Follow him without getting seen?"

Without getting killed?

"I think so," Ben says.

"I'll take the other line."

Crowe and Hennessy have to be freaking. They know they're on thin ice. They're going to reach out.

And up.

It's a good situation, Chon thinks. If Crowe and Hennessy had flipped on each other, Ben would have gotten his "justice," but it would still have left the higher-ups out there, and they would have him killed.

Better this way.

"Ben?"

"Yeah?"

"Keep your head down."

"You, too."

"Always."

Recent evidence to the contrary notwithstanding.

224

Duane Crowe goes home long enough to pack a few things.

Because this could go either way.

He folds his Old Guys Rule shirt into the duffel bag and thinks about the phone conversation that was less than reassuring.

Yeah, we have judges, but this is federal, Duane. That makes it tough. Say you get twelve—you serve twelve. You can do twelve. I've done it. You're still a young man when you get out.

I'm not a young man *now*, Duane thinks. He grabs a couple of pairs of jeans out of a dresser drawer and throws them in the bag. I have a daughter going to college. I have tuition to pay. I can't do one year, never mind the cost of the trial, the defense.

And that's just the drug charge.

The other thing . . .

. . . *is a problem. If the other guy gets weak in the knees . . . You fucked up. You know, with the girl. It's a problem.*

Yeah, thanks a fucking heap. Tell me something I don't know. Just like the Powers That Be, you work your ass off for them, make them money, and then when there's a "problem" they leave you on an island.

But Duane gets the message.

The Powers That Be will take a chance on the drug charge, but the homicides?

If I don't do something about Brian, they're going to do something about me. They're going to clean house—Brian, Leonard, me.

If they're not on their way already.

He puts the revolver in his pocket and heads out.

225

Ben sits in his car and calls Chad Meldrun.

The bored, too-cool-for-school receptionist puts him on hold. Comes back on a few seconds later and says, "Chad said to say he can't represent you anymore."

"Did he say why not?"

"Conflicted."

"You or him?"

She hangs up.

But Ben knows what he wanted to know—Chad is in the office.

Which works out, because Ben is in the parking structure.
All the President's Men.

226

O is conflicted as to what to wear.

She walks into her closet, surveys the hangers full of clothes, and tries to decide how to go, sartorially speaking.

I mean, what does the style-conscious South Orange County Princess wear to meet her father for the first time?

Dress it up, or caj it down?

Go older, or younger?

She thinks about a polka-dot dress and pigtails, but decides it's *waaaay* too creepy because maybe Paul Patterson doesn't have a sense of satire or irony.

She looks at your basic "little black dress"—like, look at what a lovely lady the daughter you threw away turned out to be—but worries about crossing the paper-thin line between sophisticated and sexy.

She thinks about not going at all.

This is a girl who has stood in front of a vending machine—torn between F-3 (Peanut M&Ms) and D-7 (Famous Amos chocolate-chip cookies)—for fifteen minutes and then walked away with nothing rather than make a choice.

O knows she doesn't have that luxury here. She has to wear *something,* she can't just go naked as the day she was born, as symbolically appropriate as that might be.

You might be able to walk naked in Laguna without raising alarm—or an eyebrow—but Newport Beach? They don't get undressed to have sex. You could get arrested in Newport for wearing white after Labor Day.

Okay, this is getting you nowhere, O thinks.

But maybe that's just where you should go.

Maybe you should lie down, fire up a blunt, and forget it.

227

Chon pulls over near Crowe's place up Laguna Canyon and looks at the driveway.

Crowe's car isn't there.

Chon gets out, slips his pistol into his waistband, and goes to the front door. It's locked.

The man has taken off.

Chon doesn't blame him, but it's a problem.

Not a big problem, but a problem.

228

Chad "No Worries" Meldrun comes into the parking structure like he has a problem.

Worries.

Has that "places to go, people to see" look on his face as he strides to his Benz, gets in, and peels out.

Ben follows him.

West on Jamboree.

North on the PCH.

All the way to the Newport Beach Yacht Club.

Which figures, Ben thinks.

Money is a pigeon.

It always finds its way home.

229

This is, like, Republican Central. The party could hold its California convention right here, and Ben feels like he should have a visa to even get in.

A twenty slipped into the doorman's palm

("Are you a member, sir?"

"No, but he is.")

is sufficient documentation, but Ben feels Out of Place and a little hostile as he makes his way through the lobby and watches Meldrun go out onto the patio, overlooking the harbor, overlooking the yachts, where on this late Friday afternoon the elite are there to have a drink and to see and be seen.

Ben's working hard at being Joe Detective, trying to blend into the crowd and still keep an eye on Meldrun without being seen when he hears—

"Ben?"

It's a woman's voice.

"Ben? Ophelia's friend? Is that you?"

Ben panics momentarily because

(a) he doesn't want to lose sight of Chad, and
(b) he can't think of her actual name, only "Paqu."

"Oh, hi. Mrs. . . ."

He damn near says "Four."

"It's Bennett, now," she says in a tone that manages to combine self-deprecating charm with a warning not to push the subject. (Indeed, she's here cruising for his replacement. Four is about to become Four*mer*.)

"Mrs. Bennett."

She's statuesque, sexy, beautiful, with all the genuine human warmth of an ice sculpture.

(Except, Ben remembers, O swears that she will not melt. O has watched *The Wizard of Oz*, like, twelve thousand times to get tips.)

"What brings you here?" Paqu looks a little surprised, as if she either can't understand why a friend of her daughter's would be at the club, or forgot that they let Jews in now.

Ben catches sight of Chad's back. "Oh, you know—Friday . . . the patio."

Paqu glances at his left hand. "Yes, it can be quite the place to meet eligible young ladies."

Subtext: you'd better not be doing my daughter.

"Is O with you?" Ben asks, aware that if she is, she's in handcuffs and leg irons, because O would rather sip cat urine straight from the cat than iced tea with her mother on the patio.

Paqu lets the "O" reference slide. "No, I believe she's out seeking employment."

And I believe, Ben thinks, that bin Laden is hitting open-mike night at the West Akron Holiday Inn.

He watches Meldrun go up to someone—Ben can't make out his face—along the railing bar.

"What do *you* do?" Paqu asks.

"Sorry?"

"What do you *do*, Ben?" Paqu asks. "For a living?"

"I'm an environmental consultant," Ben says, still unable to get a good look at who Chad is talking to.

"What does that mean?"

It means I have to tell the IRS something, Ben thinks. "When a big building or a complex is going up, I advise the landscape architects what kinds of trees, plants, and grasses to put in."

"That sounds fascinating," Paqu says. "Very 'green.' Is that the word?"

"That's one of them."

"What's another?" she asks.

That's when Ben realizes she's a little drunk.

"Bullshit," Ben tells her. "It's all bullshit, Mrs. B."

She looks him straight in the eyes. "Ain't *that* the goddamn truth, Ben."

Yeah it is.

Because some people move out of the way and Ben sees who Meldrun is talking to.

Stan.

231

O—wearing a blue knee-length dress—walks up to the distinguished older home on Balboa Island and rings the bell. When the man comes to the door, she says, "Hi. Would you be my sperm donor?"

The man blinks and says, "Could I just take three boxes of Thin Mints, please?"

232

Brian Hennessy opens the door of his apartment to a nasty surprise.

Chon.

Who lays a shotgun stock into the base of Brian's skull.

233

Places Ben Would Expect to See His Father Before He Would Expect to See Him on the Patio:

1. A Republican National Committee Fund-raiser
2. Dollywood
3. Wines R Us

4. A Monster Truck Show
5. Rush Limbaugh's Small Intestine
6. Anywhere

Ben fucking reels.
Turns and walks away.
The truth always comes home, but not to
his home.

234

When Brian comes to, he's duct-taped to a chair.
Chon sits across from him.
"What did I tell you?" Chon says. "What did I tell you I'd do if you laid another hand on one of our people?"
Brian remembers the answer. "Don't. Please."
"Say it—what did I tell you?"
"That you'd kill me."
"Did you think I was kidding?"
"No."
"Do you think I'm kidding now?"
"No. Please. Jesus."
"I'm going to give you one motherfucking chance," Chon says. "One. To tell me the truth. If you lie, I'll know it and I'll kill you. Tell me you understand, Brian."
"I understand." His legs are shaking.
"Who pulled the trigger on Scott Munson and that girl?"
"Duane."
"Duane Crowe."

Brian nods.

"What did you tell the cops?"

"Nothing."

"Here's what you're going to do," Chon says. "You're going to call Crowe, tell him you want to meet."

"He won't come."

"Tell him he comes or you tell the feds everything," Chon says. "What's his number?"

Brian tells him.

Chon takes Brian's phone, punches in Crowe's number, and holds it up to Brian's mouth.

235

"I meant 'sperm donor' not as in 'would you give me some sperm, please,' " O says, "but would you be the man who made a sperm deposit with, or rather with*in,* my mother that resulted in, well, me?"

Paul Patterson recovers his poise quickly and says, "Come in, please."

He ushers O into a beautifully furnished living room that looks, well, old.

Old Newport Beach money.

Photos of sailboats on the wall. Wooden models of boats in glass cases.

"Do you sail?" O asks.

"I used to," Patterson says. "Before I got . . . well, before I got too old."

He is older than he was in her fantasy.

In her fantasy he was in his late forties maybe, handsome, of course, with just a streak of silver in the temples of his otherwise jet-black hair. In her fantasy he was athletic, he'd kept himself in shape, maybe he was a tennis player or a surfer or an iron-man triathlete.

The real man is in his early sixties.

His hair is wispy, a weird kind of yellow and white.

And he looks frail. His skin is translucent, like thin paper.

Her father is dying.

"Please sit down," he says, pointing to an upholstered, wing-backed chair.

She sits and feels uncomfortable.

Small.

"Would you like something to drink?" he asks. "Iced tea or some lemonade?"

O loses it

totally

blows.

All that pent-up emotional lava just freaking explodes.

236

INT. PAUL PATTERSON'S HOUSE - DAY

<u>O</u>

Iced tea? Lemonade? That's it?! After nineteen fucking years, that's it? No hug, no kiss, no it's so won-

derful to finally meet you, I'm so sorry I abandoned
you before you were born and broke your heart and
totally fucked up your life?

Patterson looks sad. Even sadder as he answers—

                    PATTERSON
My dear Ophelia . . .

                      237

Patterson goes Counter Darth Vader on it—
"I'm not your father."

                      238

Ben pulls into the driveway of his parents' house in the canyon,
gets out of the car, walks up to the door, takes a deep breath, and
rings the bell.

What the fuck do they have to do with all this, Ben wonders.
For all their goofy, reconstructed-hippie bullshit, they're essentially
kind, loving people. Caring therapists, good if overbearing parents.

It feels like it takes forever, but his mother finally answers the
door.

She looks shaken.

"Ben—"

Stan walks up behind her. Puts his hands on her shoulders and says, "Ben, what are you involved in?"

"What am *I* involved in?" Ben asks. "What are *you* involved in?"

239

They pull into the parking lot.

A warehouse complex in the canyon.

Old C trains scattered around.

Empty. Quiet.

Crowe's Charger is already there.

Chon lies on the floor of the van behind Brian. He pushes the shotgun barrel into the back of the seat. "You feel that, Brian? It will go right through this seat into your spine. The best you can hope for is a helper monkey."

"I feel it."

"Pull up beside him and get out."

Chon feels the van slow and then stop.

The door opens.

Brian gets out.

Crowe rolls down his window

And shoots Brian in the head.

"I was aware," Patterson says, "that your mother married me for my money. I was in my forties, she was in her twenties and beautiful. I knew—everybody knew. I married her anyway."

O sits and listens.

Patterson continues, "I knew that I was her second husband but wouldn't be her last. It was all right with me—I was happy just to borrow her beauty for a few years."

Borrow, O wonders, or rent?

"We didn't have a prenuptial agreement," Patterson says. "My family was furious, my lawyers more so, but Kim wouldn't hear of it. I knew what I was doing, but money has never been my problem in life. One agreement that we did have, however, is that there would be no children."

O winces.

"I was too old," Patterson says, "and didn't want to cut that ridiculous figure of the middle-aged father trying to keep up with a toddler. But there was more to it. I knew the marriage would never last and, as a child of divorce myself, I didn't want to inflict that on another child."

But you did, O thinks.

"I knew that she was unfaithful," Patterson says. "She would be gone for long, unexplained hours. She would take little trips. I knew but I didn't want to know, so I never pressed the issue. Until she informed me that she was pregnant."

"With me," O says.

Patterson nods.

241

Ben follows them into the study, the walls lined with book-shelves filled with psychology texts, sociological studies, economic histories, evidence of their belief that the truth of the world is contained in books, if only you could read enough of them, and the right ones.

Now Ben wants a truth that can't be found in books and says, "Please, I need to know."

"We came here in the fresh bloom of our idealism," Diane explains. "We thought we would change the world."

Ben's about to object to the whole "Diamonds and Rust" monologue he senses is coming, but then his mother starts talking about a guy giving away tacos.

242

Chon watches Crowe get out of the car and stand over Brian's body, making sure.

There's not a lot of doubt. Brian's lifeless eyes stare up at the moon and a pool of blood forms beneath his head.

Chon slides the van door open and drops to the ground. Belly-crawls around until he sees Crowe swinging his gun at the sound.

Crowe sees him and fires.

But Chon has already dropped into a low crouch. Can't shoot the man, can't take a chance on killing him, so he drops the shotgun, lunges, and tackles Crowe at the waist, driving him into the sand.

Fifty-eight thousand fucking times he practiced on the sand south of here, down on Silver Strand, but he's weak now, and rusty, so he lets

Crowe's gun hand come around as he tries to jam the gun barrel into Chon's head and the shot

is *deafening,* a roar like a big wave going off and Chon feels the burn and his head roaring as he gets his knee up and drives Crowe's arm to the sand and traps it there, but Crowe is

big and strong and he pounds his left fist into Chon's ribs, then the side of his head, bangs his hips up and bridges his back, trying to buck Chon off, but Chon

slides up and gets his other knee on Crowe's left forearm and now he kneels on the man's arms, feels the blood running hot down his face, his pulse slamming in his neck and he takes his thumbs and presses them into Crowe's eyes.

Chon's forearms quiver with exertion, he's trying to hold it until Crowe screams and drops the gun and yells, "Enough!"

Chon grabs Crowe's pistol and gets off him, holding the gun on him.

Crowe rolls onto his stomach, presses his palms into his eyes, and moans, "I can't see, I can't see."

Chon walks over to his shotgun and picks it up. He feels blood seeping out of his left leg where the wounds have opened up from the fight. When he comes back, Crowe is on his knees, trying to get up.

Chon kicks him back down.

Presses the shotgun barrel into his neck.

"Who do you work for?"

"They'll kill me."

"They're not your worry right now," Chon says. "I am. Who do you work for?"

Crowe shakes his head.

Chon's out of wind and his leg starts to throb. He says, "They wouldn't die for you."

Crowe gives him a name.

It hits Chon like a blow to the chest.

He leans over and says, "Tell me the truth. Did you kill those two kids?"

Crowe nods.

Chon pulls the trigger.

Sorry, Ben.

He drags Crowe's body over by Hennessy's, then puts the shotgun in Hennessy's hands and lays the pistol by Crowe's.

Justice or revenge.

Either way.

Taking his knife, Chon cuts a strip off his shirt and presses it against the open wound on his leg.

Then he notices that it's raining.

243

"What happened?" Ben asks when Diane finishes her story.

244

Chon starts to run.
A steady, disciplined trot.
It's only six or seven miles.
Nothing to it.
The rain grows heavier now.
Thick, heavy drops fall on his shoulders, run down his side and
his leg.
The blood mixes with the water.

245

John 14:2
"In my Father's house there are many mansions—if it were not
so I would have told you.
"I go to prepare a place for you."

246

What happened? Stan repeats.
To us?
To the country?

What happened when childhood ends in Dealey Plaza, in Memphis, in the kitchen of the Ambassador, your belief your hope your trust lying in a pool of blood *again*? Fifty-five thousand of your brothers dead in Vietnam, a million Vietnamese, photos of naked napalmed children running down a dirt road, Kent State, Soviet tanks roll into Prague so you turn on drop out you know you can't reinvent the country but maybe you reimagine yourself you believe you really believe that you can that you can create a world of your own and then you lower that expectation to just a piece of ground to make a stand on but then you learn that piece of ground costs money that you don't have.

What happened?

Altamont, Charlie Manson, Sharon Tate, Son of Sam, Mark Chapman we saw a dream turn into a nightmare we saw love and peace turn into endless war and violence our idealism into realism our realism into cynicism our cynicism into apathy our apathy into selfishness our selfishness into greed and then greed was good and we

Had babies, Ben, we had you and we had hopes but we also had fears we created nests that became bunkers we made our houses baby-safe and we bought car seats and organic apple juice and hired multilingual nannies and paid tuition to private schools out of love but also out of fear.

What happened?

You start by trying to create a new world and then you find yourself just wanting to add a bottle to your cellar, a few extra feet to the sunroom, you see yourself aging and wonder if you've put enough away for that and suddenly you realize that you're frightened of the years ahead of you what

Happened?

Watergate Irangate Contragate scandals and corruption all around you and you never think you'll become corrupt but *time* corrupts you, corrupts as surely as gravity and erosion, wears you down wears you out I think, son, that the country was like that, just tired, just worn out by assassinations, wars, scandals, by

Ronald Reagan, Bush the First selling cocaine to fund terrorists, a war to protect cheap gas, Bill Clinton and realpolitik and jism on dresses while insane fanatics plotted and Bush the Second and his handlers, a frat boy run by evil old men and then you turn on the TV one morning and those towers are coming down and the war has come home what

Happened?

Afghanistan and Iraq the sheer madness the killing the bombing the missiles the death you are back in Vietnam again and I could blame it all on that but at the end of the day at the end of the day we are responsible for ourselves.

What happened?

We got tired, we got old we gave up our dreams we taught ourselves to scorn ourselves to despise our youthful idealism we sold ourselves cheap we aren't

Who we wanted to be.

247

Paqu lies on the sofa.

Bottle of gin, bottle of pills on the coffee table.

The effects on her face, in her eyes. She sees O come in and says, "You look uncharacteristically nice."

"Where's Four?"

"That's very amusing," Paqu says, her words a little slurred. "Four is gone."

"I went and saw Paul."

"I told you not to."

"I know."

"But you did it anyway."

"Obviously."

Paqu sits up, pours the last of the bottle into her glass, and says, "And are you happier now? Did you gain an epiphany? One that might propel you from this perpetual adolescence of yours?"

"He said he wasn't my father."

"The man is a liar."

"I believe him."

"Of course you do," Paqu says. "You believed in the tooth fairy until you were eleven. I considered having you tested."

"Who was he?"

"Who was who?"

"My father," O says.

Just tell me.

248

He knows his old man.

Knows him in the way that only blood can.

The shared secret code hidden deep in deoxyribonucleic acid.

DNA.

Fathers and sons are really brothers
Twins of the double helix
Fates twisted around each other
Inseparable
Inextricable
He knows his father
would not have come unprepared to this feast
because *he* wouldn't
Knows that his father
cannot let it end here
Because *he* couldn't
Knows that he now has to do
The one thing
That will cost him more than he can pay
And that he would never do for anyone
Not even himself
But will do
For Ben
Go to his father's house
And ask
For mercy.

249

INT. PAQU'S LIVING ROOM - NIGHT

PAQU takes a long sip of her drink and looks over the glass
at O, who stands there, furious and determined.

                    PAQU
Look at you, my little girl, all forceful and reso-
lute. You look ridiculous. Do you want your face to
freeze that way?

O says nothing, just holds her glare.

                  PAQU (CONT'D.)
I wish you were this determined to find a job.

Same.

Paqu is really out of it now—the effects of the alcohol and
pills have hit her.

                  PAQU (CONT'D.)
Of course, I should talk. I've done absolutely nothing with
mine. Nothing. Except give birth to you. And, no offense,
please don't take this personally, but you're such a . . .
disappointment. Very well. You want to know who your father
is? Who he was?

                    250

Elena sips a sherry and watches the evening news.

A small pleasure before dinner at an empty table, as Magda
refuses to come out of her room, leaving Elena to dine with memories and might-have-beens.

She is just finishing her drink when her guards let Lado in.

"I heard there was a slaughter at the Revolución Club," she says.

"I heard the same thing."

"A terrible thing," she says. "We live in terrible times."

"Someone whispered a name to me," Lado says.

"Whispered or screamed?"

She looks out the window into the courtyard, where she still expects Filipo to pull up in his car and twirl her in his arms.

"*Buen viaje,*" she says.

Have a nice trip.

251

"This guy John," Ben asks. "What did he look like?"

"Why?" Diane asks.

"I need to know."

She rummages around until she finds a scrapbook. Opens it up and the results are almost comical—his mom and dad as hippies— long hair, leather fringes—almost as if they're at a costume party.

Diane turns to a picture of a bunch of people on the front steps of an old bookstore and points to a young man, bare-chested and in jeans.

"That's John," she says.

"I have to go."

252

His name was Halliday, Paqu says, and they called him "Doc."
And when he found out I was pregnant with you he
put a gun to his head, pulled the trigger, and ruined the interior
of a very expensive car.
I don't know if my pregnancy was the . . . causal factor . . . but
there you are.
Happy now?
O runs out of the house.

253

Ben drives down the canyon and hits Chon's number.
There's no answer.
Where the fuck are you? Ben thinks.
Chon was following the line up from Crowe and Hennessy. If
he's succeeded, the line leads to his own father.
Ben can't let him do it.
He lets the phone ring and ring.
Chon doesn't answer.

Chon's gassed out.

Blood flows freely down his leg as he lumbers up the hill to John's house.

He stops down the street to catch his breath and recon the scene.

There's a car parked in the driveway, and he can make out three men inside—two in front, one in the back.

Chon takes three long breaths, drops to his stomach, and crawls across the neighbor's yard to the back. Then he climbs the fence into John's yard, tears another strip off his shirt, wraps it around his hand, and punches the bathroom window.

He reaches in, unlocks the window, slides it open, and climbs in.

Walks from the bathroom into the living room.

John is standing there.

Old denim shirt, jeans.

"Surprised to see me?" Chon asks.

"I thought you were in Iraq. Someplace like that." John turns and walks into the step-down living room, walks behind the bar, and starts to make himself a drink. "You want something?"

Chon doesn't.

"A joint?" John asks. "You want to smoke up?"

"Keep your hands above the bar."

"You don't trust your old man?"

"No," Chon says. "You taught me that, remember? 'Never trust anybody'?"

"And I was right."

John takes a sip of his drink and sits heavily on the sofa. First time Chon notices that he has a gut.

"Sit down."

"No thanks."

"Suit yourself." He leans back into the cushions. "Who gave me up? Crowe?"

He looks almost amused.

"Crowe and Hennessy are both dead."

"You did us a favor," John says. "They had to go, anyway."

"I thought you were out of the business."

"And I didn't know you were in it," John says. He holds a hand up. "Swear to God, son. But I guess the apple don't fall far from the tree, huh? Though I guess you're some kind of war hero? Is that true?"

"No."

John shrugs. "So what brings you here?"

"Believe me, I didn't want to come here."

"But here you are."

256

Ben goes to Chon's apartment.

He's not there.

Ben drives the streets—the PCH, the Canyon, Bluebird, Glenneyre, Brooks—Chon is nowhere to be seen.

Of course he is, Ben thinks.

When Chon doesn't want to be found, he's not going to be found.

Ben hits his number again and again.

257

INT. JOHN'S HOUSE - NIGHT

SOUND OF CHON'S PHONE RINGING.

He doesn't answer it.

> CHON

> I've never asked you for anything.

> JOHN

> But you're going to now. What do you want?

> CHON

> A pass for Ben Leonard.

John shakes his head.

> JOHN

> Walk away from him.

> CHON

> I'm not that guy.

John laughs.

                    JOHN

You going to tell me who you are and who you're not?
I know who you are.

                    CHON

You don't know a fucking thing about me.

                    JOHN

Your mother wanted to flush you down a sink. I know
that.

                    CHON

Yeah, she told me.

                    JOHN

She would. (Beat) I wouldn't let her do it. I dunno,
I was feeling sentimental, I guess.

                    CHON

I'm supposed to, what, thank you?

                    JOHN

You're the one asking for the favor.

                    CHON

You going to do it, or not?

                    JOHN

The fuck you owe this Leonard guy, anyway?

                    CHON

He's family.

John takes this in—seems to hear the truth of it. He doesn't
have an answer.

CHON (CONT'D)

This isn't about me and Ben—it's about me and you. I'm
asking you for something. You want to give it to me,
great. You don't . . .

JOHN

What?

CHON

We go a different route.

JOHN

I can't do what you're asking me to do. I don't mean I
"won't," I mean I can't. I can do *this* for you—I can
tell you walk away. Trust me, I know what I'm talking
about. I wish I'd walked away twenty years ago. You
still can.

CHON

You go after Ben, you have to come through me.

JOHN

Then we have a problem, kid.

John reaches under the sofa cushion and pulls out a pistol
and points it at Chon.

258

"I'm not a kid anymore," Chon says.
"You never were."

"I can rip that gun out of your hand and shove it down your throat before you can blink."

"Yeah, I forgot, you're Superman," John says. "You're a cold enough little prick to kill your own father, I'll give you that, but you think I'm the top of this thing? You think this is as high as it goes?"

Chon's tiring. The world starts to dance a little in his eyes.

"Anything happens to me," John says, "the order is already out. Your buddy Ben is dead."

Leveling the pistol at Chon, he gets up. "Outside. We're going someplace."

He moves Chon out the door.

259

The gunmen come up from Mexico, but they aren't Mexican.

Schneider and Perez are as American as apple pie, trained veterans of their country's wars, underemployed and so working for the Berrajanos.

Now they're on loan-out to John McAlister back at home.

Walking up the beach, hoodies over their heads, they look like druids in the mist.

They've come for Ben.

260

They get in the backseat with one of the gunmen.

He looks to Chon like a refrigerator.

Or a cop.

And he says to Chon, "I don't care whose fucking kid you are. You try anything, I'll put two in your head."

"Easy, Boland," John says.

"Just so he knows," Boland says.

"Where are we going?" Chon asks. "A ball game? Chuck E. Cheese?"

"Mexico," John answers.

261

Mexico, Chon thinks.

Because you can only dump so many bodies in South Orange County before the cops really get fed up and come after you.

The OC is very strict on littering.

Mexico?

Not so much.

262

Ben's doorbell rings.
Please let it be Chon, he thinks.
He goes to the door.

263

Lado is walking across the gravel parking lot to his car when
Magda steps out of the shadows and grabs his elbow.
"Lado," she says, "do something for me, please?"

264

It's O.
Standing in the rain.
Her hair wet, water
running down her neck.
Tears in her blue eyes.
"Can I—"
"Come in," Ben says.

266

265

"I don't have anyplace," O says.

"It's okay."

"I don't have anyplace to go."

"It's all right," Ben says. "You can be here."

He pulls her into his arms and holds her.

266

They come to the border.

(Yeah, well, everyone does, sooner or later.)

"Don't be an asshole," John says.

A little late for fatherly advice, Chon thinks, but he knows what John means. If there was a moment to make a break for it, this would be it—start yelling at the checkpoint, staffed with heavily armed Border Patrol agents, and there's not a damn thing John or the two thugs could do about it.

"Your buddy Ben is still alive," John says. "Get stupid here and he won't be."

That's my dad, Chon thinks.

A real Boy Scout.

Always prepared.

267

O says, "It turns out that Patterson isn't my father."

"Sorry."

"Oh, it gets better." She takes a pull on the joint, holds in the smoke, and exhales with, "My real father was a guy called—you're going to love this—'Doc Halliday,' and—get ready for it—he killed himself while I was baking in the oven."

"Jesus, O, that's terri—"

Then he does the math.

His parents said that Halliday committed suicide in 1981, but O couldn't have been born until—

"What's your birthday?"

"August twenty-eighth, why?"

"What year?"

"1986. Ben—"

But he's already punching the phone.

268

The BP agent asks them why they're going to Mexico.

"Boys' night out," John says.

"Don't come back with anything," the agent advises.

"We won't," John says.

After they pass through the checkpoint, Chon hears John mumble, "The end of America."

269

Dennis picks up the phone.

"What do you want?"

"Have you ever heard of a guy named Doc Halliday?" Ben asks.

"I'm a DEA agent," Dennis answers. "Have baseball players heard of Babe Ruth? Have gunfighters heard of Wyatt Earp? Of course I've heard of Halliday. Why?"

Ben tells him.

270

Looong drive down through Tijuana.

Short on conversation.

What's there to talk about, really?

Old memories?

Good times?

Chon is more focused on something his father said back at the house. *I can't do what you're asking me to do. I don't mean I "won't," I mean I can't.*

Why not, Pops?

Down the old highway into Baja.

Past Rosarito, Ensenada, the old surfers' run.

South into the empty country.

Moonlit night.

Sagebrush and the

eyes of coyotes

glowing green in the headlights.

They could do it anywhere here, Chon thinks, by the side of the road in any ditch.

A seminal fuck and a terminal shot.

Two bursts

in the back of the head

The Lord giveth and He taketh away

The old Bill Cosby joke—"I brought you into this world, and I can damn well take you out of it."

You just disappear and that's all.

The crows take your eyes and the peasants take your shoes and commend your soul to God, but who can say with any certainty that crows don't pray over carrion flesh? They are the smartest of birds; perhaps sensitivity comes with intelligence, maybe they feel for the dead that sustain them.

He's trained for this moment, of course.

Escape and Evade School, a name so redolent with irony it makes him want to weep. The second they open the door to take him out his muscle memory will take over, but he knows that he's still weak from his wounds, freshly injured by his fight with Crowe—his chances are bad, but he'll take the chance—the opportunity— to bring more meat with him to the crows.

I can damn well take you with me.

The car turns off the highway onto a dirt road, and Chon feels his muscles stiffen and forces them to relax.

The old man has a gun, which will be mine in the half second it takes to grab it. Shoot the gunman through the back of the seat, then the driver, then John.

He runs this film clip through his mind until it's smooth and perfected and his body has memorized the sequence.

The car pulls off onto a narrower road, and Chon sees the glow of lights that must come from a house. As they bounce up the rocky road to the top of a hill he sees that it's more accurately a compound.

A high adobe wall snakes up and down the hillside.

Shards of broken glass on top of the wall reflect off the spotlights.

Two armed guards, machine pistols slung over their shoulders, stop the car in front of a wooden gate. The driver says something to one of the guards in what sounds to Chon like an eastern European language, and the car goes through into the compound.

The house is large, two-story, of very basic rectangular Mediterranean design. The west windows look out over the bluff onto the ocean.

John gets out of the car.

"Don't try any of your Special Forces chop-sake bullshit," he says to Chon. "It's Mexico. You don't have anywhere to go."

Chon isn't so sure about that.

He isn't so sure he couldn't kill the two guys in the car, make it over the wall, and walk the hundred or so miles through the Baja desert.

The bigger problem is Ben.

Effectively a hostage.

Maybe O, too, if she's with him.

He watches his father walk into the house.

272

"Leonard," Dennis says, "does your boy Chon have a cell phone?"

Ben doesn't answer.

"Jesus Christ," Dennis says, "for once in your life, trust somebody—even a narc. Does he have a cell phone?"

Ben doesn't name names.

He names numbers.

273

Another guard opens the door for John.

John steps into the foyer as

Doc comes down the stairs.

Yeah, Doc.

Laguna Beach
1991

John walks down Ocean Avenue toward the beach and feels strange.

Strange to see the ocean, strange to walk outside and not see coils of barbed wire and guard towers, strange to not think about who is walking behind him and what they might want.

Ten years in the federal lockup in Indiana, and now he's back in Laguna.

A free man.

Ten years of a fourteen-year sentence before the pardon came through, but now he's out—no parole officer bullshit. No one to report to every time he wants to drain a beer or take a dump.

He walks over to the lifeguard tower, then up the boardwalk.

Roger Bartlett is already there.

"Hi, John," Roger says. "Welcome home."

"Yeah."

"And thanks for meeting me here," Roger says, "instead of in the office."

Yeah, John thinks, banks are morally sensitive.

John snorts. "We've put money in every bank in Newport, Laguna, Dana Point, you name it. Shit, I was fifteen I was delivering bags of cash to you assholes. Nobody complained. Wasn't for us, you wouldn't have the funds to lend to anyone."

We built this city on rock-and-roll bull*shit*.

They built a good chunk of this city on dope. Cash that went into the banks and came out as mortgages for houses, stores, businesses. Built it up pretty good during the ten fucking years he spent in the hole for selling something somebody wanted to buy.

Comes home, there's a ten-year-old stranger sitting on the couch, Taylor tosses him the keys, says *He's your kid now,* and walks out the door. Hasn't been back since and it's been two weeks.

He looked at the kid and said, "Hello, John."

Kid answered, "My name is *Chon.*"

Fuckin' little asshole.

And thanks for all the cards and letters and visits, *Chon.*

Of course, he puts that on Taylor. Divorced him eighteen months into his stretch. He signed the papers—what difference did it make?

Now he looks at Roger, who seems a little nervous, a little edgy, and says, "I want my money."

"It's all there for you, John," Roger says quickly. "It's been earning interest, performing nicely."

"How much?"

"Fifty-two grand."

"The next words out of your mouth better be 'April Fool's,' motherfucker."

"You think pardons are cheap?" Roger asks. "Check it out with Meldrun, he's logged every fucking hour. Not to mention judges, congressmen. Everyone has their hand out. And Taylor? You think she doesn't come around every other week? I've never seen her in the same dress twice, by the way. Christ, I thought my wife could shop. And you have a kid, John, in a private elementary school—"

"Yeah, well, that's going to stop."

"Whatever," Roger says. "I've done my best for you. We all have. You're free. Enjoy your life."

"Cash me out."

"John, you don't want to—"

"Cash me out."

John moves to a smaller house and puts "Chon" into public school.

Then he looks up an old buddy and goes back into the marijuana business and reaches out to another former associate to leverage thirty grand into three hundred g worth of product.

It takes time to lay that much off, though.

Time to get back in the market.

John was back in the dope trade for about three weeks when Chon was walking down Brooks Street, a car rolled up, and a guy told him to get in. They drove him to an old ranch out in Hemet and kept him there until John paid what he owed.

Three hundred K.

Chon was out there for a month, having a pretty good time looking at *Penthouse* magazines, sneaking roaches, and driving an ATV around the place, then Big John came to pick him up personally.

"See how much I love you?" Big John asked when they were in the car.

"See how much I care?" Chon answered, holding up his middle finger.

Big John slapped him across the face.

Hard.

Chon didn't fucking flinch.

A week later, John's walking down the street when a car pulls up, they tell *him* to get in, and they drive him down to Mexico.

276

Way the fuck down past TJ, Rosarito, and Ensenada, down along the Baja Peninsula.

John is thinking he's going to get a bullet in the back of the head, but then they pull up this hill, then over the top, and there's a big house surrounded by an adobe wall, and they pull through the gate into the compound.

Doc comes out the door.

No shirt, baggy khaki cargo shorts, huaraches.

Hugs John like his long-lost son.

"You could have just called me," John says.

"Would you have come?"

"No."

"That's what I thought."

Doc looks good for a dead man. A few strands of white in the hair, which has retreated off his forehead a few inches. John hasn't seen him in over ten years, not since the faked suicide and Doc's disappearance into the "program."

"I thought you'd be selling aluminum siding in Scottsdale," John says.

"Fuck that shit," Doc says. "I bailed the first chance I got, came down here. Freedom is precious, my son."

"Tell me about it," John says. "You ratted me out, Doc."

Doc shakes his head. "I *protected* you. Bobby, those other pricks, they were going to kill you. I took you out of it, somewhere safe."

"Ten *years,* Doc. My wife is gone, my kid is a stranger—"

"You never wanted either of them in the first place," Doc says. "Be honest."

"What do you want, Doc?"

"I want to help you," Doc says. "Make it up to you."

"How?"

"You kept the faith, Johnny," Doc says. "You're like my own blood. I want to bring you in on something. Shit, I *need* to bring you in on something."

277

You're fucking up, Doc tells him, doing it the same old way. That's how we got busted, how we got jammed.

It's a loser's game, it always ends the same.

We don't want to be in the drug business.

We want to be in the turf business.

278

"What do you need me for?" John asks after Doc lays it out for him.

"I need someone I can trust up there," Doc says. "Someone to run the day-to-day. I mean, I can't come *el norte,* I'm freaking Napoleon down here."

"I have a record," John says.

"As John McAlister," Doc says. "Get a new ID. Get five of them, who cares? It's easy enough to do. Set up a shell business, look gainfully employed, and fly under the radar. John, we're talking real money."

"And how do I move the money to you?" John asks. "I can't be running down to Mexico without attracting attention."

"The system's all set up," Doc says. "There'll be sort of a board of directors, you know, some of the old 'gang,' for major decisions. But you'll be the CEO. It's all set up. All you have to do is plug in."

John plugs in.

279

As soon as John's car leaves, Kim comes out of the house. She's beautiful in a white caftan with embroidered flowers, her hair long, her feet bare.

"What did he say?" she asks Doc.

"What do you think?" Doc asks.

Kim shakes her head.

"What?"

"I don't like him," Kim says. "I never have."

"I love him," Doc says. "He's like a son to me."

"You have a child."

"That I never see."

"I'm not living in Mexico," Kim says. "I'd go insane."

"I'd like to see her sometime."

"It's better this way," Kim says. "I have to get back soon. Shall we go in?"

They go into the house and upstairs to the bedroom. The shades are pulled and the thick walls keep it relatively cool.

Still, they are sleek with sweat as they make love.

Baja, Mexico
2005

Well, Papa, go to bed now, it's getting late,
Nothing we can say will change anything now.

—BRUCE SPRINGSTEEN, "INDEPENDENCE DAY"

280

The room is big and perched on a bluff overlooking the ocean. Spotlights illuminate the beach and the breakers.

A foot trail runs from the compound down to the beach, and John sees a quiver of long-boards leaning against the wall of the deck.

Doc wears a Hawaiian shirt over an old pair of khaki shorts and huaraches. A ball cap even though it's night.

He's vain, John thinks, covering up the receding hairline.

"How's life?" John asks.

"Life is the same," Doc says. "Luxurious exile. I surf, I fish, I grill the fish, I watch shitty Mexican TV, I go to bed. I get up at least once in the night to piss. I'm not going to ask how life is with you."

"Things have gotten a little out of hand."

"No shit?" Doc asks.

Doc has a deep tan that looks darker against his snow-white hair. It hangs down to his shoulders, but it's still white. Deep lines in his face, deep lines under his eyes from squinting into the sun. He looks like an old surf bum.

"I've got enough fucking agita down here right now," Doc says. "This whole thing with the cartel."

"I still think siding with the Berrajanos was a mistake."

"They're going to win," Doc says, "and I have to live down here, whoever's on the fucking throne. You want a soda? I got Diet Pepsi and Diet Coke."

"I'm good."

"When did people start saying that?" Doc asks, going to the refrigerator and taking out a Diet Coke. " 'I'm good,' instead of 'No, thanks.' "

John doesn't know. He doesn't care.

Doc pops open the can and takes a long drink. Then he sits down on the couch and says, "We had us some times, didn't we, Johnny?"

"Yeah, we did, Doc."

"Those were some days," Doc says, shaking his head, smiling. "*Good* times. Your kid, what do they call him . . ."

Chon.

" 'John' wasn't good enough for him?" Doc asks.

"You remember the sixties?" John asks. "Everybody was 'Rainbow' and 'Moonbeam.' "

"This ain't the sixties," Doc snaps. "It's two-thousand-and-fucking-five, and whatever the hell your kid's name is, he's a problem. Let me tell you something—I'm spending my last years sipping a drink on the beach and watching the sun go down, not in some cell in Pelican Bay."

"I told him to back off."

"He killed two of our guys tonight," Doc says. "That sound like backing off?"

"He saved us the trouble."

"They were still our guys," Doc says. "We can't let people think it's okay to do that."

He finishes his soda, crumples up the can in his big hand, and tosses it into a little blue plastic wastebasket with the recycling logo on it. "You know what has to happen here."

"We're talking about my *kid*, Doc."

"Why I wanted to talk with you," Doc says. "Get a sense of, you know, where you are with this."

"What do you want, my permission?"

"I don't need your permission, Johnny," Doc says, fixing him with a stare. "It's going to happen. The only question is whether it happens to just him and his buddy, or to you, too."

John just looks at him.

"We're not asking you to pull the trigger," Doc says.

John stares at him for a few seconds, then he gets up. "I'm not even that sure he's my kid."

He walks out the door.

DON WINSLOW

282

Of all the corkers God pulled off in the Old Testament, the real howler was Abraham and Isaac.

Had the angels rolling on the floor

Moaning

Stop. My ribs. Stop.

283

John opens the passenger door and says, "Someone wants to talk to you, see if we can work something out."

He takes Chon into the house.

Boland goes in with them.

284

To Chon, Doc Halliday looks like any middle-aged geezer hanging around the beach hoping against hope to pick up a young chick.

"I thought you were dead," Chon says.

Doc grins, looks at John, says, "He's *so* much your fucking kid."

John nods.

"I want my friend left alone," Chon says. "He can't hurt you."

306

Doc walks up close to Chon. Looks for a long time into his eyes and then says

285

INT. DOC'S MEXICAN HOUSE - NIGHT

                DOC

Look, kid, I brought you down here to try to talk some sense into you because I love your father. When he hurts, I hurt, do you understand that?

Chon doesn't answer.

              DOC (CONT'D)

So if you can look me in the eye and *promise* me—that you'll walk away and *let this go*—then *vaya con dios.*

               CHON

What about Ben?

                DOC

What about who?

Chon stares at him.

              DOC (CONT'D)

So, do we have a deal? I'm giving you the gift of life here, kid.

               CHON

Keep it.

286

Doc turns to John, shrugs, and says, "Maybe you're right. Maybe he isn't your kid."

"No, he is."

He pulls the pistol and shoots Doc square in the forehead.

287

In the words of Lenny Bruce—
"Into the toilet—for *good,* this time."

288

Doc totters for a second.
A statue pushed off a plinth
Then falls
And as he topples
Boland swings his Glock up to blow John off the earth.
And would, except
The room goes suddenly black
And there is only
Darkness and chaos.

chaos (n., from the Greek *kaos*) The formless or void state preceding the creation of the universe.

Highly trained Baja state policemen who know their work, Lado's men blow the generator, plunging the compound into darkness, the only light now coming from the lamps on their helmets and the night-vision scopes on their rifles as their teammates blast a hole in the compound wall.

Then they make small, tight, leapfrogging rushes toward the house, one team covering the other as they move.

This is not a war in which prisoners are taken, this is a war in which prisoners' entrails are used as message boards, so while the Berrajano men defending the compound couldn't give a shit about Doc, they do give a shit about their own lives and so they fight like hell.

And they're good.

All are veterans of Mexico's long drug wars, and some fought in Bosnia, Congo, Chechnya. They are, in short, *survivors,* and now they fight to survive, to get through another night to eat another breakfast, smoke another cigarette, fuck another woman, hug their children, drink a beer, watch a *fútbol* match, feel the sun on their faces, just get out of this dark cold night.

Lado has other ideas.

Other orders.

Kill the man called Doc who approved the assassination of Filipo.

Slaughter the Berrajanos who guard him.

Leave a message.

He gives terse commands but knows they are superfluous—his men know their job, they have performed dozens of these missions, they move forward in small knots, firing short, efficient bursts, and the trained ear can distinguish the two sides by the firing patterns as some of the Berrajanos fire from the wall and slip over to the outside to try to make their way through the chaparral to safety, while others retreat into the house and fire from the windows, hoping to make the house a fort where they can make a stand.

Lado has no intention of allowing that. He'll take no unnecessary casualties but he will take necessary ones, and now he sends men rushing to the main door with a satchel charge. Two fall in the exposed space in front of the door but one makes it, leaves the satchel, and crab-scuffles away, flattening himself to the ground as the charge goes off and shatters the heavy wooden door.

It hangs on its hinges like a drunk man leaning in the doorway as Lado's next team surges forward into the house.

291

Schneider and Perez come up the stairs at Brooks Street and find Ben's apartment.

Perez sends Schneider around the back and then goes to the door.

Holding his pistol behind his back, he rings the bell.

292

Chon belly-crawls across the floor.

Focusing his eyes fifteen degrees to the left cuts off the cones that try to distinguish colors and lets him see a little better in the dark, just well enough to make out the form of Boland lying on the floor, his hands on his machine pistol.

Chon reaches him, throws one leg over the man as if mounting a horse, and then rolls so that he's lying on his back with Boland on his back on top of him. Chon gets his forearm across Boland's throat, his other hand locked behind his neck. He wraps his feet around Boland's ankles like a snake, then arches his own back, stretching Boland out as if on a rack.

Then he chokes him.

Chon's muscles strain and quickly tire as Boland bucks and thrashes and tries to tear his arms away, but Chon holds on until Boland's sphincter and bladder let loose and what was a man becomes a corpse.

Chon takes the Glock and feels better now that he's armed, but armed against what? Against whom? Bullets zip over his head he hears them *thunk* into wood and plaster he hears shouts and groans and it's all so familiar but he's used to being on the other end of this lethal equation on the outside coming in not on the inside trapped like a civilian a collateral casualty in a war between unknown adversaries. He doesn't know a Berrajano from a Lauter, they're all Mexicans to him he's in the dark figuratively as well as literally he only knows that this darkness gives him the chance to *get the fuck out of there* except he remembers that he isn't alone in this chaos and he makes out his father lying face-first on the floor his forearms covering his head against the splinters of wood shards of glass flying around the pistol still in his right hand his

finger reflexively tightening pulling the trigger shots going off at
random the muzzle flashes bolts of red lightning Chon thinks for
a second his old man might kill him after all accidentally and he
crawls over, wrenches the gun from his hand, sticks the barrel into
the side of his father's head, and says—

293

"Call it off."

John fumbles in his pocket and pulls out his phone.

Funny these days how life or death can come down to cell
phone service.

294

Ben opens the door and a guy is standing there with a cell
phone in his hand.

"Hi," Ben says.

"Hey," the guy says. "I must have the wrong place. I'm looking
for Jerry Howard?"

"I think you do have the wrong place."

"Sorry to bother you."

"No worries."

295

Chon yells over the din *Time to go do what I do* and he starts
to crawl, his old man crawling behind him, the general rule being
if you can stay low you have a chance, and the truth is we didn't
walk out of the formless primordial ooze, we crawled.

296

In the dark of course there is not sight but sound, so
Follow the fight from the rhythm of its fire
Like most battles
It doesn't end in a thundering crescendo
But in sporadic spurts
then desultory single shots
then silence.
There is no climax
just anticlimax, or more properly speaking
nonclimax.
Lado's men work their way through the house
Hallway by hallway
Door by door
Room by room
Methodically killing, just as
Methodically dying
And then it's over.

297

Chon makes it out into the courtyard.

His father crawling behind him.

There is a chance, just a chance, that they can get to the car and make a break through the chaos, although Chon hears the firefight dying down and knows that the confusion will quickly end and the window is closing. But there's still a chance and he's just about to gather his legs under him and lunge for the car when the hears the *chomp-chomp-chomp* of the helicopter rotors and then the light hits him.

298

From above

the searchlight from a helicopter

hovering

illuminating the scene of slaughter.

The light is *blinding*, Chon can barely see, chokes on dust as the rotors whip up the dry dirt around him and he hears the amplified command, in English—

"Freeze! Drop your weapons and stand up with your hands over your heads!"

Chon does it.

Struggles through the wash to his feet, drops his gun, and raises his arms above his head.

Sees John do the same.

Looks around at a scene of execution, as black-clad men dispatch the wounded with shots to the back of the head, while others work on their own wounded.

The helicopter lands, kicking up a whirlwind of dust.

A man gets out, bending low beneath the rotors. Straightens up and walks toward them, holding a badge ahead of him.

"Special Agent Dennis Cain, DEA. Come with me, please."

They follow him into the helicopter.

299

Lado stands over Doc's body.

Then bends over, slices the dead man's stomach open, pulls out his intestines, and carefully forms them into the word

"P-A-P-A"

Magda's request.

300

Sitting in the chopper before it takes off, Chon says, "Give me your phone."

John gives it to him.

Chon punches in Ben's number.

Ben answers first ring.

"Thank God," Ben says.

"You okay?"

"I'm good," Ben says. "You?"

"Yeah, good," Chon answers. "O?"

"She's here with me. What the—"

"I'll tell you all about it," Chon says, "when I see you."

He clicks off.

301

"I wanted him alive," Dennis says, looking down at Doc's body. "Biggest bust of my career."

Lado shrugs.

"So you're on the cartel's payroll," Dennis says.

Lado looks at him.

Says, "Just like you."

Five hundred K for a walkaway, and Filipo had it all on tape.

"You work for us now," Lado says. "I'm moving north. With my family. I want a green card and a CI designation."

Dennis nods.

Granite countertops aren't cheap.

302

INT. HELICOPTER - DAY

        JOHN

Just so we're clear—this doesn't change anything
between us.

        CHON

Didn't think it did.

        JOHN

You do your thing, I do mine. We see each other on the
street, we nod, go our separate ways.

        CHON

Sounds about right.

They sit and watch as DENNIS climbs into the chopper and
supervises the loading of Doc's corpse in a body bag.

        JOHN

We let the past stay in the past.

303

Okay with Chon.
But he knows
The past isn't the past.
It's always with us.

In our history.
Our minds, our blood.

304

July Sky.
Bright-blue sunny California.
Happy tourists.

Like, this is the California you pay for. This is the California
you saw on TV and in the postcards. This is more like it.

Ben, Chon, and O sit in the Coyote and watch Dennis's press
conference on the television above the bar.

It's *genius.*

Dennis—rock star—poses beside a blown-up photo of Doc
taken back in the sixties.

"Doc Halliday," he says, "was killed resisting arrest as he tried
to flee across the border. This represents the final breakup of one
of America's oldest and most powerful drug rings, one with con-
nections to the vicious Mexican cartels."

"You okay?" Ben asks O.

"Absolutely crunchy," she says, looking at her guys.

Knows you get two chances at a family—the one you're born
into and the one you choose.

She has hers.

Her dad was always dead to her.

Now Dennis's mouth twists into a somber frown. "Sadly, a corrupt policeman, William Boland, was involved in the ring and also

killed. Two others, Duane Crowe and Brian Hennessy, apparently killed each other in a gunfight. Both are believed to have been involved in the murders of Scott Munson and Traci McDonald."

Karma, Ben thinks, is a bitch.

Theirs, and mine.

I might not be guilty of Scott's and Traci's murders, but I am responsible. Lot of karma to pay off.

Maybe set up some kind of foundation, help out in the Third World. Start paying it back.

There are some things you carry alone, Chon thinks, looking at the two people in the world who he loves.

Inside you.

Heavy but bearable.

Like your own DNA.

He looks back up at the television.

"The final breakup of the Association," Dennis says, looking into the camera, "is a major victory in the War on Drugs."

305

"I thought I looked pretty good on TV," Dennis says. "Didn't you?"

"You're a handsome man," Ben says.

Chon doesn't say anything.

They're meeting in the usual spot at Los Cristianitos. Dennis takes a spicy chicken sandwich from the Jack in the Box bag. "Lunch on the run. You have something for me?"

Ben slips him an envelope.

"First of every month," Dennis says. "Your girlfriend can be late, you can't."

"As long as you keep DEA off our ass," Ben says.

"Yeah, that's the idea."

"Guaranteed?"

"You want a guarantee, go to Midas," Dennis says. He sees Chon's frown, takes a bite of his sandwich, and says, "Jesus, cheer up."

He wipes his mouth with a paper napkin, looks them up and down, and says, "What I wouldn't give to be you. You have your youth, money, the cool clothes, the girls. You have it all. You're kings."

306

That's us, Ben thinks.

ACKNOWLEDGMENTS

I want to thank Jonathan Karp for his support and belief in me and this book, Jofie Ferrari-Adler for his thoughtful editing of the manuscript, and Richard Rhorer and his team for their work launching *Savages* and *The Kings of Cool*. I also want to thank everyone at Simon & Schuster for their hard work and support of this novel.

My thanks also go out to The Story Factory and Joe Cohen, Matthew Snyder, Todd Feldman, Risa Gertner, and Jon Cassir at CAA.

I want to also thank Deborah Randall, Toni Boim, Chris Kubica, and Emily Horng for their work behind the scenes with business, legal, and social-media matters, and with my website.

A number of people shared their stories about the old days in Laguna, and I can best express my appreciation by not naming them. I also want to acknowledge two nonfiction books, *Orange Sunshine* by Nick Schou, and *The Brotherhood of Eternal Love* by Stewart Tendler.

Appreciation, always, to my son, Thomas, and to my wife, Jean,

ACKNOWLEDGMENTS

for their patience, encouragement, support, and the occasional meal delivered to my desk.

Finally, I want to thank my fans, both loyal readers who have supported me for two decades now and new readers. Please follow me on twitter at: @donwinslow.

ABOUT THE AUTHOR

Don Winslow is the acclaimed *New York Times* bestselling author of fifteen novels, including *The Gentlemen's Hour, Savages, Satori, The Dawn Patrol, The Winter of Frankie Machine, The Power of the Dog, California Fire and Life,* and *The Death and Life of Bobby Z.* He lives in Southern California. To learn more, follow him at twitter.com/donwinslow or visit www.donwinslow.com.